Wisdom Seeds
reaping what love sowed

a novel by
Patrice Wade Johnson

urbanpress

for my Aunts –
Velma Lewis, Sheila Johnson, Marion Germany
I remember everything

Prologue

As I parked along the dirt road in the cemetery, I could hear the singing even with the windows up. I felt numb. "If His eye is on the spa-a-a-rrow, then I know, He is watching o-o-over me" – that was Nana's favorite song. "God," I sighed, "I don't feel like you're watching over me right now and I need you. I can't do this anymore."

My stomach knotted as my eyes followed Joshua moving through the crowd. He walked to the front row and stood next to the grandmother he had only known for two days. Joshua reached over and held her hand during the prayer.

Staring at the faces of those around the casket, I easily identified Greg's brother. They looked just alike. His sisters resembled their mother. I avoided all of them at the church. What was there to say?

Joshua stood facing the casket with his back to me. I knew he really didn't hate me, he was angry. My dad was right, my secret had come back to haunt me. The whispers in my shadow were now screaming. Joshua had the best of everything, including memories of a loving father. Jason loved him. Greg left him – and me. The moment felt surreal. I attempted to get out of the car for air, but the door was too heavy. I let the window down and let myself sink down in the seat.

'I have planted seeds of wisdom in you.' Nana's words resonated in my head. What had I learned? Life hurts. I hadn't learned that from wisdom, I learned that from pain. The sparrow had fallen and I wasn't sure God was watching.

ONE

My summers during college were spent in Wheeling with my maternal grandmother. Nana told me about the Youth Investment Program at West Virginia University when I was a senior in high school. I applied for a counselor's position during my freshman year at Penn State and looked forward to spending my summers close to Grandma Ida, affectionately called Nana. Even knowing my Sunday mornings and Wednesday evenings would be spent at Memorial Park AME Zion Church, I still looked forward to spending my summers in West Virginia.

Ida Pearl Holloway. I loved everything about her and cherish every memory from my visits to Wheeling. By the time I was in high school, only Mom and I were visiting her regularly and Nana was only coming to visit us during the Christmas holiday. It was always evident in the silence between them that my dad didn't particularly care for Nana and I never understood why. Nana was a country girl and had a love for life that was contagious. It was absurd that anyone could not love Ida Pearl. Even during the height of his obstinence when he hated everyone, my brother, Noah, still loved Nana.

I remember everything about her. She loved Jean Naté and put it on every morning after her bath. Even her towels smelled like Jean Naté! She had a collection of hats and shoes to match every dress and she meticulously coordinated her outfits, never wearing more than three colors at a time. I only remember her wearing pants twice. Both times she was visiting us and it was bitter cold. Nana even wore sundresses while she worked in her yard because she said after growing up on a farm, she would never wear anything made of denim again.

When I was sixteen Nana showed me the letters she and Grandpa Booker exchanged during their marriage. For thirty-eight years they wrote each other love letters on Valentine's Day. Nana and Grandpa Booker loved each other second only to the Lord — it was Nana who taught me about love.

It's her stories of the wisdom seeds that I remember most. She told me the first one when I was five. It was the fall of 1963, the day after Grandpa Booker died. I found my grandmother sitting in her room and I climbed on the bed, laying my head in her lap.

"Dani," she whispered.

I answered with my face still in her dress. "Yes Ma'am."

"Do you know what it means to have love in your heart?"

"Yes Ma'am." I sat up next to her.

"Well, I'm going to tell you about the love of Jesus and I want you to promise me you will always remember," she said braiding my hair. "I always want you to have love in your heart."

"I promise."

"Love God with all your heart because He first loved you and died so you could have eternal life."

"Okay," I smiled.

"No matter what happens in your life, always remember Jesus loves you. That's a wisdom seed."

"A wisdom seed?" I squinted, turning to look up at her.

"Baby," she smiled, "a wisdom seed is something someone plants in your heart so it will grow one day."

"How's it going to grow inside my heart?"

"Because life will water it, and when you grow up the seed will bloom."

"Like a flower?"

"Just like a pretty flower."

She started singing her favorite song and I sang along with her. From that day, whenever I was visiting her, or she was visiting us, she made me recite John 3:16 every morning.

"For God so loved the world that He gave His only begotten Son, that whoever believes in Him should not perish but have everlasting life."

As we were getting dressed, we always sang "His Eye Is On The Sparrow". I memorized the scripture and the song because I loved her. It would be years before I would come to understand the significance of what I committed to memory.

Several years passed before Nana planted the wisdom seed of kindness in my life. It was the spring of 1969 and one of the last times we went to visit Nana as a family. During this particular visit, my mom took her second and final stand to my dad. The first was in naming me. My dad named my brothers and wanted to name me Sarah Elizabeth. I am eternally grateful she insisted my name be Danielle, even though she tacked that on to appease him.

Anyway, my dad was doing his usual 'fuss thing' with Noah, scolding him for acting like a heathen. Mom motioned for us to follow her into the kitchen where Nana was squeezing lemons. Joey and I proceeded out to the back porch because we weren't permitted to sit under adults while they were talking. I sat on the swing by the radio that was holding the window open so I could see my mom and Nana standing at the sink.

"You used to be care free," Nana said, as Mom filled the pitcher with water. "I sure do miss her," Nana continued. "My Judy was a girl who always carried a song in her heart. Then she got married."

"Mother, you promised we wouldn't talk about this," she answered speaking just above a whisper.

Although I was very good at eavesdropping, I had to concentrate because their voices were muddled behind the static on the radio. I wanted to turn it down, except that would have given me away. The secret to good eavesdropping was to make people think you weren't interested in what they were saying.

It was hard to imagine my mother as carefree. She was a dutiful wife who made sure she took care of my dad, the house and us. She was the picture perfect preacher's wife, well dressed and always smiling. At age eleven, I knew she wasn't carefree and was beginning to wonder if she was happy.

"He never dealt with his own pain," Nana's voice was raised. "He spent years trying to pretend those things never happened."

I didn't know what she meant, yet I listened intently.

"Judy!" Dad called Mom from the side of the house where I suspected he had whipped Noah. Joey looked at me and I took his silent cue to keep my mouth shut and stay glued to the swing. Before I had time to think about it, my dad came up the back porch steps pulling Noah by the arm. Sweat was pouring off his face onto his starched white collar. I tried to make eye contact with Noah — he was looking at Joey who was pretending to play a piano and sing along with the Temptations. There was no time to warn Nana or Mom.

My dad's voice was stern as he flung open the back door. "I refuse to condone his belligerence as teenage angst." His veins protruded from his neck and his eyes were fixed on Nana.

"You're angry with yourself David, not Noah and not me." Nana's voice remained calm as she continued to squeeze lemons. Mom continued to stir the sugar water in the pitcher. Noah looked at the floor.

My dad cleared his throat, raised his voice and banged his fist on the counter. "Woman, that's what's wrong with the world — everybody wants to do their own thing with no accountability! And I will not. . ."

Before he could finish, my mom's neck jerked and her head turned ten seconds before her body. She stepped between her mother and my dad, maintaining eye contact with him. With the spoon less than half an inch from his nose, she reminded him that yelling and addressing her mother as 'woman' was unacceptable. It sounded like my mom was crying.

I wanted to go in the kitchen and was trying to work up the courage to get off the swing when Nana came outside with Noah and hurried us down the steps. Noah and Joey mocked my parents as they went running up the hill behind the house. Nana and I started picking flowers. It was April and the flowers were beginning to bloom.

We were walking in silence and then without breaking her stride she said, "Dani, never say things you will live to regret." With that serious look I had come to know, she asked, "Do you understand?"

I said yes even though I didn't. Her wisdom seeds were still only good stories. I followed her along the fence as she continued to pick flowers. Without looking back she said, "I'm going to plant the wisdom seed of kindness in your heart." She stopped, leaned against the fence and looked up the hill where Joey and Noah had run. "Words spoken in anger can never be taken back. Although someone may apologize, the scar of their words will remain forever." She paused. "And how do you remove a scar?" She asked, looking down at me.

I looked up squinting because the sunrays came through the leaves on that big oak tree like a spotlight in my eyes, and shrugged my shoulders.

As she bent down to pick up another flower, she said, "You can't, but if you focus on the scar, you'll be miserable for the rest of your life. Miserable people have no love in here." She pointed to her heart. "Love and hate can't live in the same heart. Hate makes you mean, but love makes you kind. The only way to have love is to forgive. God said we must be willing to forgive people when they hurt our feelings. God forgives us when we sin and hurt His feelings." Nana turned and began walking back toward the house. "Repeat after me," she said without turning around. *"And be kind to one another,"* she paused and waited for me to repeat after her. I obediently obliged through the verse, *"tender hearted, forgiving one another even as God in Christ forgave you, Ephesians 4:32."*

Nana planted the third wisdom seed in my heart during the summer before my sophomore year at Penn State. One Saturday morning while we were sitting on the front porch snapping beans, she said, "Dani, hand me my Bible." Nana never lost her pace snapping beans and, without looking, tossing them into that old tin bucket. The same bucket she said she used to wash my mom when she was a baby. I tried not to think about that as I watched it fill up with beans. We had to eat them for dinner.

Nana wiped her hands on her apron and took the

Bible from me. She turned to 2 Corinthians 6:14:

*"Do not be unequally yoked together with unbe-
lievers for what fellowship has righteousness with lawlessness? And what communion has light with darkness?"*

She read as if she were a famous orator, pro-
nouncing each word with emphasis.

"Remember that scripture." She handed me the
Bible and put two handfuls of beans on her lap. "You're
away at college and you've got to make good choices
about people. Not all people are good, even though they
might look nice on the outside. Everyone smiling at you
is not going to like you and some people will take advantage of you."

It felt like a lecture, but I was captivated. Nana
spoke with authority.

"No one likes to be alone – the happy, the sad,
the good or the bad. Look at people who are loved, you
will see that they are loving and they surround themselves with others who are like-minded – just as the
scornful like to avoid joy and keep a disdain for those
who are happy. If you find people who are unhappy and
unable to maintain friendships, stay away from them.
And since we are known by the company we keep, then
you must make a decision. What kind of people do you
want to be around – the friendly or the scornful?"

She resumed her beat snapping beans. I stopped
to concentrate on the question I had never thought about
before.

"Dani, who are you walking with?"

Unsure of what to say, I sat there with a dumb
look on my face. Childish as it seems, I was thinking I
wasn't walking with anyone. I was sitting on the front
porch snapping beans with her.

"Make sure you surround yourself with good

people, Dani," she said breaking the silence. "Walk with good people. That's a wisdom seed for goodness."

I understood, although not clearly. There was some big life lesson in what she said and I was sure I was missing a piece. My mind raced to respond, but I had no words.

Nana sat up to get another handful of beans off the table. "You like Tony, don't you?"

"Yeah, he's nice." I tried not to smile.

"You can smile," she teased. "I already knew."

"It's not like that Nana, we just went to the movies."

"Are you going out again?"

"Bowling on Saturday," I tried to say with a straight face.

"He's a nice kid. He and his friend, Jeffrey, left New York to give themselves a chance."

"I know, he told me," I replied.

"That shows he has a good head on his shoulders. A good man knows how to get away from and stay out of trouble. Sometimes when boys grow up without a father, it's hard for them to learn how to be good men. But God done blessed them two with good men who cared about them." Nana smiled. "God done planted a lot of good men all over the country," she paused, "so you don't have to settle."

"Yes Ma'am."

"You just wait on your blessing from God. Keep your ears open so you can hear God talkin' cause your own eyes might deceive you."

"Yes Ma'am."

"Everything that looks good is not good for you," she hesitated and added, "but that don't mean your blessing can't be cute!"

Nana knew how to make me laugh, even when she was serious and teaching me a life lesson.

Tony met Nana when he volunteered to help paint the church. Nana prepared lunch for the students and Tony complimented her cooking. She invited him to dinner the following weekend and he volunteered to cut her grass. In return, Nana began cooking for him all the time — sometimes cakes and pies and sometimes dinner.

Although Tony had asked me out a few times, I wondered if he was doing it for Nana. Even though he was very nice, and cute, I wouldn't allow myself to believe that I was his type. He wore his short Afro tapered around his face and rolled the sleeves on his tee shirt to display his muscles. His jeans were always starched and creased. I was still waiting for my body to develop and wore my hair pulled back into a ponytail. My cotton sun dresses and matching short sets from Sears made me look fourteen. Anyway, it made Nana happy to think she matched me up with a nice young man.

The summer with Nana ended too soon and I wished I didn't have to leave. Nana promised to visit me in the spring. I believed her, but still cried on the bus.

My sophomore year started out dragging. I wrote Nana diligently every Saturday, anxious to return to see her again. She replied insinuating that my anxiety was in seeing Tony, not her. I wrote many letters trying to convince her otherwise. Even her stationery smelled like Jean Naté.

Eric Wilson came along during the first week in October and I fell in love with him by the end of the month. I was looking for that magic love Nana had with Grandpa Booker. Eric was a romantic and wrote me poems. He even wrote me a song and sang it to me in the cafeteria. I shared pieces of the poems with Nana because I wanted her to know how romantic he was. Nana wrote back telling me she doubted his sincerity. It took me two weeks to write asking her why. Eric said everything I wanted to hear. He thought I was cute and I wanted to be in love.

By the time Nana wrote me again, I was ready to burn Eric's sonnets. He had shattered my heart, broken up with me because I wouldn't have sex with him and lied to his friends telling them he had. I thought about the wisdom seeds – never saying something I would later regret and walking with the right people. I surmised the seeds must not have taken root because I regretted having said I loved Eric and had totally misjudged his character.

My letter to Nana was pitiful. Penn State no longer seemed like the place for me and I wanted to transfer to West Virginia. I suggested we discuss how to tell my parents when she came to visit.

Spring break came but Nana didn't. Her arthritis made walking difficult and she thought it best to stay at home. Our visit would have to wait until summer.

As the end of my sophomore year approached, I made plans to join Nana in West Virginia. I was able to get my counseling job at the Youth Investment Program again, too.

I arrived in Wheeling in time to help Nana bake sweet potato pecan pies for the Memorial Day Veteran's Luncheon. Nana's weight loss was startling and I consciously avoided staring at the limp which replaced her once graceful stride. She was dismissive about the hip replacement suggested by her doctor and her fragility frightened me. During my senior year in high school, I requested an application to West Virginia University and now regretted never completing it.

West Virginia was my summer respite where Nana and I enjoyed a ritual of activities. We attended prayer meeting and Bible study faithfully, every Wednesday evening. Most of the fifty-member congregation also attended and Deacon Grady opened with the same three songs each week – "Jesus on the Main Line", "Blessed Quietness" and "What a Friend We Have in Jesus".

Our Monday evenings were spent with the Home Missionaries, of which my grandmother had been the president for fifteen years. We prepared dinner and provided a hot meal and fellowship for all who came. Some were homeless, some were poor and some were just lonely. There were families, children, young adults and the elderly. During my first year, I stayed in the kitchen serving and cleaning. My second year was spent playing games and reading stories to the children. I studied Nana as she sat with her visitors, talked with them, prayed with them and sometimes hugged and cried with them.

Nana could talk for hours about the earthly ministry of Jesus and how He showed His love through compassion for people. As she taught the Beatitudes, I committed them to memory.

"Blessed are the poor in spirit, for theirs is the kingdom of heaven. Blessed are those who mourn, for they shall be comforted. Blessed are the meek, for they shall inherit the earth. Blessed are those who hunger and thirst for righteousness for they shall be filled. Blessed are the merciful, for they shall obtain mercy. Blessed are the pure in heart, for they shall see God. Blessed are the peacemakers, for they shall be called sons of God. Blessed are those who are persecuted for righteousness sake,

for theirs is the kingdom of heaven, Matthew 5:3–10."

I had yet to come to a full understanding of the wisdom seeds Nana taught me.

Nana masked the severity of her pain well. She was up every morning making breakfast, even after I would hear her moaning at night. On my second Sunday back in Wheeling, she invited Tony, Jeffrey and Vicky to dinner. We spent most of the evening listening to Nana's tales about the 'good ol' days'. Her stories were never complete without making us repeat scripture and sing her favorite hymns.

Two weeks after I arrived, Tony left for Hartford, Connecticut to complete his internship. My social life plummeted from minimal to nil. I let books consume my time and leisurely read the New Testament.

One Saturday Nana taught me how to make black-eyed peas and rice with ham hocks, sweet potato pies with a shortbread crust and stewed turkey legs. These were her favorite recipes that she had never shared with anyone else except my mother.

On our way home from church, Nana asked about my plans after college. I hated admitting not having any. My goal was to graduate and do something and I promised to begin exploring my options. Graduate school at West Virginia seemed like the perfect choice.

After dinner, we retreated to the porch swing and the cool night air. It was then that Nana began to tell me her time to rest was near. I refused to believe her because I wanted her to live forever.

"Nana, don't talk about dying."

"Danielle," she replied in her serious voice, "nobody lives forever."

"You probably could." I felt like I was five and wanted to bury my face in her dress. "My wisdom seeds need you to help them."

She lifted my chin. "Sometimes people leave us, no matter how much we wish they wouldn't. And sometimes we think we can't live without them."

I could feel tears welling in my eyes – no words would come. I wanted to put my hands over my ears. I needed her and words were inadequate to explain how much.

"We find the strength to go on," she continued as the tears streamed down my face. "Tears are the watering from sorrow, crying is good – it's like rain." She wiped my tears with her fingers. "The next time something makes you cry, just know it's growing you. Without rain nothing would grow and without tears you won't grow either."

"I want my children to know you."

"They will know me through you."

"Nobody loves me like you do," I said almost whining.

"Jesus loves you much more than I ever could, don't you ever forget that."

"I love you so much Nana. I can't imagine you gone."

"When you see the rain, just know you're not alone in your sorrow, and when you see the sun, remember my smile. I'll always be watching you from the balcony of Heaven." Nana held my hand and pushed my hair back off my face. "Remember this, too," she said making sure I maintained eye contact with her, "God sees the sparrow when it falls."

"Then why does He let it fall?"

"You just remember that if God takes the time to watch the sparrow, you can rest assured He's watching you."

I awoke the following Saturday to the strange sound of silence — nothing frying, no coffee perking and no humming. I found Nana sitting on the porch swing. It was an overcast morning. The clouds appeared pensive and swollen like they were too heavy to move.

Still in my pajamas, I sat at her feet on the front porch. "Are you okay, Nana? Can I get you anything?"

Nana stopped swinging and smiled at me.

"Will you take me to Oglebay Park?"

"Of course," I smiled back at her, "and let's go to the IHOP for breakfast."

Nana wore her favorite red dress and the straw hat with the big red carnation. She said Grandpa Booker always liked her in red. While we waited for our food, Nana reached across the table and took my hand.

"Dani, do you remember the three wisdom seeds?"

I was proud to recite them to her. "The seed of love is to love God with all my heart because He first loved me and died so I could have eternal life. The seed of kindness is to forgive others because God forgives me and the seed of goodness is to walk with good people."

"Child, this is the fourth seed — the wisdom seed of peace."

I nodded with anticipation. Nana looked so beautiful — at seventy-five her skin was flawless. Her smile was still the same, too.

She quoted Proverbs 15:1. "*A soft answer turns away wrath, but a harsh word stirs up anger.*"

"You will always catch more with honey than you will ever catch with vinegar," Nana continued. "Do you know why?"

"I'm not sure," I told her feeling like I was seven

years old again.

"Honey is very sweet to the taste. It is also sooth-ing. Anything I am trying to catch will be lured by honey. Vinegar, on the other hand, is only good with greens and does not attract anything – not even the hungriest creature. They gave Christ vinegar to drink on the cross to burn His insides. Words spoken in anger are like vinegar, they burn your insides." And with that look I had come to know so well she asked, "What do your words do?"

This time I had an answer. "I hope they make people happy, Nana."

"Let your words be pure and kind. Make sure your words speak peace." Nana squeezed my hand. "Love, kindness, goodness and peace. That's my prayer for you. Remember that."

At that moment, I realized the wisdom seeds might be more than just stories.

Nana passed away three weeks into my junior year. I dropped the phone when Mom called. What would I do without her? Who was going to love me like she did?

Tony met me at the Greyhound station in Wheel-ing and hugged me when I got off the bus. "Are you okay?"

I shook my head no, trying not to cry.

We rode in silence to Nana's house. As we pulled in the driveway, I noticed the flowers and cards decorat-ing the porch. My hands began to shake just thinking about Nana not being there to greet me at the door. I exited the car and stood at the bottom of the steps fumbling in my purse for the keys.

"Want me to go with you?" Tony asked, standing behind me.

All I could do was cry. He let me ramble on about missing my grandmother while he held me.

"I'll miss her, too," he said trying to comfort me. "I loved her. She was the grandmother I never had."

Tony and I held hands and walked slowly across the porch. The hinges on the front door squeaked as he opened it. I stepped into the living room and closed my eyes. The smell of Jean Naté greeted me.

"I need to get the letters," I announced, breaking the silence as I walked toward Nana's bedroom.

"What letters?"

"Nana and Pappy's love letters are in the basket," I said pointing to the corner beneath the picture of my grandfather.

We sat in the living room and I began to read the letters, passing each one to Tony – expecting he would want to read them, too. Their letters told of a wonderful love – better than *Mahogany* or *A Star is Born*.

"Do you think she'd mind?" Tony asked.

"This is true love," I said remembering Nana's smile as she told me about the letters. "These are portraits of love. She wouldn't mind."

It was raining and they kept trying to make me walk under an umbrella as we lined up to go in the church. I was numb and didn't feel the rain. Noah and Joey arrived in time to join the family processional into the church. Noah put a rose in Nana's hand before they closed the casket.

"She always liked flowers," he said sitting next to Mom and holding her hand.

Joey struggled through "His Eye Is On The Sparrow," Nana's favorite song. She had given him a hymnal when he was ten and it was the first song he learned to play.

I sat next to my dad wondering if he was being strong for Mom. He put his arm around me and held Mom's other hand. She cried through the entire service. Everyone did, except my dad.

As they lowered my grandmother into the ground, the clouds began to part. The sun was trying to sneak through to kiss Nana's casket before they covered it with dirt. I thought about what she said. In the rain she felt my sorrow and the sun meant she was smiling. Driving back to the church for dinner, I was comforted by the thought of her smile.

"She's happy now," I said to Tony as we sat outside the church. "She's with Pappy."

"They really loved each other. I can tell from the letters."

"I hope someone loves me like that."

Tony smiled at me. "They will if you let them."

Mom looked out the church door and motioned for me.

"Dani, come and eat."

"No thanks Mom. I'm not hungry."

"Maybe you should eat," Tony said getting up from the bench where he, Jeffrey, Vicky and I had been sitting.

"No, I'm okay."

Jeffrey and Vicky got up and gave me a hug.

"Think you might feel like a movie later on?" Vicky asked.

"Sorry, I can't," I told her. "I'm leaving in a few

hours. I have a class Monday morning."

"I'm sorry you have to leave so soon," Tony said from behind me.

I turned to face him. "Me too."

"I hope this doesn't mean I won't see you anymore."

"It doesn't have to."

Tony smiled and took my hand. "Can I take you to the bus station?"

"I'd like that." I tried not to blush. "Can you pick me up at six?"

"See you at six o'clock." He waved and then walked away with Jeffrey and Vicky.

I joined my family in the Fellowship Hall.

Mom greeted visitors and reminisced with old friends in the church basement. Noah and Joey stood with her like bodyguards. She had not seen either of them in over a year and it felt good to see her smiling.

A week after the funeral I contemplated taking a leave of absence. My mind was blank and I doubted my ability to get through the semester. The sparrow had fallen and I wondered if God was watching. I thought of the seeds Nana planted in my heart and wondered if they had started to take root. Love, kindness, goodness and peace seemed far away and out of my reach.

Tony came to visit me the following spring. I was no longer in denial that time and distance were not on our side to have a relationship, so I would savor the memories of the weekend for a very long time. The first time he kissed me, I felt swallowed up in his arms.

"I've wanted to kiss you for a long time," he said, still holding me. "I like your lips." He traced my lips with his index finger.

Not knowing what to say, I just let him hold me because it felt good. Nothing prepared me for the moment and even my fantasies were miniscule by comparison. I wanted to give myself to him. If he had asked, I would have said yes.

Over dinner Tony told me about his plans to pursue his MBA at New York University. He was looking forward to graduating and would be returning to Hartford to work over the summer. Graduate school would consume him over the next two years and he didn't know where he would end up after that.

"You're beautiful," he said smiling. "It would be selfish to ask you to wait for me."

"Yeah, it would." I lied knowing that I would have waited.

"I hope we keep in touch."

When he left on Sunday, I knew I would never forget him; he was the first one who told me I was beautiful.

I went to school through the summer to make up for the withdrawals from first semester. Apathy replaced my enthusiasm about graduation; I studied to consume my time. I knew enough psychology to know idleness was depressing. My senior year was a blur that came and went very quickly.

On a sunny afternoon in May, I walked across the stage to receive my degree and thought about the wisdom seeds. Love, kindness, goodness and peace – I wanted them to bloom in my life. I could see Nana's smile in the sunlight and knew she was watching from Heaven's balcony just as she promised. Looking up as I took my seat, I whispered, 'thank you.'

Nana was gone. A part of me wanted to be in love with Tony, but he was gone, too. School was over and I was headed home. My summer would be spent in Pittsburgh where I would be interning with a research team. I was hoping the experience would help me decide what to do with my psychology degree – I still had no idea. My dad repeatedly expressed his disappointment with my indecisiveness. I would only be home for three weeks and that would be palatable for both of us, I hoped.

Packing the last box in my dorm room, I realized my best memories were from my summers in Wheeling. My degree said Penn State University; however, my life lessons were from Nana. I carefully packed each letter she sent me in the box on top of the love letters she and Pappy shared with each other. I was daydreaming and was startled by Mom standing in the doorway.

"Dani, your father's waiting in the car."

"Here I come."

I put the top on my box of memories and walked out of the room without looking back.

Two

Smithtown, New Jersey is a small family town. You need a detailed map of the Blackhorse Pike to find it. I knew just about everyone and those I didn't know, they knew me. My dad had been the pastor at St. Luke's Baptist Church since I was three. He always said a good shepherd never leaves his flock.

During the sixties and seventies, places like Smithtown flourished with African Americans who welcomed small-town life that mirrored Ward and June Cleaver. There was a town picnic every summer and everyone served Kool-Aid. New homes were being built by successive generations that had come to appreciate the hominess of Smithtown — especially to raise children. Most Central High graduates went to Rutgers, the University of Pennsylvania, Temple or Rowan University. Community and family values were not just slogans or campaign issues, they were truly the way of life.

Growing up in Smithtown seemed scripted. I sang in the choir because my mother wanted me to. Although she has a beautiful voice, she was told that the pastor's wife should teach Sunday school. She vicariously participated in the choir through me. I did all the other PK (Preacher's Kid) things too — I was in Young Life, I went to prayer meeting every Wednesday and I never missed Sunday School or Baptist Training Union. It was expected of me, especially since Joseph and Noah were prodigal sons who hadn't come home.

My oldest brother, Noah, diverted from my dad's number-one son path when he started high school. Being a good basketball player and good-looking led to his swift demise. He was being groomed to be a preacher, but for as long as I could remember, he hated going to church. I remember him taking money out the offering plate, skipping Sunday School and going to the Carvel to spend his offering money. It was almost like he lived each day to be passively obstinate. His obstinance became complete defiance and his passivity turned into overt aggression against the man who had prayed for a son to follow in his footsteps.

By the time Noah was sixteen, he had been kicked off the basketball team, was on probation in school and was hanging out in Atlantic City every weekend. In fact, by that time he never came in from Saturday night until after we left for church. My dad would tell him every Friday that his heart would be defiled if he didn't stop going there. He stopped a year later after he met Tashika. It was 1971, he was seventeen, she was nineteen, had twin girls and her own project apartment in Brooklyn, New York. I always knew he wasn't going to be a preacher — no matter how hard my dad tried to make him one.

My father was in denial and remained convinced for years that Noah would return home seeking his forgiveness and ready to assume his pre-appointed role as the Assistant Pastor of St. Luke's. My mother was an enabler because she didn't know what else to do. She vacillated between blaming herself and blaming my dad, yet always remained partial to her first-born — it was never as bad as my dad made it sound.

My other brother Joseph was a good kid and a good student and the brother could sing. I always loved listening to him and wished he had left a piece of that voice in Mom's womb for me. His voice was naturally engaging; it kept you on the edge of your seat, never wanting him to stop. He sang from his soul, as if he composed each song himself. Joey started a youth choir when he was fourteen years old and even the kids who didn't come to church joined. That choir rocked the church when they sang but my dad complained it was too worldly. Musically, Joey was ahead of his time.

It was Joey's love of all types of music that became the issue between him and my dad. Joey had a sincere dedication to his dream of starring on Broadway. He did all kinds of odd jobs — cutting grass, pulling weeds, walking dogs — to earn money to see a Broadway play. Mom worried about him going to New York, especially when he went alone, but Joey had a plan and a mission. When he was a junior in high school, he informed my parents that he intended to go to Julliard. My dad responded by trying to make Joey feel guilty about liking sacred and secular music. He would remind him daily that secular music was the devil's music.

The following summer, Joey quit directing the youth choir. He took a job at a casino in Atlantic City, hoping to meet a celebrity who would give him a big break. Joey always managed to work on Sunday and avoided having to explain why he couldn't go to church anymore. A week after he graduated from high school, he bought a plane ticket to Los Angeles.

And then there's me. I was motivated to do as I was told by the fear of disappointing my mom, and the need for my dad's approval. Noah's moving in with Tashika and Joey, leaving home with no forwarding address, broke my mom's heart. With two prodigal brothers, I tried to be everything I thought my dad wanted but it was never enough. When I didn't get the solo, he said I didn't try hard enough, and when I got a 'C' in chemistry, he said I didn't work hard enough even though all my other grades were A's and B's. I was crushed when I came in third in the hundred yard dash at the state track and field finals — my dad said I didn't want it badly enough. I was his only daughter, but I could never redeem the legacy of his sons.

Sleep monopolized my first day home, which allowed me to avoid my dad's questions about my future. On day two, my parents, assuming I was asleep, were discussing me in the dining room.

"That girl's going to make you very proud one day," Mom said as I eavesdropped on their conversation from the top of the stairs.

My dad's response was flat. "She needs to be serious about the Lord. Without God there is no true success. God blessed her with a good mind and a good education and she couldn't find time once a week to thank Him."

"You sound like you've given up," was my mom's standard reply. "She does love Jesus."

His reply was sarcastic. "If she loved Him, she would go to church."

Mom came to my defense. "She didn't like any of the churches on campus."

"In four years, she found plenty of parties, attended every football game and couldn't find one church to worship God once a week. I don't think she tried too hard!"

Meet my parents, Reverend David and Judith Allen. My dad was still stewing in his suppressed disappointment about his children, and Mom was still trying to convince him of the good she saw in us.

The Sunday morning humidity seemed to shroud me as I descended the steps. At 7:30 the heat was already hanging in the air like the smell of fried chicken in Nana's kitchen. It was only May and my dad never turned on the air until June first.

"Morning, Mom." I hugged her taking the cup out of her hand. "Good morning, Father." I put the cup down on the sports page hoping he would look at me. "I'm going to church with you guys this morning. I've got a lot to be thankful for and I'd like to personally tell God thank You," I announced hoping to get his undivided attention.

"Tell me, Dani," he asked looking over the newspaper. "What are you so thankful for?"

"I got the internship in Child & Adolescent Psychology at Western Psychiatric Institute in Pittsburgh," I blurted out. "I'll be leaving in three weeks."

Mom got up and hugged me.

My dad moved the cup and picked up the sports section. He never said a word.

"I'm staying with Andrea and Alicia. They don't live far from the University," I added since no one asked.

"You never mentioned any plans to leave. What made you decide to go to Pittsburgh?" Mom asked as she placed her cup in the sink.

"I don't know," I said turning to face her. "It's an opportunity that should open up some doors for my career." I humored myself with that one, as I had no idea of what I wanted to pursue.

Mom tried to smile as she cleared my dad's dishes. Her smile was practiced and her eyes were sad, just as they had been for years. This was one more feather in her unhappy cap. The boys were gone and now I was jumping ship. I promised myself I would make her very proud of me. My dad never looked up or thanked her for clearing his dishes. I wondered if he even noticed her unhappiness. He had not changed, and I was sure church service would be just as I remembered.

The pin stripes in my dad's black suit matched the leather upholstery and he seemed to sit up a little taller.

I sat up between the seats. "Nice car."

"Thank you," my dad stated flatly.

"This is what your father always wanted."

"Seek ye first the Kingdom of God and His righteousness, and all these things shall be added to you," I said hoping to impress him.

My dad looked back at me as he turned the corner. "Matthew 6:33." He never smiled.

We rode the rest of the six blocks in silence. Three weeks, I thought to myself, twenty-one days and counting.

From my usual second seat in the second row, I stared at my dad during the church service as I listened to each hallelujah and amen that could have been scripted into his weekly sermon. I wondered if Reverend Allen would ever really get to know me and love me for who I was. He was good at making everyone at home miserable and I was convinced he was miserable, too. My dad proclaimed himself to be a scholarly preacher and intended to redeem the preacher family line from the shame he felt my grandfather cast upon it.

In one of my psychology classes, I studied people with my dad's profile. He would never accept the fact that his external, narcissistic behavior was in complete conflict to his role as a pastor. It was almost as if my dad was schizophrenic. He was a completely different person at the church. I realized at a very early age that I wanted

Reverend Allen as my dad.

Much of what I knew about David Allen was through the eyes of others. His congregation loved him and saw him as an outstanding member of the community. He remained married to my mom, his only sweetheart. They raised three children who were parented by both of them in an era where blended families were becoming common place. He spearheaded the Big Brother program and hosted their annual picnic in our backyard. In spite of how the community revered him, my dad's heart remained wrenched. Although he had ordained twelve young men from his Big Brother program, he had two sons who walked away from the church.

Mom summed him up by saying he was a very good man who was disappointed about a lot of things in life. "He loves us," Mom told me several times, as if she needed to convince me — and maybe herself.

My life changed forever on a sticky, hot Saturday in June of 1980. I arrived at the Trailways bus station in downtown Pittsburgh at 6:45 p.m. My cousins were wearing sorority tee shirts, like we planned. Andrea wore white jeans with white canvas sneakers that looked new. Her hair was flawlessly curled in spite of the heat. Alicia's hair was pulled back into a ponytail. She looked more like a high school student with her cut-off jeans and green flip-flops. Andrea was taller and Alicia was thinner.

"Danielle Allen," Alicia said hugging me. "You look exactly the same."

"I'll take that as a compliment, but I like this hairstyle better than the Shirley Temple curls." I was a little unsure of who was who, and consciously did not address them by name.

"You look like me," Andrea smiled. "You must favor your dad. I'm Andrea," she said pointing to herself. "I'm the twin that looks like the Allens."

Andrea and Alicia were fraternal twins. I remembered them looking a lot more alike than they did now.

Pittsburgh was much nicer than I had imagined. Its steel-town image of dusty mill clouds was not evident as we drove along Penn Avenue. Bloomfield was the Italian community and Garfield was a picture of urban America. We drove through the business district in East Liberty and turned onto Linden Avenue in Point Breeze. It was a professional community that had once been a statement of prominence for African Americans who were able to move in.

Their street was a one-block cul-de-sac and their house was third from the corner. We pulled into the driveway of their red brick house and after a quick tour of the essentials – bathroom, kitchen, game room – Andrea showed me to the guest room. I decided to unpack later and joined my cousins in the living room.

"There's a PUMP meeting tonight." Alicia threw the flyer onto the coffee table as I sat on the couch.

"What's PUMP?" I asked, reading the acronym Professionally Upward Mobile People.

"It's a nice crowd, business cards are passed, opportunities are made, you know networking kind of stuff," Andrea added.

"And they party a little, too!" Alicia smiled and winked at me. "Just don't go in looking for a man. Keep it social Baby Cuz – you'll have fun."

Even though I was tired from the bus ride and hadn't unpacked, I decided to tag along with them. My social life over the past two years had been dismal and going out didn't seem like such a bad idea.

Gregory Henderson caught my eye as we entered the Student Union. He was a gorgeous hunk of chocolate sculpted into a priceless masterpiece. His tapered haircut and mustache accentuated his cheekbones and his eyes. The short sleeves of his knit shirt cuffed his biceps, and his tailor-made pants showcased his physique.

"Stop staring," Andrea nudged me. "Let me introduce you to some people."

She introduced me to the group of people gathered by the window. William Christopher was in the Doctoral Education program at Duquesne University and his wife, Marcella, was a production engineer; Yvonna Thomas was a theater major at Carnegie Mellon University; Connie Brown owned a chain of child care centers; Dave Jenkins owned a remodeling company; Kim Lewis was an attorney; Jeanette and Victor Gardner owned a chain of hair salons that offered apprenticeships in hair care; Brandon Mitchell was an orthodontist; and Deanna Sanford was a medical student. She never introduced me to the chocolate brother.

I was trying to decide between cranberry juice and apple juice when he came up behind me.

"So you're new too?"

"Does it show?"

"I saw you being overwhelmed with all those introductions."

"So you've met?" Alicia interrupted, joining us at the snack bar.

"Well, not really," I told her. "Hi, I'm Danielle." I extended my hand to him. "And you are?"

"Gregory Henderson." He smiled showing two

rows of perfect teeth.

Before I could respond, Andrea was standing between us.

"Girl, I've been looking for you. I want you to meet someone." She led me by the arm away from Gregory. "Baby Cuz, you're looking a little goo-goo eyed."

"I am not!" I pulled away from her, mindfully trying not to show the attitude I felt coming on.

We stopped outside the double doors in the hallway.

"You are so," she stated with her teeth clenched tightly. "And we told you don't come in here looking for a husband. This is just social."

"I'm trying to be social," I replied being conscious of my voice level. "I just met the brother, his name is Gregory."

"Dani," Andrea turned to face me, "you're from a small town where everybody knows everybody."

"Andrea, I'm not fourteen," I snapped.

"I know." Her tone softened as she put her hand on my shoulder. "I don't want you to get hurt. I don't know this Gregory — he's new here too. Be careful."

One of the women I had just met opened the door and called her. Andrea walked toward the door but stopped and turned to look back at me.

"Please be careful, Cuz."

"I'm not trying to marry the man," I said out loud to myself.

The rest of the evening was spent sipping cranberry juice, smiling and holding superficial conversations with people whose names I couldn't remember. The lights were dim and there were too many people to look for Gregory.

On the way home, Andrea talked about PUMP

being a meat market. My stomach tightened because her comments were indirectly aimed at me.

The alarm clock rang and I thought I was dreaming.

"It's eight o'clock, Dani. Do you want to eat before we leave for Sunday School?" Andrea's voice was bubbly.

"Sunday School?" I mumbled.

"Do you think you're the only one who knows about Sunday School?"

"I haven't been to Sunday School since the twelfth grade," I confessed. "When did you start going to Sunday School?"

She turned up the tape player.

"I don't have anything to wear, I haven't unpacked yet." I tried not to sound like I was whining.

Alicia came out of the bathroom and stood in the doorway. "That's okay, the Lord says come as you are and so did the pastor."

They laughed and I thought about my dad. He demanded we dress meticulously for church on Sunday.

"You can wear something of mine," Alicia added before I could come up with another excuse to stay in bed.

"You'll be blessed by the service," Andrea told me as I headed for the shower. "Our church is a home for everyone who is sick of the foolishness of man interfering with the sacred things of God."

I wasn't sure what she meant and didn't feel like asking her to explain.

I could hear my cousins talking in Andrea's room as I came out of the bathroom. Hard as I was trying to eavesdrop, I couldn't make out what they were saying over the music. Wrapped in a towel, I detoured to the kitchen for a glass of orange juice before heading back to my room. Alicia's brown pants suit was hanging on the door waiting for me.

As we were getting in the car, I tried to hide my disappointment about the pants suit. The pants were tight and the jacket was fitted. It felt too small.

"What about you?" Alicia asked as we pulled out of the driveway. "Where do you stand with Christ? Are you saved?"

"My dad reminds me, every chance he gets, that I need to be more serious about Jesus. I'm not even sure I know what being 'saved' means," I confessed, trying not to sound cynical.

"Stop playing girl!" Alicia turned in her seat to look back at me.

"I'm not playing. I really don't know."

"What?" Alicia responded in disbelief. "Miss Gotta Go To Church at least four days a week, sing in the choir, usher, and do everything else cause I'm the Preacher's Kid."

"Alicia!" Andrea cut her off. "It's okay, Dani. A lot of people don't really know what salvation means. And some might never know because people assume they already know and don't tell them."

Andrea glanced at Alicia several times, seemingly to give some message that Alicia didn't get or was choosing to ignore. Then she continued, looking at me in the rear view mirror as she drove.

"Being saved means accepting Jesus as your Lord and Savior, admitting you are a sinner and you're sorry for those sins. It's believing that Jesus was born of a virgin, died on the cross for your sins and rose after three days. It's believing that God forgives you and has washed you clean with the shedding of Jesus' blood at Calvary." Andrea spoke with sincerity. *"If you confess with your mouth the Lord Jesus and believe in your heart that God raised Him from the dead, thou shall be saved, Romans 10:9,"* she added smiling.

"For God so loved," Alicia began and I finished with her, *"the world that He gave His only begotten Son, that whoever believes in Him should not perish but have everlasting life, John 3:16."*

"Nana taught me that when I was a little girl." I smiled thinking of her and the memory of learning that scripture.

"It's in there," Andrea smiled. "Stop fighting it."

"Girl, being saved is knowing you don't have to do this life thing by yourself." Alicia's tone softened. "It's knowing Jesus is always with you."

We arrived at The Sanctuary and it was huge compared to St. Luke's. I noticed some of the people from the PUMP meeting in the parking lot and scanned the crowd for Gregory. He wasn't there. That was okay, I was wearing Alicia's pants suit and it wasn't something I would have bought, but it matched my shoes.

As the service began I thought about St. Luke's. Mom would be sitting in the second row, aisle seat, left of the pulpit. She would be humming "Blessed Assurance" with her eyes closed. I thought about Nana and closed my eyes to thank her for teaching me scriptures so I didn't feel like a complete dunce. I thought about the previous night and wondered if I would see Gregory again.

The preacher talked about the Lord being our keeper. He read from Psalms 121:5–8:

"The Lord is your keeper; the Lord is your shade at your right hand. The sun shall not strike you by day, nor the moon by night. The Lord shall preserve you from all evil; He shall preserve your soul. The Lord shall preserve your going out and your coming in from this time forth and even forevermore."

Nana used to talk about Jesus being the perfect keeper. I wanted to be kept by Him and decided to take going to church more seriously.

My cousins and I spent the evening trying to get caught up. Alicia was a high school math teacher. Her boyfriend, Dennis, accepted a job in New York in April and she was unsure of where the relationship was going. She admitted she loved him.

Andrea was a high school guidance counselor and was pursing her doctoral degree in Educational Administration. She contacted me during my senior year when she attended a conference at Penn State. The three hours we spent on the phone trying to catch up seemed to pass like minutes and we promised each other we would re-connect. My coming to Pittsburgh gave us the opportunity to get to know each other again. I hadn't seen or talked to my cousins since my Aunt Sharon's funeral twelve years ago. My dad rarely mentioned his brother, Paul, and the last I remembered they were living near the base in Quantico, Virginia.

"It was hard being a teenager without my mother," Alicia said opening a bottle of nail polish. "I used to dream she was still alive."

"It's like a part of you is missing, and no matter what you do you can't get it back." Andrea stopped doing crunches and faced me. "You're so blessed to have your mother."

"You know, like when you went to the prom, the first time your heart was broken," Alicia began.

"And little things like when your bras are too small, when you wanted to use tampons instead of pads, and when you have cramps. My dad didn't understand," Andrea added.

"My mom isn't easy to talk to," I stated flatly.

Alicia seemed puzzled. "What do you mean? From what I remember, your mom is very nice."

"We never really talked about stuff." I answered searching for the right words.

"Why not?" Andrea wanted to know.

"We just never did." I could feel tears welling in my eyes. "I was really close to my grandmother – Ida, my mother's mother."

"There's nothing like a mother." Alicia said, fighting back her own tears. "I really miss mine."

"My parents met at a party at Dartmouth." Andrea intentionally shifted the conversation.

"Oh, I didn't know that."

"She should have been a doctor," Alicia added.

"What happened?"

"Love," Andrea smirked. "Two weeks after she graduated, she married my dad. When he completed his basic training, they moved to Japan where he was stationed for three years."

"What did her parents say?"

"Her parents were killed in a car accident when she was a teenager. She lived with her aunt who was not happy."

Andrea and Alicia spent their summers in Cambridge, Massachusetts with their great aunt, Virginia Baltimore. They had many good memories of their time with her, even though she never liked their dad. It was just like Nana and me; Nana didn't particularly care for my dad either.

I shared with them the four wisdom seeds Nana taught me. They shared with me about dream stealers who doubt you and say your dreams are too big and impossible. The evening was good, but it was also like a spear. I resolved to do better at connecting with my mother. I envisioned that one day she and I would sit and talk and get to know each other, really know each other. I would be able to tell her about my fears and pains and I would ask about hers. One day, I hoped, we would share ourselves with each other.

My first day at work was exciting and intimidating. Equipped with my Bachelor of Science degree in Psychology, I thought I was ready to take on the world. My first week was a reality check that there were many things I needed to learn. The stories some of the women told were incredible. Years of abuse and neglect, poor choices, drug dealing boyfriends, herpes, venereal diseases, broken noses and ribs — and I thought I had it bad growing up with my dad. By the end of my first week, nothing shocked me, not even the multiple partnerships in which some of the women delighted in knowing their children would be siblings by the same father.

As a Research Associate in the Department of Epidemiology, I was assigned to a team that assessed pregnancy outcomes and infant bonding with substance-abusing women. The number of women who were eligible for the program was overwhelming and we always maintained a waiting list. A major incentive for the participants was the positive recommendation to Child Welfare for all women who abstained from using drugs during their pregnancy. We also paid five dollars for completing each questionnaire and those who completed four questionnaires were given a fifty-dollar certificate to The Kid Store and a basket filled with layette items.

My workday was exhausting and I was glad Andrea was taking classes at the University of Pittsburgh over the summer. The obstetrical clinic was on the far side of campus and each evening Andrea and I met in front of the campus library to ride home together. Alicia usually had dinner waiting and hurried us as we came in the door. We held hands to bless our food and discussed the daily devotional. Andrea said it was good to discuss positive things over dinner because complaining about the day only gave you indigestion. Spending time with my cousins made me wish I had sisters. I had never thought about that before and, in fact, had often wished I was an only child.

"How's your dad?" I asked one day after dinner.

"He says he loves France. It's where he and my mother planned to live after he retired," Alicia shrugged. "He calls for birthdays and Christmas. We haven't seen him since we graduated from Hampton."

"I keep praying for him," Andrea said. "He's very misguided about who Jesus is. My dad thinks everyone is like Grandpa Tim."

"I thought my dad was the only one who didn't get along with Grandpa Tim."

"Girl, let me tell you," Alicia piped in with excitement.

"What?" She had my full attention.

Alicia sat up in her chair. Andrea sighed and began clearing the dinner dishes.

"Now this is the story my dad tells." Alicia rested

her elbows on the table. "Your dad was the favorite grandchild and always wanted to be a preacher like our great-grandfather, William Allen. When your dad was about eight, he asked to go live with our great-grandparents and Grandpa Tim had a fit. After that, Grandpa Tim wouldn't let Grandma Rita take our dads and Uncle Matt to visit them anymore. Our great-grandfather died a year later of a massive heart attack. Your dad grew up believing that our great-grandfather died of a broken heart because his only child, Grandpa Tim, was the prodigal son who had no interest in finding his way home." Alicia sat back in her chair and took a deep breath. "Girl, ain't that a mess?"

"Yeah," I shook my head. "I had no idea."

"Girl, there's more." She smiled like she was about to tell a secret and yelled into the kitchen. "Hey Annie, would you make some iced tea?" Alicia scooted her chair back a little. "Our great-grandmother, Louise Allen, never acknowledged Grandpa Tim at the funeral except to deny his request to speak. Grandpa Tim was infuriated and refused to stay for the family dinner. Great-grandmother's final words to her son were, 'Let the children stay. They're here to mourn their loving grandfather — a good man.' Grandpa Tim turned to walk away and everyone followed except your dad. He never looked up at them, but held tightly to his grandmother's hand. Grandpa Tim left Emmanuel Baptist Church and returned to the Bronx fifteen years later to bury his mother."

"Oh Alicia!" Andrea rolled her eyes before putting the glasses of iced tea on the table. "The rest is just family gossip." She stood behind Alicia with her hand on her hip.

I was on the edge of my seat. "What happened?"

Alicia crossed her legs, letting her right foot swing. "My dad was a PK Player."

"Until this girl he really liked turned up pregnant and said my dad was the father," Andrea finished sarcastically. "Grandpa Tim wanted my dad to marry her, but he knew the baby wasn't his."

"What? Get outta here!" My mind was working hard to process this family history.

"It was a life lesson for my dad and it took years for him to admit that his behavior was merely attention seeking." Andrea seemed sympathetic.

Alicia sipped her tea. "Girl, remember Uncle Matt?"

"Alicia!" Andrea's tone was chastising.

"She needs to know." Alicia was flippant with Andrea.

"My dad never speaks of him unless he's talking about damnation," I stated finally having information to add.

"Girl you know he started spending his summers touring the country with some gospel group when he was sixteen. My dad said about a year later, he became secretive and distant."

"Actually," Andrea added, "my dad always said Uncle Matt had a lot of unresolved issues."

"I haven't seen him since I was about seven," I added, still feeling the need to share some family history. "He came to visit us and my dad wouldn't let him play the piano in church. He never came back. I don't even see Grandpa Tim and Grandma Rita that often even though they live in New York."

Alicia continued her saga defining our grandmother, Mrs. Rita Allen, as the best-dressed woman in the church. Grandma Rita strategically removed herself from the gossip about her husband by becoming a social-ite who supported every well-known community cause. Alicia said that our grandmother defined pretentious and, in her quest for fashion fame, she emotionally neglected her children.

Andrea joined in the conversation and relayed how Grandpa Tim made Matthew the minister of music when he was only fourteen years old. It wasn't long before music became Matthew's god. There was nothing more important to him than being able to bring people to their feet with his music. The gospel message in the music became secondary to the emotionalism. Andrea said Uncle Matt had been chasing fame and fortune for most his life. She said her dad refers to Matthew as a gifted musician who can make a piano talk.

Alicia concluded the family history lesson with how her father, Paul, swore that he would never be in-volved in any type of organized religion because it was just a game. Her dad credited his success to being a good person and treating people with respect.

I knew my dad believed his father, Grandpa Tim, was a product of his era, the result of too much liberalism invading the church and too many hustlers hiding behind the cross. Although Grandpa Tim says he is a preacher, my dad maintains that it wasn't God who called him. To my dad, Grandpa Tim was nothing more than an embarrassment while he was growing up. I also knew my dad blamed Grandpa Tim for his brother Paul leaving the church and his brother Matthew not having a true understanding of being a Christian.

What I learned from this family history lesson was that my dad had been just as stoic with his parents as he had been with us. He spent most of his youth at the Peace, Love and Joy Fellowship trying to prove to his father, the community and himself that he would not be a part of the pseudo-religious madness Grandpa Tim created. Just like my brothers, my dad was estranged from his family.

Each day I realized how much I missed not growing up with my cousins. We were family and we were a lot alike. Our fathers had let their anger keep us apart and we made a vow to always be there for each other — no matter what. It felt good to know I had them to lean on. I let myself imagine a family reunion where everyone got to know each other. Pipe dreams.

Three

The PUMP flyer was on the kitchen counter. I hadn't thought about Gregory for a week, but the notice triggered images of those perfect white teeth set precisely in the deep chocolate of his face. Maybe he would attend the meeting, maybe I would see him again, and maybe we could get to know each other.

My heart sank when Andrea said she had to finish a paper and couldn't go to the PUMP meeting. My hope was renewed, however, when Alicia told me she was meeting some of her sorority sisters there.

As we were getting out of the car that voice greeted me. "Well hello stranger."

"Hello stranger to you, too," I said, trying not to sound excited as Greg walked over to us.

"I was hoping you'd be here tonight." His smile was perfect.

Alicia cleared her throat.

"Gregory, this is my cousin Alicia," I said introducing them.

"Call me Greg — Gregory is so formal." He shook Alicia's hand, keeping his eyes on me.

Alicia smiled at him and turned to me. "Meet me at the double doors at one o'clock." She walked ahead of us and turned to look at me again after she crossed Fifth Avenue.

"Where've you been hiding?" Greg asked as we took our time walking to the Student Union.

"Around, working, getting acclimated."

"Is that all?" His voice was deep and sexy.

"That's it," I shrugged.

"Sounds exciting."

I smiled realizing his closeness made me nervous. "I looked for you at The Sanctuary on Sunday."

He held the door for me. We found two seats in the lobby.

"Church?" he smirked. "Haven't been since Mother's Day — but I had to work. I'm on every Sunday."

"On? What do you do?"

"Stock shelves at the Giant Eagle," he stated with a straight face.

"Stock shelves?"

"I'm just kidding," he began to laugh. "I'm a resident at Children's Hospital."

My response should have been sarcastic, but my nervousness would only let me smile.

He took my hand. "You believed me."

"No I didn't." I couldn't stop smiling.

Greg was staring at me and then asked, "What about you? What brings you here?"

"I'm interning at Western Psych."

"Interesting. What department?" He played with my fingers as we talked.

"Epidemiology," I stated matter-of-factly.

"Sounds different — I can tell that's your MO. You're different, that's what I like about you."

"You don't even know me," I responded trying to maintain my composure, but his hand was warm and his presence engulfing.

Greg kissed my hand. "I'd like to."

It was a line and I knew it. I didn't care, he was absolutely gorgeous. Greg noticed everything about me — my earrings, my shoes, he made me laugh — and that made me feel special. Hard as I tried to dominate some of our conversation, he only wanted to talk about me.

Greg gently pulled me to my feet and we followed

the music down the hall to the PUMP meeting.

"Where are you from?" he asked, holding the door open and smiling at me.

I responded without looking at him, "Smithtown."

"Who?"

"Smithtown, New Jersey. Don't tell me you've never heard of it," I teased, feeling a little relaxed.

"Never heard of it. I confess."

We found a table by the door and sat down across from each other.

"How many boyfriends are waiting for you to come home?"

"I don't have any love stories about a high school sweetheart waiting for me to return home. There were only two kinds of boys in Smithtown — the ones who wanted to say they were first and the ones who were afraid of my dad."

"Is your dad the sheriff?"

"He's in charge of everybody's soul — he's the pastor."

"So you're a church girl?"

"What's that supposed to mean?"

"No offense," he said laughing. "I'm just trying to get the playing rules straight."

"What are we supposed to be playing?"

"Come on now, don't get serious on me."

"You haven't answered the question."

Greg reached across the table and took my hand. "No games. I can tell by your smile we might be able to have something good."

His flattery made me blush. We left the party and went for a walk around the Cathedral of Learning.

Alicia and I were in the car going home when I

realized I didn't know much about Greg.

"I didn't see you all night," Alicia stated with raised eyebrows.

"Greg and I went for a walk."

"So what's his story?"

"He's a resident at Children's Hospital. He's from Harrisburg." I recalled the only two things I knew about him.

Although Greg and I exchanged numbers, I waited to see how long it would take him to call. He called the next day and invited me to a movie that evening. That was the beginning of seeing Greg regularly. We talked on the phone almost every day and went out three or four times a week, when his schedule permitted.

"I'd like to meet your family," I announced on our way to dinner three weeks later.

His tone flattened. "That's not a good idea."

I was confused by his response. "Why?"

"I'm not ready for you to meet them!"

"What does that mean?"

"It means," his tone became even more direct, "when I'm ready for you to meet them, I'll let you know."

His tone made me angry and I pressed him. "Well, when will that be?"

He never answered or looked at me. We rode to the restaurant in silence.

"Dani, it's complicated." His tone was apologetic as we turned into the Red Lobster parking lot.

Sitting with my arms crossed and staring out the window, I remained silent.

Greg parked in the back of the lot, then he took my hand and kissed it gently. "I never know what's

going on at home. My little brother is a gangster wan-
nabe who's always got trouble with him — he's either in
jail or working his way back. Police, gang bangers, ghetto
girls, drug dealers — you never know who's looking for
him and who's at the door."

"I'm so sorry," I said, regretting my anger.

"My mother cries a lot and my father drinks a
lot," he continued. "My sister Jackie moved to California
when she was eighteen, said she couldn't take it anymore. Gwen had her first baby when she was fourteen,
she now has three kids and she's only twenty. I do the
best I can."

Holding back tears, I squeezed his hand. I understood family dysfunction very well.

"I'm sorry." He smiled and softly kissed my cheek.
"This was no way to start our date."

"We don't have to stay," I told him

"Are you sure? I did promise you dinner."

"I'll be okay, will you?"

"Be better if you'd come by my place for a while."

Greg lived a few blocks from Carnegie Mellon University in a one-bedroom apartment on Forbes Avenue.
There were flyers from several pizza places posted over
the mailboxes. The wood banister to the second floor had
been preserved and was the only reminder that this had
once been a single-family house. He lived in apartment
three.

Greg confessed to being a fan of Richard
Roundtree and we settled on the couch with *Shaft*, iced
tea and chipped ham sandwiches. By the middle of the
movie, we were snuggled on the couch. I was holding
Greg's left hand to keep it out of my shirt and his right
arm was wrapped tightly around my waist. I could feel

his heart beating. His body was warm and it felt good being so close to him.

When I turned to smile at him, he kissed me. First lightly on my lips and then he was kissing me down my neck. I melted at his touch and then he was on top of me. His warm hands were on my back, pulling me closer to him.

"Stop!" I pushed him away and scooted back so I could sit up. He felt good, but I didn't want to lead him on.

"No pressure," he smiled. "That's not why you're here."

He kept his hands to himself for the rest of the movie and then drove me home. Standing at the door, he whispered in my ear, "I had a great time. Can we do this again?" Then he kissed my forehead.

I smiled, knowing I would see him again and again and again.

Our dates typically began with dinner or going to the mall and seemed to always end up in his apartment. I was so comfortable with him. Five weeks into the relationship, on a balmy Friday night at the end of July – too humid for the drive-in and too late to go anywhere else – we were lying on the couch in front of the fan watching my favorite movie, *Love Story*. Everything in me shouted warning signs that I was putting myself in a compromised position. I foolishly convinced myself that I could say no but then I didn't want to say no and I didn't want him to stop. While the movie played to the living room furniture, we played house in the bedroom.

My feelings frightened me, but being with Greg like this was new and different and exciting. My parents would kill me if they found out. Nana had told me that my special gift was only to be shared with my husband. "No other man should ever know you intimately." I could hear her voice and see that serious expression on her face. "I could marry Greg," I thought to myself, "I think I love him."

It was almost noon when I rolled over to the whispers of my cousins talking in the other room. Then the front door closed and I heard the car start. Assuming they were gone, I decided to get up.

"Late night?" Andrea asked in a maternal tone as I came out of the kitchen.

"Yeah."

"I heard you in the shower this morning."

I didn't respond.

"Dani, what do you really know about Greg?" The pitch in Andrea's voice escalated. "Rumor has it he's married."

"He's not married," I disputed. "He doesn't wear a wedding ring and there are no pictures of anyone in his apartment. And if he's married, where is his wife?" I stated in defense of his reputation.

"Dani, I just don't want you to get hurt," Andrea said, following me back to the bedroom and over annunciating her words. "First, you start spending all you time with him, when he's available, and now you're sleeping with him. You're better than that."

"He has a crazy schedule. I told you he's a resident."

"Do you love him?" Andrea asked point blank.

"Yes," I answered confidently, even though I wasn't sure.

"Does he love you?"

"Yes."

"Enough to marry you?"

"We never talked about it." I felt like I was being interrogated.

"Well if you're having sex," she stated sarcastically.

"Making love," I corrected her.

"Having sexual intercourse outside the bonds of marriage," Andrea continued, "then you should get married. If it's that real, make it right before God."

"You sound like my dad." I plopped down on the bed, burying my face in the pillow. I knew Andrea was right.

I was starving but my efforts to avoid conversation with Andrea kept me in my room. Guilt began to set in and regret began to pollute my memory of the previous night.

Greg called later that afternoon – he wanted to go to the movies after his shift. I didn't care about seeing a movie, I needed to talk to him and tried not to let my anxiety show in my voice.

It was almost nine o'clock when Greg picked me up. "You're glowing," he told me as I got in the car.

My bottom lip began to quiver. "We need to talk."

"What's the matter?"

I began to cry. I was confused and angry with myself.

"Hey, hey, hey." Greg pulled over and came around to my side of the car. He opened the door, knelt down and took my hand. "What's the matter? What happened?"

"I'm not that type of person. I don't sleep around."

He wiped my tears. "This is real girl. I love you."

"Really?" I asked, needing to be sure.

"Yes, really," he smiled. "I love you."

"Do you love me enough to marry me?"

"Yes." He bit his lower lip. "When the time is right. I need to get through my residency before I start planning the rest of my life." Greg stood, pulling me to my feet and into his arms.

"I love you," I said with my face buried in his chest. I never wanted him to let me go.

My relationship with Greg intensified and I was going to his apartment after work almost every day. I started leaving clothes at his place so that I could shower and change before going home. Andrea seemed to always know. No matter how hard I tried to convince her that I knew what I was doing, she was adamant that I was going to get hurt. It became a source of contention between us, and she made it very clear she did not approve at all.

Alicia refused to discuss Greg. "Sometimes when people that love you are trying to tell you something for your own good, you need to listen," she said standing in my doorway one morning after one of my many late nights. "Everything that looks good is not good for you. Too much chocolate will rot your teeth." She walked away and I heard her bedroom door close.

Alicia was leaving for New York to see Dennis. As far as I was concerned, she had no room to talk. I knew she would be staying with Dennis and assumed she was sleeping with him, too. She loved Dennis, I loved Greg.

Greg was on call the following Friday and I didn't have anything to do – Andrea was meeting with her study group, Alicia wasn't coming home until Saturday and I hadn't made any other friends because I never socialized with my co-workers outside of the clinic. Andrea frequently pointed out that Greg monopolized my time, but I was in love and I was happy. However, realizing that I had not spent much time with my cousins over the past few weeks, I made plans to spend Sunday with them.

"Let's go to dinner," I announced in the car on our way to church. "My treat."

"Sounds good to me," Alicia smiled. "Can I suggest the Southern Platter?"

"Yeah," I told her. "That does sound good."

Andrea continued to drive. Alicia turned and winked at me.

"Annie," Alicia poked her in the arm, "don't you want to come?"

"Yeah, I'll come," she said with a straight face. "The Sunday School teachers have a short meeting after church. I should be done by two o'clock."

"We'll wait," Alicia told her. "You're driving!"

Mom sent me a picture of the three of us that Uncle Paul had taken during the summer of 1969 on the beach in Atlantic City. I had the picture copied and framed to present to my cousins as a small token of appreciation.

"This is for you," I said tearing the paper off the picture after we ate.

"Where did you get that?" Alicia asked.

"My mom sent me the picture in one of her letters. I thought it was cute and wanted you guys to have a copy."

"Thank you," they said in unison.

"I really appreciate your letting me stay here," I told them. "I had a great summer."

"Would it have still been great without Greg?"

Andrea smirked with a raised eyebrow.

"Yeah."

"Well, what about Greg?" Alicia asked.

"What do you mean?"

"What's up with the relationship now that you're going home?"

"I know how to get to Harrisburg," I smiled. "He's trying to get a job at the Hershey Medical Center. He wants to stay near his parents so he can help them."

"He's so perfect," Andrea stated sarcastically.

Alicia changed the subject to their upcoming vacation. She and Andrea were going on a seven-day cruise to the Grand Cayman Islands the week after I left.

August had come too quickly and my internship was ending. I hadn't applied to any graduate programs before leaving Penn State, and it became necessary to make some decisions about what I was going to do next. I was sure of my love for Greg, and decided to wait until he found a job before applying to graduate school. In my mind, our wedding was imminent. My boss was applying for another grant to support additional staff and said she would be pleased to have me on her team. I promised to keep in touch with her — it was something to fall back on if Greg stayed in Pittsburgh.

Greg was interviewing in Harrisburg and I was selfishly disappointed. He promised to come back on Tuesday so we could spend the rest of the week together, but Greg called Tuesday night apologizing for feeling torn between coming back to see me and spending a few days with his parents. We made dinner plans for Thursday — that was the last day of my internship and we planned to meet when I got off work at four-thirty.

I was feeling a little tired and had every intention of going home after dinner. When we left Red Lobster, Greg drove to his apartment. He said he needed to feel me in his arms before I left. Although I didn't feel like it, it seemed like the natural order of things.

"I'm going to miss you," he said as I lay snuggled against him. "Fourteen days until I meet Reverend Allen." He paused and coyly asked, "Will I measure up?"

"I'm sure Mom will like you."

Greg changed the subject, "Let's savor these moments."

He pulled me closer to him and I slept wrapped in his love. The next morning I woke up in his arms.

Andrea was making coffee when I came in the door at seven o'clock on Friday morning. She shook her head but didn't say a word. Alicia was sitting in the dining room, and didn't say anything either. There was no need trying to rationalize my decision to spend the night with Greg – I knew they wouldn't understand because they didn't believe he loved me.

I went to my room and couldn't decide what to do next. I needed to pack my clothes because my bus was leaving at nine the next morning. I also needed something to wear to the luncheon reception for the interns at noon. I set the alarm clock for ten-thirty and stretched out across the bottom of my bed – packing would have to wait.

I missed the morning bus and it was one-thirty before I left Pittsburgh. Alicia agreed I might be coming down with a summer flu, Andrea thought my body was sleep deprived. My headache wouldn't let me dispute her, and I didn't want to leave on a bad note, so I let her fuss as she drove down Penn Avenue. We promised to write, call and visit, and then we took pictures in the booth in the bus station. I thanked my cousins again and hugged them before boarding the bus.

Thoughts of Greg consumed me on the bus ride home. Love had never been real before him. Mrs. Gregory Henderson, I thought to myself — the doctor's wife. There was no doubt of our love. Mom had no idea of the seriousness of our relationship, but it would be apparent in Greg's eyes when he looked at me. Nana would have been disappointed that I gave myself to Greg before marriage; still I believed she was happy for me. I thanked her for the wisdom seeds — love, kindness, goodness and peace — they were all mine. One day Greg and I would be writing love letters to each other on Valentine's Day just like Nana and Grandpa Booker. I would share the letters with my daughters and granddaughters just like Nana shared her letters with me. My eyes were closed and I smiled at the thought of being in love. I woke up as the bus pulled into the station in Camden.

Mom was leaning on the hood of my dad's Benz reading an *Ebony* magazine. Her hair was pulled back into a French roll and the orange of the evening sun highlighted her yellow linen dress. She looked up and smiled as I got off the bus. My mom was classy and looked like a model posing for a photographer.

Mom wanted to talk in the car but I needed to put my head back and close my eyes. I had chills and could tell I was coming down with something. Mom sang a medley of hymns as we rode back to the house.

The aroma of my mother's honey barbeque sauce greeted me as I came in the back door, but the hoagie

I had eaten on the bus was bubbling in my stomach. It took everything in me to make it upstairs to the bathroom. After spending twenty minutes with my face in the toilet, Mom came to the door with a glass of warm ginger ale.

"Get those nasty clothes off before you get in the bed." Mom's disdain for street clothes on the bed overshadowed her sympathy.

"Mom," I whined getting up off the bathroom floor, "please let me lay down for ten minutes."

"I'll make you some tea. You need to get out of those clothes; you don't know who sat in that seat on the bus before you. And you'll feel better in a clean nightshirt."

There was no need trying to persuade her. No street clothes on the bed had been a long-standing rule in the Allen home. I put on a tee shirt and collapsed onto my bed. When I woke up it was after midnight – I called Greg anyway. There was no answer. I assumed he was still at work.

On Wednesday, I was still unable to keep food in my stomach, and Mom suggested an appointment with our family physician. Dr. Morant suspected I was pregnant and I reluctantly consented to an internal exam. Greg was careful to use protection, except the first time. Dr. Morant smiled and said congratulations – I was horrified. My twenty-minute exam turned into a ninety-minute visit. I left the office with a prescription for prenatal vitamins and the names of three OB-GYNs. I was glad I borrowed Mom's car and she hadn't come with me.

Unsure of what to say to my mother, I drove down to Atlantic City and sat on the beach until the sun set. Greg would have to marry me. We would struggle, but we would make it. I could begin graduate school when the baby was about two. This was workable.

There was a message from Greg when I got home. His schedule had been switched and he wasn't able to come to Smithtown the following weekend, but wanted to know if I would come to Pittsburgh for a few days. I returned the call and said I would. He asked me to stay with him and not let my cousins know I was in town – I agreed. My heart fluttered thinking that Greg knew I was pregnant via some type of paternal intuition. I found moments of solace assuming we would spend our visit planning an October wedding. As there would be no time to get a dress made, I resigned myself to buying one. Greg would have to make time to come to Smithtown so we could tell my parents of our plans.

The chirping of the birds in the tree outside my window greeted me on Thursday as I kicked the sheet off of me. Although it was a humid morning, there was a slight breeze that made the window sheers dance. I heard my dad's car drive away and met Mom in the kitchen.

She poured water in a teacup as I sat on the stool behind the counter.

"Good morning. Do you feel any better?"

"A little." I avoided eye contact and played with the sugar bowl.

"What did Dr. Morant say?"

"It's nothing to worry about," I answered before changing the subject. "I'm going back to Pittsburgh."

"Why? You're still not feeling well. I can see it in your eyes."

"My boss from the internship program may have a full-time position for me," I lied. "I need to meet with her next Friday."

"How long will you be gone?"

"Probably until Sunday."

Before I could get out of the kitchen she asked, "Who's Greg? Will you be seeing him while you're in Pittsburgh?"

I tried to sound nonchalant. "I think I can fit him in."

"If he misses you so much, why hasn't he come to visit?"

"He's a resident at Children's Hospital. His schedule is crazy."

"A doctor — you never mentioned him. Will we be meeting him any time soon?"

Mom was unusually persistent. I could feel myself blushing.

"Of course, Mom."

"Seems to be serious. Is it love?"

"Yeah, I really think so."

Mom looked at me over her glasses. "Just remember, Dr. Morant is your doctor."

I felt transparent — it was as if she knew.

Out of guilt I took the bus to the Greyhound station in Camden. I had lied to my mother and, on top of that, anticipated the five-hour bus ride making me nauseous.

Greg met me at the bus station and I cried when he hugged me.

"It hasn't been that long," he teased.

Not wanting to discuss being pregnant in the bus station, I tried to smile.

"What's the matter?" Greg asked when we got in the car. "I thought you'd be happy to see me."

I answered without looking at him, "I'm pregnant."

We rode in silence to his apartment. He never looked at me and intentionally fumbled with his keys while we walked up the steps to his apartment. He opened the door and set my bag down. I proceeded to the couch and sat on the arm. I needed Greg to hold me, but he sat at the other end looking out the window.

"What are we going to do?" I emphasized the word *we*.

He continued to stare out the window.

"I can't have a baby by myself Greg. I'm scared. My dad is going to kill me." I could feel myself rambling.

"Dani, this complicates everything," he said slowly. "It's a big step — a major commitment."

"A major commitment?" I snapped, jumping up off the couch and standing in front of him. "What about me being pregnant? Is it more major than that?"

Greg got up from the couch and stood facing me. Expressionless and void of compassion, he mechanically stated, "I can't marry you."

"Why? What's the matter? I love you! I thought you loved me?"

He put his head down, took a deep breath and put his hands in his pockets. Sweat was dripping off his forehead. Looking at the floor, he whispered, "I do love you, it's just complicated."

"What do you mean complicated? Being pregnant without a husband is complicated!" I could hear myself yelling.

"I already have a wife. We were going to get an annulment — then she got pregnant."

Greg spoke without taking a breath, almost as if he were reciting a memorized passage. His words left me dumbfounded.

"We can take care of this tomorrow." He spoke

with an air of cockiness.

The air in the room thinned out and I felt like I was suffocating. I had to get out of his apartment and walked toward the door.

"Dani, we need to talk about this. I fell in love with you. I am in love with you. This is not something I anticipated. Not right now."

He had a list of pathetic excuses. His voice was no longer recognizable, it became an annoying drone. With nothing left to say, I picked up my bag and reached for the doorknob. I don't know how far I walked. I stopped at a phone booth on Forbes Avenue and called Alicia. I'm not sure how she understood what I was saying, but she came to get me. I told her everything on the way to the house. We sat on the couch and she held me while I cried. Then I put my head back and went to sleep.

"Dani," Andrea was shaking me, "we need to talk."

Alicia was on the floor doing sit-ups. Her weak smile let me know she had already told Andrea what happened.

I sat up next to Andrea. "You were right." I buried my face in my hands and began to cry. "He's married. He has a wife and we're both pregnant."

"We need to pray." Andrea motioned Alicia to join us. "Lord, we need you right now. Danielle needs You in her life. Touch her heart; let her feel your presence. Touch her mind, give her peace. Lord, help me to know how to help her."

While Andrea prayed, I thought about Nana — the wisdom seeds were choking on the weeds of my stupidity and withering in the heat of deception.

"I don't know what to do," I said still holding their hands. "He wants me to have an abortion. Can you believe that?"

Alicia gently squeezed my hand and spoke softly. "There's always adoption."

"I can't give my baby away." I started to cry again. "I feel so stupid."

The guest room was a reminder that Andrea was right. She was too gracious to say I told you so and I regretted not listening to her. Guilt and embarrassment kept me awake until almost two o'clock, and the first time I made love to Greg played over and over in my thoughts. Love wasn't supposed to hurt.

I pretended to be sleeping until after my cousins left the next morning. It was almost noon before I got out of bed with my mind still racing and a migraine looming in my left temple.

As I let myself sink down in the tub, I hummed Nana's favorite song. I began to cry, again – Nana probably wasn't smiling. My tears were not growing me, they were drowning me. Do not be unequally yoked. Nana told me that when I was eighteen years old. Not all people are good, even though they might look nice on the outside. She described Greg without ever having met him.

After the bubbles started melting, I wrapped myself in Andrea's robe and detoured to the kitchen to turn on the tea kettle.

The August sun was bright so I closed the blinds. How could I be pregnant? What was I going to do? Why did I fall in love with a married man? Stupid, that's what I was, just plain dumb stupid. I didn't deserve to be anyone's mother.

The phone interrupted my mental pity party. It was Alicia.

"Hey girl, feeling better?"

"Yeah," I lied. "I'm okay — just fighting a head-ache."

"Dani, we're here for you. Whatever we can do, really."

"I know." I took a deep breath. "It's appreciated."

After drinking my tea, I decided to get dressed and make dinner to give my mind something else to think about. The blue jean outfit made me sick. Greg bought it because he liked the way it looked on me. I wished I had something else to put on.

Getting dressed proved to be overwhelming and I was taken hostage on the couch by my headache.

"Dani!" Alicia was shaking me and her voice was panicked.

"What?" She startled me because I hadn't heard her come in.

"What are you doing? You got three bottles of pills on the sink, you're here in the dark, blinds closed, lights off — did you take any of those pills? Girl, get up!"

The shrill in her voice became more piercing with each question.

"I'm up." I interrupted her. "And no, I did not take any of those pills. I was looking for something to take for my headache and decided to sleep it off. The sun was too bright. I closed the blinds so I could sleep."

Alicia had one hand on her hip and massaged her temples with the other one. "You're probably hungry. Did you eat today?"

"No."

Alicia sighed, took a deep breath and then joined me on the couch.

"Get dressed," she said without looking at me.

"We're meeting Andrea for dinner."

The best way to tell my parents about the pregnancy dominated our dinner conversation. Mom would be hurt, Dad would be angry. There was no good way to tell either of them, and I admitted being afraid my dad would put me out. My cousins agreed he would be furious, but were confident my mom would never let that happen.

The thought of loving Greg made me sicker than the thought of telling my parents. Greg lied and probably never loved me. It was a game and he won. I got tagged and I was out. He could say he was first.

Four

After I returned from Pittsburgh with my secret, I busied myself job hunting in Atlantic City, Camden and Philly. I had a collection of applications from psychiatric departments and social service agencies – both of which I felt I had a need for. Fatigue made sleeping difficult and the fear of telling my parents consumed me. Two weeks later, I forced myself to go downtown to complete an application at the Community Health Center. The classified ad listed the position as an entry level Case Manager. Although I didn't feel capable of helping anyone, I desperately needed a job.

The heat had taken a temporary hiatus and the weather was a welcomed eighty degrees. I got off the bus and walked down Fourth Avenue. As I turned left onto Main Street, I heard a voice calling me.

"Danielle Allen." It was Rhonda Porter.

"Hey, how are you?" I hadn't seen her since we graduated from high school.

"Good," she said hugging me. "What's going on? How was Penn State?"

"Had a good time. What about you? How was Rutgers?"

"I got what I went for – it was alright." She never paused. "I'm surprised to see you; I heard you were in Pittsburgh."

"Just an internship," I answered, hoping there were no more questions. "What's up with you?"

Her excitement was obvious. "I'll be opening my own pre-school next month. The renovations are almost done, I'm so excited!"

"That's great, Rhonda, congratulations." I hugged her.

"I just put an ad in the paper for two teachers and an administrative assistant," she told me. "Are you looking?"

"I'm pounding the pavement," I sighed. "Haven't decided what I want to do as far as grad school."

"Girl, you were an honor student and editor of our yearbook — I know you're organized. If you want the administrative assistant position, you got it."

"I don't know much about preschool, but I was an administrative assistant in the Dean's office during my freshman year at Penn State."

"I can't pay much," Rhonda smiled, "but it will be a little something until you decide what you're going to do."

Rhonda and I talked for almost an hour before exchanging numbers and promises to call.

Riding home on the bus, I decided to take Rhonda's offer. At least I wouldn't have to continue looking for a job.

Mom was sitting on the porch.

"Hi baby," she greeted me as I walked up the driveway.

"Hi Mom." I nervously smiled.

"Come, sit with me." She motioned for me to join her on the swing. "You've been distant since you came back from Pittsburgh. What's the matter? What happened with your interview?"

It was a beautiful sunny afternoon and the trees shaded the front porch. Mom was drinking lemonade. She put her glass on the windowsill as I sat down.

"I'm pregnant," I blurted out, burying my face in my hands.

Mom didn't say a word. She held me and let me

cry.

"I'm sorry," I said wiping my eyes with a napkin. "I didn't mean for this to happen."

"Who is he Dani? Your boyfriend Greg?"

"He told me he loved me. We spent the summer together. When I went back to tell him I was pregnant, he told me he was married."

"Oh, mercy Jesus!" Mom was momentarily speechless. She stopped swinging and she stopped stroking my hair. "He's married?! Where was, I mean did you know he had a wife?"

I sat up and shook my head no.

Mom turned my face towards hers. "Is he going to help you with the baby?"

"He wants me to have an abortion," I answered through tears. Then I whispered, "His wife is pregnant, too."

"Lord, Lord, Lord, Lord, Lord," was all she said. Then she contemplated for a moment. "Your father is going to have a fit."

"Do you think he'll put me out?"

"Oh, no!" Mom's tone was adamant. "You're going to need my help with the baby." She hugged me and for that moment I felt secure.

Another week passed and Mom continued to remind me that I needed to tell my dad. I role-played scenarios — there was no good way to do it.

When we returned from church on Sunday, I let him settle in the recliner with the paper. Mom was preparing salmon steaks, his favorite, but my news was going to ruin his appetite.

"Daddy, can I talk to you?" I asked, feeling like he could see me through the crossword puzzle.

He sat up in the recliner and folded the paper. "What is it Danielle?"

"I'm pregnant," I said, squinting as if the words hurt.

"So you need to be married." His tone was matter-of-fact. "Who's the father? I will speak with his parents about having the wedding next month."

I plopped down on the couch wishing I could disappear behind the pillows.

"Who is it Danielle?" His voice was now demanding. "Is it Quincy Jordan?"

"No," I quickly told him. "It's nobody you know."

"Then who is it?"

"His name is Greg. Dr. Gregory Henderson."

"Well, I need his phone number. I will handle this with his parents."

I hesitated and then whispered, "He's married."

"He's what?" My dad threw the paper down and began to yell. "Married! You mean to tell me you're pregnant by a married man? Is that what you were doing in Pittsburgh?"

"He told me he loved me," I tried to explain. "He never said he was married."

My dad got up from his chair and kicked the paper, wildly scattering the pages across the floor as he walked to the couch and stood over me.

"You weren't raised like that," he snarled between clenched teeth. "You kids get a mind of your own refusing to go to church, loving the worldly pleasures and allowing sin to reign in your life. I raised all of you to love God!"

"You chased us away from God because we didn't fit into your perfect mold!"

My dad's veins protruded from his temple and his

neck, and I felt like he wanted to hit me.

He turned and walked toward the stairs, "You all turned away from God."

"You turned away from us," I retaliated, as I stood in front of the couch, afraid to move but too angry to back down.

Without looking at me, he went upstairs. I heard the study door slam and I fell apart, again.

On Thursday, I called Rhonda and invited her over for lunch to discuss the job. It was a nice day and I set the table on the back porch.

"Hey girl," I greeted her in the driveway. "Let's go around back."

"Sounds good," she smiled. "Is there a blind date back there, too?"

We both laughed as I took a seat on the bench and Rhonda sat at the table.

"Rhonda, I'd like to take the job as your administrative assistant."

"Oh good, "she interrupted my practiced monologue.

"I'm pregnant."

"Oh," she replied with a look of disbelief. "You're pregnant?"

"Yeah," I sighed. "I'm due in April."

"You don't seem too happy about it."

"He left me," I began to explain, biting my lip and refusing to cry, again. "Told me he loved me and left me."

She joined me on the bench and held my hand. "Dani, I'm sorry. Are you okay?"

"I just need a job." I tried to smile and hoped she wouldn't ask any more questions.

"No problem girl — the job is yours."

On Saturday morning, Mom and I went car shopping. When we left Camden that afternoon, I was the proud owner of a 1980 white Chevette. I parked in the driveway, careful to leave room for my dad to enter his side of the garage. When he got home that evening, he never mentioned the car.

I began working as the administrative assistant at Little Wonders Preschool in October of 1980. We started with twenty four-year-olds and by the end of November, we had a waiting list of thirty-two. Preschools were new, but the concept was catching on like fire. I was happy for Rhonda.

My position evolved into administrative assistant/ social worker and I became Rhonda's right hand. My energy was better spent helping Rhonda succeed than focusing on my failure. I worked diligently at my job and assumed the lead in managing the compliance monitoring and social service referrals. What I learned about networking and resources for children and families was beneficial to my own circumstances.

Rhonda and I became close friends and should have been good friends during high school. It was one of those hindsight kind of things and I assumed she would have been the best friend I always wished for.

By November, I needed maternity clothes — which I dreaded. I had done well avoiding my reality but maternity clothes would be a daily reminder.

"What are you doing tomorrow?" Mom asked as I was leaving for work.

"I don't know," I shrugged. "Nothing I guess."

"Good, we're going shopping."

"For Thanksgiving?"

Mom smiled. "No silly, for maternity clothes."

"Do you want a boy or a girl?" Mom asked as we entered the baby department at Sears.

"I don't know. I never think about it."

"Do you have names picked out?"

"No, I haven't thought about that either."

"You better start thinking – you're really having my grandbaby," Mom said and smiled.

I tried to force a smile, for her.

"Looking for a gift?" Mrs. Walters, the town gossip, asked as she approached us from the main aisle and stood between Mom and me.

"Good morning, Mrs. Walters," Mom replied with her bubbly First Lady voice. "How are you doing today?"

"Just fine Sister Allen, just fine. Danielle," Mrs. Walters turned to me, "haven't seen you in the choir stand since you came back. If you're not interested in singing anymore, you know we're always looking for ushers."

"I'll keep that in mind," I said with a forced smile.

"I didn't know anyone was expecting," Mrs. Walters snooped. "Who is the gift for?'

"It's no gift Mrs. Walters," Mom was still bubbly. "Danielle is having a baby."

Mrs. Walters paused, looking at my stomach and then at Mom.

"You have a good day," Mom told her as she pulled my hand down the aisle. "Usually the truth will shut them up, at least temporarily." Mom was almost giddy and we both laughed.

Shopping for maternity clothes was difficult. In

addition to being a reminder, the clothes were ugly, but I managed to buy enough to get through the winter. Mom suggested I do more shopping in February to get through my last few months.

"You'll be a lot bigger by then," she stated softly, again smiling broadly.

Before leaving the store, we went back to the baby department. Mom and I looked at cribs, high chairs, play pens, strollers, changing tables – there was so much stuff, and it was all so cute. I couldn't decide if I wanted white or brown furniture, so I told Mom we'd have to come back. She agreed and we went to lunch.

Mom sat across from me and I played with my napkin to avoid making eye contact.

"Dani, it's okay to be nervous about having your first baby. And it's okay to talk about it."

"I've been trying to pretend I'm not pregnant."

"You don't have to do that." She took my hand and gently squeezed it. "Have you felt the baby move yet?"

"All the time." My emotions were out of control and I began to cry.

"The next time the baby kicks, will you tell me so I can feel it?"

"It's usually after dinner."

"And I'll go to the doctor's office with you, if you want me to. I'm here for you, Dani. You don't have to do this alone." She lifted my chin. "Let me help you. I want to."

"Mom, I'm so nervous about everything. I don't even know what to ask Dr. Thompson. She wants me to go to a Lamaze class – I'm embarrassed because it's for couples. I'm getting fat, I can't stand the smell of hot sauce and I cry all the time. I'm falling apart." I was whining. "Do you think Nana would be mad at me?"

"No, she wouldn't be mad." She paused. "And yes, she would still love you just as much."

I wondered if she was still smiling.

Just as I imagined, there was pointing and mumbling when I entered the Women's Sunday School class. Mrs. Walters had done well informing everyone of my pregnancy and my maternity dress confirmed it. Mother Jones motioned for me to sit next to her as I stood looking for a seat. She opened the class with prayer and told Sister Beth to read the lesson. I was nervous and fumbled through the Old Testament.

Mother Jones took my hand. "You're not the first one, or the last one, to have a baby without a husband. Some of them staring and squawking don't want me to start tellin' it."

I faked a smile as she turned to the book of Daniel for me.

Thanksgiving passed quietly. My parents spent the day with my dad's friends in Philadelphia and I spent the day eating and sleeping. Noah called and said he hadn't heard from Joey in a few months. He didn't mention my being pregnant and neither did I — no need to have to go through the whole story. His family was doing fine. Tashika was thinking about getting a job. Noah was still working at the phone company.

Christmas was just as uneventful. We had dinner after church and then my parents spent the afternoon visiting the sick and shut-in members. Rhonda and I exchanged gifts at her house and ate some of the sweet potato pie her grandmother made. Later that evening, I called Alicia and Andrea to wish them a Merry Christmas and thank them for the gifts. Then I ate again and slept for the rest of the night.

We were getting dressed for New Year's Eve service when Joey called. It was nice hearing from him and Stormy who was now six. He suggested the family get together. I agreed, knowing my dad would be a task for Mom to handle, especially since he had said very little to me since I informed him of my pregnancy.

Mom told me I would be much bigger by February and my reflection in the hall mirror confirmed it. We took our second trip to Sears for more clothes and I picked white baby furniture. The baby's room would be decorated in mint green and ivory.

"I asked your dad to move my sewing machine and hat boxes to Noah's old room," Mom told me on our way home from Sears. "That way the baby's room will be next to yours."

"Do you think he will?"

"Of course he will. He loves you Dani, he's just disappointed," she replied, trying to be reassuring.

"Thanks Mom, I really appreciate everything."

"Are you excited yet?" she asked, changing the subject.

"Yeah and still nervous," I admitted.

Mom smiled and took my hand. "This is my first grandbaby I'll see at birth."

I hadn't thought about the fact that my mom hadn't seen any of her grandchildren until they were at least six months old. It made me happy that this was going to be special for her — in spite of the circumstances.

Joshua Boaz Allen was born April 5, 1981, three hours after I arrived in the labor suite. I was alone, but pain superseded my fear. My body trembled so hard that it shook the bed. I was cold but perspiring. My screams seemed like they were coming from outside of me. Panting like a dog was useless.

God answered my prayer when the anesthesiologist gave me an epidural. I didn't know what it was, but he said it would take the pain away, so I agreed. My body was exhausted from the two hours of trauma and I closed my eyes to rest. Ten minutes hadn't passed before a nurse came in to check me. She rolled my bed down a hallway and into another room. Dr. Thompson pulled her mask off and told me I was going to be fine. She told me to push. That was the hardest part. Then I heard him cry — so I did, too. It was for real, I was a mother.

Exhaustion doesn't adequately express how I felt after delivery. Even the adrenal rush of motherhood didn't mask my sudden need for sleep. I was dozing when Mom and Rhonda tiptoed into the recovery room to meet my son. Although my dad wasn't there, I hoped it would make him happy that I picked biblical names for his grandson. Joshua was a valiant leader who carried out a mighty task in spite of obstacles, and Boaz was a perfect gentleman. My son would be a valiant leader and a perfect gentleman.

I thought about the wisdom seeds. They would now be critical and I would have to do better at helping them grow.

Motherhood was a difficult transition and my feelings vacillated between my fear of being a good mother and my contempt for Greg. I resented being single and hurt for my son who would never know his father.

My dad continued to say very little to me — he never said congratulations or even asked to hold Joshua. His only acknowledgement of the baby was an unwrapped monitor left on my dresser.

Mom proudly took her grandson to church on Mother's Day. Having just gone back to work, I needed sleep and stayed home. Mom was cooking when I awoke to her singing "Amazing Grace" and the aroma of her baked chicken. She should have been a singer; she has a beautiful voice.

I knew everyone was trying to figure out who was Josh's father and would be waiting to see who came to church with me on Father's Day. It was more than I felt like dealing with. I had managed to avoid talking to people after church over the past three weeks by going to my dad's study after service. I would again seek solace there before the benediction.

After church, I put Josh down for a nap and contemplated calling directory assistance in Harrisburg to let Greg know he had a son. I changed my mind and concluded that Greg didn't deserve to know — if he cared he would have called. Greg probably never gave us a second thought after the day I walked out of his apartment. I surmised he went home to his wife and continued his life as if we never met. I wrapped my dad's ties and took a nap with Josh.

During dinner I asked my dad to bless Joshua on the first Sunday in July. In his familiar stoic tone he agreed, after making it clear the blessing would have to be done privately at our house on Saturday. He had a long-standing rule that babies born out of wedlock could not be blessed during Sunday service.

Rhonda was honored to be Joshua's godmother and she helped Mom plan a cookout. Alicia and Andrea drove down and spent the weekend with us. Several of the church members, who Rhonda told about the private blessing, stopped by with gifts and Mom invited them to stay. No one asked about Joshua's father and several of the women offered to babysit so I could have a day out. Mother Jones came by and gave me a box of Calgon.

"I knew you would get a lot of gifts for the baby," she said hugging me. "This is something for you. Don't forget to take time for you."

"That's going to be hard," I tried to smile. There was not enough time in my day and there was no room to add anything else. My bedtime was thirty minutes after Josh's.

"You're no good to him if you're no good to yourself." She squeezed my hand before going over to give Mom a hug.

Throughout the afternoon, my dad reminded everyone that he expected to see them in church the next day. In spite of that, the day was a memorable one. For the first time in a long time, I felt happy. Nana was smiling – I felt it in the sun's rays.

The brilliance of the sun greeted me as I rolled over to my son lying next to me on that third Sunday in August. Against all the advice, I sometimes let him sleep with me. I recited John 3:16 to my sleeping son and then picked him up and imitated Nana singing her favorite song. It was comforting to tell myself that God was watching me because sometimes I felt like the sparrow that had fallen. I should have been flying — not lying on the ground.

The realities of my situation played over in my mind as I dressed Joshua for church. My son would never know his father and probably never have a relationship with his grandfather. Noah and Joey were estranged from the family and wouldn't be around as role models either. My son would not be a statistic. My son would be a leader and a gentleman, maybe even president. Greg would be sorry he had chosen to ignore him.

Mom, Joshua and I were already in the kitchen when my dad came down for his morning coffee. She poured coffee in his cup and devotedly set it on the table next to the leather-bound Bible. I purposely sat across from the cup so he would have to look at us. My intention was to engage him in conversation, although I didn't know what to say. He thumbed through his Bible as he drank his coffee and then announced, "I'll be in the car."

Mom took his cue that he was ready to go. She dutifully cleared his cup and saucer before getting her purse and Bible.

The morning scripture was 2 Kings 4:1–7. The woman with the oil thought her situation was helpless until she learned to use what she had. Living with my parents was not going to change the fact that I had joined the ranks of women across the country who, for whatever reason, were raising children without a husband. I loved my job, but the idea of making $20,000 was not what I had in mind for my household income. The tension with my dad was thickening and often over-bearing. It wouldn't be long before Joshua came to understand my dad's comments about his father being a married man and me being an adulteress. It was time to move on and my desire for a master's degree was reignited.

After church, I put Josh down for a nap and then developed a one-year plan. I decided to submit applications to Ohio State, Rutgers, Pitt and old faithful, Penn State. I needed to begin a life for my son and me, I needed some faith, and I needed those wisdom seeds to take root.

Although disappointed, Mom continued to support and encourage me. She forced herself to be excited about my plans for graduate school in spite of the obvious — her heart was wrenched.

"I've enjoyed the time with my grandson and my daughter," Mom told me one Saturday afternoon.

"Me too, Mom," I smiled. "I'm going to miss you."

Mom and I spent many hours talking and hard as I tried to convince myself, there was no pretending she was happy. Mom witnessed such a great love between her parents and I couldn't understand why she settled for so much less with my dad.

"Do you still love Daddy?" I asked over tea.

"Love never stops, Dani. Once you love someone, you love them forever."

Not knowing what to say next, I paused and allowed her to break the silence.

"Why do you ask?"

Risking hurting her feelings, I had to say it. "Sometimes you don't seem happy."

"I've been with your dad a long time," she explained. "People get used to each other and each other's ways. They understand each other, even when no one else can."

"What do you mean?"

"Your dad carries a lot of pain from when he was a child. A lot of pain and disappointment."

I sat patiently waiting to hear the tale that might convince me that my dad was more than the stoic character I had come to know.

"Your dad looked up to his brother Paul and he really wanted to follow him to Dartmouth. He only went to Howard because he could work his way through school and wouldn't need any of his father's money. He has always admired Paul."

While the door was open, I had to ask. "Is he jealous of him?"

"I don't know if jealous is a good word." Mom was almost defensive. "Your Uncle Paul had a very successful military career, travelled around the world, his girls went to college." She paused, as if searching for the right words.

I knew my dad was disappointed in his children, but I was more concerned about my mother and her increasing unhappiness.

"How did you meet Daddy?" I asked, moving the subject back to her.

"We met at a summer Christian youth retreat in Maryland when I was seventeen-years-old. He carried my bags from the bus to my room and then he came back that evening to escort me to dinner. We spent the entire two weeks together, and before he left, he told me I would be his wife. I believed him. We kept in touch by letter and the next year, after I graduated, I followed David to Howard. He was the only boyfriend I ever had."

Her story seemed so romantic. I wanted to imagine my parents as a happy, fun-loving couple, but I couldn't.

"I used to dream about being a First Lady," Mom continued. "When David was called to the ministry during his junior year, I took that as confirmation I was to be his wife."

"What about you, Mom? What about your singing? Didn't you ever want a career?"

"Things were different, Dani. I watched my mother scrub floors and take in laundry. She worked so hard that sometimes she fell asleep at the dinner table. My father worked in the mill all day. He left before I got up and sometimes didn't come in until I was in bed. The only time I spent with him was when he was dying. I promised myself I wouldn't work if I didn't have to."

"Why'd you go to college?"

"My parents wanted me to. They saved everything so I could go to school."

"What was your major?"

"Education. I wanted to be a teacher."

"Mom, you'd be a wonderful teacher."

"I taught at a school in Maryland while David finished at the seminary. My salary wasn't much and your dad always said better days were ahead."

"Why'd you stop?"

"I had Noah and your dad told me I didn't have to work. He said he would take care of me if I stayed home to raise his children. I did the best I could."

"You did fine, Mom." I tried to reassure her as tears slowly made tracks down her face.

"I miss my mother," she said getting up from the table. "I never understood why David didn't like her. I needed her to help me."

Mom suddenly appeared vulnerable and exposed as she stood solemnly looking out the dining room window. My feeble attempts to comfort her were marred by the overwhelming guilt I was feeling for messing up.

"I love you, Mom," I said getting up and going over to hug her. Then I held her while we cried.

Five

Joey and Noah promised Mom they were coming home for Thanksgiving, and I was excited about seeing them. Although Mom swore she didn't need any help with Thanksgiving dinner, I was looking forward to helping her. She was sitting at the table writing a grocery list when I came into the kitchen with Joshua on my hip.

"Who's Grandma's baby?" She stopped writing and extended her arms to Josh. He reached for her, and sometimes I felt like he loved her more than me.

"Have you heard from any graduate programs yet?" Mom asked as she sat Josh on her lap.

"No, not yet."

"Have you mentioned leaving to your dad?"

She knew I was waiting to get accepted and make final plans before telling him anything, and I shook my head no. The anticipation of being on my own with a new baby was overwhelming by itself; I didn't need any daily reminders from my dad that I brought this on myself because of my sin.

"I don't think he'll take it too hard." I took Josh from her and put him in his high chair.

"He's going to miss you and Joshua."

I never responded or looked at her.

"He really loves you, Dani. He just wants you to have the best."

"And to be a good little preacher's daughter."

"No, to be a good Christian woman and mother."

"And somebody's wife."

"And somebody's wife. Joshua needs a family."

"I am his family. I'm all he has and all he needs."

"You're his mother. He has us, too, but he needs a father."

Mom was right, Joshua needed a father. Who would want me, a spoiled woman? My dad always said that women with kids, like Tashika, get knuckleheads, like Noah. No knuckleheads and no more Gregory's. If necessary, I was prepared to do this alone.

Joey and Stormy arrived the Wednesday evening before Thanksgiving. Mom opened the door and hugged Joey as if she never wanted to let him go. He was her baby boy who used to play her favorite hymns while she sang.

"And how is Grandma's princess?" Mom hugged Stormy.

"Fine," she smiled taking off her coat. "My mother said to tell you and Pap Pap Happy Thanksgiving."

She had grown up so much since the last time I saw her. Stormy had Joey's smile, mannerisms and engaging personality. Her hair ballies were coordinated with her red corduroy jumper and her peppermint stripped Peter Pan shirt. The white tights clung to her skinny legs and her black patent leather Mary Jane's looked liked they had been shined with Vaseline. For seven years old, she was well-spoken and extremely poised.

"Aunt Dee Dee," she said hugging me, "where's the baby? Daddy said you have a baby!"

"He's sleeping, but you can come upstairs and see him."

"Can I hold him, please? I know how."

"When he gets up," I promised her.

Joey smiled as he watched us. "Looking good, baby sis." Joey hugged me for the first time in years. "Congratulations and all that."

Holding back tears, I said, "Thanks."

Joey seemed taller than I remembered. His perfectly maintained Afro was now gone. He looked like my dad in his tapered haircut. Just as I remembered, he wore khaki pants with loafers. He always liked the preppie look, even before it became fashionable.

My relationship with my brothers had, for the most part, been superficial while we were growing up. Both of them left the house before my sixteenth birthday. Joey moved to California after he graduated from high school and when his money ran out, he went to New York. He never found the fame he was searching for but ended up being a favorite at the small clubs in Harlem. He attempted college but said it wasn't him – so he quit. For the past three years, he had been the director of the Community Youth Center in Brooklyn and loved his job.

Joseph also collected girlfriends. He had at least twenty I knew of and had lived with most of them. Until moving to Brooklyn, the longest he'd ever had an address was when he lived with Lynette – the mother of his daughter. In spite of his consistent instability, he was a decent father and Stormy is a daddy's girl.

"Is Noah coming in with his crew?" Joey asked loud enough for my dad to hear as he came in the door.

Mom hesitated as my dad was taking off his coat so I answered, "Yeah, all of them."

"Joseph." My dad nodded his head as Stormy greeted him with a big hug. He actually smiled. "How's my baby?"

"I'm not the baby anymore Pappy. Joshua is the baby now."

I looked at Mom and then at Joey. Mom looked down at her clasped hands. Joey looked at Dad with raised eyebrows.

"Come on in here and sing me a song." My dad broke the silence, gently taking Stormy's hand and leading her down to the game room

"It's cool." Joey patted me on the head, just like he used to.

Mom disappeared into the kitchen and I was sure she was praying we would have a Walton Thanksgiving.

"Let's help Mom." I grabbed Joey's hand leading him into the kitchen.

Mom greeted us with cups of hot chocolate topped with marshmallows. "You two take these and catch up on things."

"Good idea." Joey took the cups and kissed Mom on the cheek.

"Thanks, Mom," I said, rolling my eyes at him. "We'll be back to help when we're done. Won't we Joseph?"

We retreated to the dining room and sat by the window. Joey slurped his hot chocolate. "I see Pops hasn't changed."

"Some things never do." I sipped my hot chocolate.

"How's Mom?"

"I'm worried about her. Do you think she's happy?"

"You tell me, you're here." Joey sat up resting his elbows on the table with his hands under his chin.

I sighed. "I'm not sure."

"It probably helps that you're here."

"For Mom, not for Dad."

"Pops give you grief? I heard the SOB left you."

"Who'd you hear that from?" I inquired, a little indignant.

"Around. That's what the talk is."

"Joey, it wasn't like that. He lied to me, told me he loved me, and never said he was married." My indignation faded to embarrassment.

"What, get the . . ."

"Joseph!" Mom cut him off, startling us as she came in with a plate of warm chocolate chip cookies. "Watch your mouth, boy."

"Mom," Joey attempted to explain.

She cut him off again. "We're going to have a nice time this weekend. Everyone." She smiled and winked at Joey before retreating to the kitchen.

"I can find him, tell his wife, start some trouble," he continued.

"No need. I've moved on."

I held the plate of cookies in front of him and he took three.

"How are you?"

"Better. Mom's been real helpful. I'm outta here in August though."

"And where are you going?"

"Grad school. Hopefully Ohio State," I told him getting up from my chair. "Be right back, I hear the baby."

When I came down the steps, Stormy reminded me of my promise to let her hold Joshua.

"Come in the living room," I told her.

"Be careful," Joey said as he came into the foyer. "Look at this boy. Are you sure he's only seven months old? What does he eat?"

"Mostly baby food, but Mom's been giving him mashed sweet potatoes, too," I stated sarcastically.

I placed Josh on Stormy's lap in the corner of the couch and posed them for a picture. They were adorable. Without thinking, I said, "Joey, go get Mom and Dad so they can take a picture with their grandchildren."

Mom sat down next to Stormy. My dad picked up Josh and put him on Mom's lap. He sat down and put Stormy on his lap. I wanted my dad to hold Josh. Still, this picture would remain fixed in my mind's eye forever; the photograph would go in Josh's baby book.

"I made banana pudding," Mom announced as she gave Josh to Joey and put her apron back on.

"Daddy, let Pap Pap hold the baby," Stormy stated with excitement.

"I'm not sure Pap Pap wants to," I told her, motioning for Joey to give me my baby.

"Yes he does." Stormy was definitive. "We're going to take a picture."

Joey handed Joshua to my dad and, for the first time that I was aware of, he actually looked at Josh. As my dad held his grandson, he couldn't contain his smile. Joey took the camera from me and snapped the picture.

"You take one with them," Joey nudged me. "Stormy come here."

"I want to get in this picture, too!" Stormy protested.

"Not this one." Joey's voice was firm. "You can't be in all the pictures."

Standing next to my dad, I hoped he would say something to Josh or me. He put his arm around my shoulders and said, "Say cheese."

It was a rare moment and Joey captured it on film.

I was in the kitchen making a bottle for Joshua when my dad came down the steps a little after seven the next morning.

"Morning Dad."

"Morning," he answered without looking at me.

He poured coffee into his favorite mug and drank it while leafing through the paper. In the moment of silence between us, I wanted to apologize for messing up. I wanted him to hug me and tell me it would be okay. He didn't, so I didn't.

As I was going back upstairs, the back door closed. My dad was driving up to the Heritage Center to get his parents.

By noon, the aroma of our Thanksgiving meal filled the house. Mom was singing in the kitchen and Joey was at home. Noah's family and my grandparents were on their way. My excitement about our family gathering was equally mixed with anticipation and anxiety.

I hadn't seen Noah since Nana's funeral. He was the most estranged of all of us and came home the least. Noah quit school in the middle of his senior year, got his GED and moved in with Tashika. They used to visit every Thanksgiving and, for the first three years, they had an addition to their family. The first year, they came with the twins - Taisha and Maisha. The next year Rakeem came along, and the year after that, Raheem. Tashika insisted that she was a housewife who balanced their budget with assistance from the state because Noah didn't make enough money. They seemed to always do okay, and their kids wore designer clothes.

When Mom and I went to visit them during my senior year in high school, I was surprised to see their apartment. It was much nicer than I imagined. The big credenza with the color television took up most of the wall space in the living and dining rooms. They didn't have a dining room set and everyone ate in front of the television. Mom was a little perturbed because 'Grace' was the lady next door and not the prayer of thanksgiving before dinner.

After we ate, we sat out on the stoop with the other kids until after midnight. Both nights we were there, Raheem fell asleep outside in his stroller. It was like one big block party and Tashika and Noah knew everybody who walked by. Some stopped to talk, others waved from cars and one of Tashika's friends across the street carried an entire conversation from her window.

On the subway ride back to Port Authority, Noah pointed out the stop where Grandpa Tim said his church used to be. Noah said he met some people who knew Grandpa Tim as Brother Love. Mom never inquired any further. I wanted to know, but knew better than to ask.

"Honey, I'm home," Noah announced as his family paraded in the front door. His huge Afro was replaced by dread locks and he looked like the lion in *The Wiz*. "I'll always love my Mama," Noah sang as he picked her up and spun her around.

"Oh, Noah!" Mom held her first born tightly.

She hugged Tashika and the kids and helped hang up everyone's coat. "Your dad will be back soon."

"Is he at the church?" Noah asked.

"He went to get his parents." Mom answered, speaking slightly above a whisper.

"He could have picked us up. He went through Brooklyn to get to Queens."

"Let me get everyone a snack," Mom quickly changed the subject, "it's been a long ride." She disappeared in the kitchen and returned with a tray of pigs-in-a-blanket and a jar of apple cider.

"What's up girl?" Tashika asked, patting my stomach as I handed Josh to Joey. "How'd you lose that already? I still got some afterbirth from all my kids." She laughed and pointed to her own stomach that was squeezed into her shirt.

"Just working nine to five."

"Girl, I'm staying home with my babies," she replied indignantly.

For the good of all, I left that alone.

Noah looked more like a football player than a former basketball player. His jeans were starched, just like I remembered, and his sneakers looked new. He always hated dirty sneakers. He wore his oxford shirt untucked — something that drove my dad crazy when Noah was a teenager. Tashika's red leather pants looked like they dared her to even drink water, her boots had a three-inch heel and matched her pants. She even wore a red leather pony tail holder.

Taisha and Maisha were identical twins. They had thinned out and were tall to be eleven. They were dressed alike in hot pink Jordache jeans with matching jackets. Their hair was parted into four perfect ponytails held by ballies that looked like oversized bubble gum. The edges of their hair were slicked straight with Tricky Sticky. Rakeem and Raheem looked like Noah. There were only eleven months between them and they could have easily been twins. Their jeans were starched and creased, and they wore their shirts untucked like their dad. Their heads were squared by the box haircuts.

We settled in the game room and Noah swore Josh looked just like him.

"Dee Dee is a Mommy," Noah said mockingly. "How did you ever get pregnant? You mean Pops let you out of the house?"

"You have four children; do I really need to explain how I got pregnant?"

We shared plenty of laughs and priceless moments. I used three rolls of film trying to capture all the memories, not knowing when we would gather like this again. The girls were playing the card game War and the boys were glued to the television. Our Thanksgiving gathering was off to a great start.

We heard the front door close. Mom greeted everyone loud enough for us to know that we should come upstairs. Noah was playing with Joshua and said to him, "Well Dr. J, let's go see the old man."

They were in the foyer and Mom was helping Grandpa Tim take off his coat while my dad took Grandma Rita's coat.

"Pappy, Nana," I announced entering the room with Joshua on my hip. "How are you?"

Grandpa Tim's arthritis had put him in a wheelchair and Grandma Rita had new teeth she hadn't gotten used to yet.

"That's my baby girl," Grandma Rita said hugging me. "And who's this?"

"Your great-grandson, Joshua Boaz," I announced proudly, sitting Josh on Grandpa Tim's lap.

Mom smiled, while my dad looked the other way.

"Hey, hey, hey, hey," Noah announced from behind me. "Hey Pops. Que pasa?"

Mom squeezed Noah's hand as she walked past him on her way back to the kitchen.

"It's nice of you to join us," my dad said looking at Noah.

"Grandpa!" All the kids followed Stormy and rushed my dad. He was particularly fond of Stormy and had to be careful not to slight the other children. He passed out five dollar bills to all of them, but had already given Stormy ten dollars. She was smart enough not to mention it.

"Hey Rev," Tashika said to my dad.

His reply was flat. "Hello."

"And who's this?" Grandma Rita asked Noah, referring to Tashika.

"This is my wife," he began to answer before being interrupted by my dad.

"Did I miss the wedding?"

"This is my wife Tashika," Noah repeated, again with emphasis on the word *wife*, "and these are our children." He called them one by one and they smiled at the great grandparents they had never met.

Joey was the last to enter the room and he took Joshua from Grandpa Tim. "Hey Pops. Hi Granny," he said hugging her. He gave Grandpa Tim a high five and went to give my dad one – my dad never raised his hand.

"Pops, lighten up," Noah stated with a hint of dismay.

My dad never answered.

Noah began singing "We Are Family" and his family joined in to sing the entire chorus. My grandparents enjoyed their rendition. My dad excused himself in the middle of it.

Joshua fell asleep just before dinner, which took away my excuse to eat downstairs with the children. My anxiety level elevated as I anticipated potential dinner conversations. There were several topics that could be explosive, among them Joshua's father.

The family gathered in the dining room and we held hands around the table before sitting down. My dad stood at one end and my grandfather was seated at the other end. Their wives were to their right.

"Let us pray," my dad bowed his head. "Lord, we thank You for this day, for Your mercy and for Your grace. Lord, we ask that You would bless this family gathering. Bless each and every person around this table, dwell in each heart. Be real to all of us. Lord, bless this food that it may nourish our bodies so that we may be used in the building up of Your kingdom. Amen."

The small talk around the table quickly became secondary to the passing of platters and the clanging of spoons against Mom's good china. Food is the universal peacekeeper and everyone smiled and laughed around the table while we piled food on our plates.

As we settled into our seats, Grandpa Tim commandeered the conversation.

"I was known all over Fort Greene in Brooklyn," he announced wiping his mouth with the corner of the linen napkin. "Everybody called me Brother Love. My congregation loved me. I spread love and compassion to hurting peoples."

"More like lust to gullible people," my dad interjected without looking up from his plate.

Grandpa Tim continued to brag. "My church was packed every Sunday. People came from all over the five boroughs. I usually had standing room only."

"It was a storefront on Fulton Street in Brooklyn," my dad corrected him, "not a church."

"All the struggling sisters loved to come and tell me about their troubles," Grandpa Tim continued, intentionally ignoring my dad. "I always took the time to listen."

I remembered Alicia telling me that Uncle Paul caught Grandpa Tim doing more than praying with the young women. It was rumored that he fathered a baby with one of the choir members.

Grandpa Tim paused to finish chewing his food. "Tell me, son," he said, looking across the table at my dad. "Do the peoples love you? Can they talk to you? Tell you about their troubles? Or do you judge them, too?"

"Timothy!" Grandma Rita slapped her hand down on the table.

My dad stopped eating to look at his father. "I was blessed to have a grandfather who was a godly man."

"David," Mom's voice was pleading, "just this once." Tears welled in her eyes and Joey held her hand.

"Old Reverend Will, Mr. Do It All Himself," Grandpa Tim retaliated. "I hope you treat your family better than he treated his."

I never knew my great-grandfather Reverend William Allen. Family talk says he worked himself to an early grave. He died when he was only fifty-one years old.

"Now Pappy," Grandma Rita reached over and held Grandpa Tim's hand. "He just didn't know how to delegate anything and tried to do everything himself."

"He did so much for everybody else that he never got around to doing anything with me."

Grandpa Tim's resentment had festered over the years and he made no attempt to conceal his disdain. He put his fork down on the table and looked at my brothers and me.

"That man never thought anyone could do anything right, not even me."

"This is not the time or the place," my dad's voice elevated. "You are out of order!"

Grandpa Tim continued. "Even my mother spent

her life gloating over the merits of her husband who, in his own eyes, met the need of his underprivileged community for thirty years."

"He was a good man," my dad interrupted. "He helped people."

"He kept people helpless so he could keep saving them day after day, week after week and month after month." Grandpa Tim was getting angry. "Until the day he died, he could tell you how many times he helped each person and how they never could have made it without him."

Noah intruded in the conversation to change the subject. "I don't know about ya'll, but I'm ready for dessert."

"I'm going to check on the kids," I announced getting up from the table and motioning for Tashika to come with me.

As we descended the stairs, she put her hand on my shoulder. "Girl, what was that all about?"

"Skeletons in the closet, and a lot of pain," I answered, not really wanting to talk about it.

"Ya'll don't do a lot of forgiving in this family, do you?"

"Mommy!" Her boys shouted when they saw her.

The old bed sheet on the carpet was covered with food.

"It wasn't me," Stormy volunteered when she saw the expression on my face.

"Me neither," Taisha stated shaking her head.

"It was the boys Mommy," Maisha tattled, pointing to her brothers.

Tashika seemed unfazed by the mess. "Ya'll are so sloppy," she casually said to her seven and eight-year-old. The boys smiled.

Hoping Tashika would help without me having to ask, I began cleaning up the mess. She sighed as she knelt on the floor to pick up some food.

"I'm not done," Raheem whined as I threw his plate in the garbage.

"Oh yes you are," I answered before Tashika could respond. "You were up playing – dinner is over."

"Was it good, Boo?" Tashika asked, extending her arms for him to come to her.

"Stormy, please get me two wet washclothes for the boys. You and the girls can go to the bathroom to wash your hands."

Thanksgiving was more of a mess than I anticipated – literally and figuratively. My dad and his father were harboring intense pain from the past and they were bitter. I felt bad for Mom. She planned the day so meticulously and bitterness robbed her of a perfect family dinner.

A dysfunctional family system – my dad was a product of it and he had passed it on.

Life returned to its normal routine after Thanksgiving. It should have been a time to reminisce, but no one mentioned it. Mom talked about making her usual pies and cobblers for the sick and shut-in members, but she didn't seem excited about Christmas. I wasn't sure if she was angry about the turmoil of Thanksgiving or just looking forward to a quiet Christmas. She seemed unusually sullen.

Mom spent many evenings in the recliner in the game room, pretending to watch television and ultimately falling asleep. I was helpless. I didn't know how to help her or what to say. My dad didn't seem to care.

He should have loved her more, held her, kissed her, anything — he did nothing. Every time I suggested they go out to dinner, Mom declined and Dad conceded.

I read Nana's letters looking for clues. There was nothing scripted about her relationship, it was just pure, raw love. There were no anecdotes to pass on — Nana said true love was a gift from God. On top of my anxiety about the possibility of relocating, I added worrying about my mom. Sometimes I wished she would leave my dad and find someone who really loved her. My motives were truly selfish — I hoped that if she left my dad, she would relocate to live with me. More pipe dreams.

Josh and I went to Christmas service and then to Rhonda's for dinner. After exchanging gifts, we had a pouting session while Joshua took a nap. How was it that we didn't have dates that dropped off beautifully wrapped packages? Why weren't we getting excited about New Year's Eve? It was dismal. Rhonda was convinced that there were no single men in Smithtown. I knew if it was hard for a single woman to find a boyfriend, then my situation with a baby was beyond hopeless. We ate another piece of pie.

My dad was in his study and Mom was in her favorite recliner in the family room when we got home that evening. I left a message for my cousins wishing them a Merry Christmas. Joey and Stormy called to thank me for the gifts. There was a message from Noah and Tashika wishing us a Merry Christmas. Joshua was fully engaged in tearing up the wrapping paper balls Mom made him. I sat under the tree playing with his toys.

SIX

It was another cold, wet March evening and my thirty-minute commute had taken almost two hours due to the flooding on the Black Horse Pike. The rain was pouring down like sheets of water and we got drenched running from the car to the back door. Joshua had just gotten over an ear infection and I remembered all too well the night I spent in the emergency room. His 104-degree temperature rendered him lethargic and dehydrated. I wanted to get him out of his wet clothes immediately, but the letters on the kitchen counter caught my attention — a letter from Rutgers was on top. I grabbed all the envelopes and went upstairs.

"Did you see the letters?" Mom yelled from the living room.

"Got em'," I answered from the steps.

I wrapped Joshua in a towel and put him in his crib. Still soaking wet, I opened the Ohio State letter and yelled so loud it frightened Joshua.

Mom was at the door when I turned around.

"I got in, Mom, I got in!" I yelled.

"I knew you would," she said hugging me. "Congratulations."

"Are you really happy for me?"

"Of course. You know I am," Mom replied.

"But?" I asked.

"Now you'll be leaving," she said half smiling, "you and Joshua."

"Mom, you knew we couldn't stay forever."

She picked Joshua up and said, "I know you need to go."

Just then we heard the front door close. "Guess I'll have to tell him," I whispered to Mom.

"I'll get Joshua dressed," Mom said, as she turned away from me and put Joshua on the changing table.

"I don't have to tell him right now," I whispered in protest still holding the acceptance letter in my hand. Mom glanced over her shoulder and gave me one of those looks.

I started down the steps, rehearsing in my mind what to say. My wet clothes were sticking to me and I intentionally didn't wipe the water dripping on my face from my hair.

My dad was standing at the counter reading the mail. His suit pants were perfectly creased even though they had to be wet. The rainwater beaded on top of his shoeshine. It was as if the rain did not dare to touch him.

"Gotta minute?"

"Uh huh," he replied, without looking at me.

I took a deep breath and blurted out, "I got into grad school."

"Congratulations," he said with little emotion.

"Ohio State," I added, thinking it would make him look at me.

"That's a long commute," he sarcastically replied.

"I'm moving to Columbus," I explained. "My acceptance letter came today and I am leaving in August."

He finally looked at me.

"Isn't that good news?" Mom interrupted from the top of the stairs.

"I'm happy for you, Danielle. I didn't know you wanted to go to grad school," he said, returning his attention to the mail on the counter.

I turned to go upstairs. My wet clothes suddenly felt colder and heavier.

Over the next few weeks, I second-guessed my

decision to leave. I had no idea what Mom would do without me. She often appeared depressed and I felt guilty taking her joy, her grandson, away from her. I thought about Nana's words – 'Sometimes we may think we can't live without people, but we go on.' I would go on, and Mom would go on, too.

"Mom, we're going shopping," I told her early one Saturday afternoon at the end of March.

She pretended to be engrossed in the crossword puzzle and looked up at me over her glasses. "Why don't you call Rhonda?"

"Because I want you to go. You can pick an outfit for Josh's first birthday party."

"I can't believe he'll be one already," she finally said.

"And, I couldn't have done it without you." I hugged her as she got up from the table.

The Saturday afternoon sun peeked through the clouds to confirm that spring was right around the corner, and even the temperature warmed up to 45 degrees. I had taken my camera along and many memories were captured that day as we went through the mall, walked in the park and went to eat. Mom was happy and she laughed with her grandson and me. I saw a glimpse of the Judy that Nana told me about a long time ago, the carefree Judy who always smiled and carried a song in her heart.

Joshua's birthday party was the following Saturday afternoon. It was another bright sunny day and the buds on the annuals in the yard were preparing to bloom. Four of his playmates from the church nursery came to the party and my cousins surprised us. They arrived with a carload of balloons, toys and a delivery slip for a racing car bed. It was a perfect day – plenty of memories and plenty of film.

By the time I put Joshua down for a nap at three o'clock, he went right to sleep. If Andrea hadn't surprised me with tickets to *Joseph and the Amazing Technicolor Dreamcoat*, I would have taken a nap, too.

"Hurry up, girl," Alicia whispered, peeking in the door, "show starts at eight."

"I just need to jump in the shower." I said. "I know what I'm wearing."

"I thought you were in here trying to take a nap with the baby," she teased.

"No, just getting his pajamas ready for tonight," I explained.

Mom came into the room. "Go get yourself together. I know what to do."

"I know Mom," I said as I put his pajamas on the dresser. "Thanks, again."

We ran into traffic at the Holland Tunnel and by the time we parked it was seven-forty. We made a mad dash to the Royale Theatre and made it to our seats just as the lights were dimming.

At intermission, Andrea and I went to look at souvenirs in the lobby while Alicia went to the restroom.

"Annie, I really appreciate the treat," I smiled at her.

"You deserve it," she smiled back at me. "They say the first year is the hardest and you did it."

"Danielle."

The voice was familiar. Almost three years had passed since Tony visited me at Penn State. He hugged me and I remembered his touch.

"How are you?"

"Good," I said hugging him back. "How are you?"

"Good, things are good. What brings you here?"

"*Dreamcoat*, and my cousins. Andrea, this is Tony." I introduced them. "What are you up to these days?" I asked, not sure I wanted to know.

"This is my fiancée, Cathy." He introduced us to the woman who walked up behind me. "Cathy, this is Danielle and Andrea."

"Hi," I turned to shake her hand. "Congratulations."

Andrea courteously smiled, said hello and stepped back to observe.

"I know you've got a husband somewhere," Tony inquired as he held Cathy's hand.

"No, not yet. I'm happy for you," I lied. "I wish you the best. Nice meeting you, Cathy." I walked away and Andrea followed.

"Girl, who was that fine man?" Andrea asked.

"Someone I met in West Virginia," I answered, trying to sound blasé.

"That's more than just someone," she teased.

"He should have been," I confessed, "but I blew it."

"Girl, what?"

"Its' a long story I'll probably always regret," I told her. "Let's not spoil the night, he's no longer available."

The next few months were spent writing letters and making calls to secure housing and childcare at Ohio State. I called so often that I befriended a grad student working in the off-campus housing office named Denise. She was extremely helpful in finding an apartment I could afford, and I couldn't wait to actually meet her.

By June, my living and daycare arrangements were settled. Denise sent pictures of my apartment with the name and phone number of the landlord. Mrs. Emma Thompson was a widow who had the second floor of her home renovated into an apartment after her daughter moved out. I called to tell Miss Emma about Josh and she said she was looking forward to having a baby around since her daughter and son-in-law were more interested in their career than in starting a family.

The movers came on an overcast August morning and loaded our bedrooms, all of Joshua's toys and our clothes. Watching them pull out of the driveway made it real — I was leaving the following Saturday. The wisdom seeds would need to be well rooted and growing; I was really going to need them.

Rhonda and I met for dinner after church on Sunday. Words were inadequate to express the debt of my appreciation. She taught me about friendship and fashion. Totally conservative is how Rhonda described the way I dressed, and all my gifts from her added color to the earth tones that controlled my closet. I was wearing the orange shell Rhonda gave me for Christmas. She was wearing a lime green dress. We looked like LifeSavers!

We cried more than we ate, but we laughed a lot, too. We had shared good times that would bind our friendship forever, and Joshua was lucky to have her for a godmother.

"Thank you," I said handing her a gift bag. "You'll never know how much I appreciate you."

"The pleasure has been mine." She took my hand. "Just promise me distance won't. . ."

"It won't do anything," I interrupted her. "I

promise."

"And I will be coming to Columbus," she said smiling.

"I'm expecting it."

She began to open the gift.

"You know, Rhon, I'm so sorry we didn't hang out in high school. You're the best friend I always wanted."

"You probably wouldn't have liked me much then. I didn't really like myself too much," she confessed.

"Then we would have had that in common, I didn't like me either."

"You didn't act out like I did," she said and paused as I sat allowing her to finish. "I messed up in school to get back at my dad for leaving us. I lied to my mom because she wouldn't stop loving my dad. I smoked weed and drank to numb my feelings. I was a mess."

"Rhon, I'm so sorry, I never knew." I squeezed her hand and before I knew it, I was being transparent, too. "I wasn't happy, it was all about approval from my dad. I knew everyone talked about my family because of my brothers, and I knew everyone thought I was corny. I didn't have any real friends."

"You always looked happy," Rhonda consoled me through her own tears.

"It was a mask I learned to wear from my mother." I wiped my eyes with the back of my hand.

"You wore it well." She handed me a Kleenex. "And you maintained your grades in the National Honor Society. Me, I was a flirt. A tease."

"Really?" I inquired, still wiping my face.

"Then Carlton won the bet." She turned away and buried her face in her hands. "I never planned on the pregnancy."

I sat next to her, put my arm around her and

listened intently because her words were barely audible between her sobs.

"On the day I went to tell him, he told me it was just a bet. All the guys laughed and cheered him on – he had dethroned me. I never told him I was pregnant. My Aunt Veda let me use her medical card to get an abortion in Philly. I went on a drinking binge for about two weeks and then my dad died."

"I remember." I searched my purse for a tissue because I had used her last one. "It was a horrible accident."

"I didn't want to end up like him wrapped around a telephone pole." Rhonda wiped her face.

"I'm sorry I missed the funeral."

"It was sheer drama," she said, forcing a smile. "I made a fool of myself acting like the girl in *Imitation of Life*, sorry I couldn't remember the last time I told my dad I loved him."

I was packing the last of Joshua's clothes when Mom came into the room.

"You need to go to bed, you have a long drive ahead of you in the morning."

"Mom, I'm nervous," I confessed putting my head on her shoulder. "What am I going to do without you?"

"You're going to get your Master's Degree and make a life for you and your son – just like you planned."

"Will you stay with me for the first year?" I asked, already knowing the answer.

"No, but I'll be out to visit Labor Day weekend – just like I promised." She kissed my forehead. "Now go on down to the game room and get some sleep."

Mom had pulled out the heavy old sofa bed and

I was too tired to go back upstairs to thank her. Joshua was spread out in the middle so I stretched out across the bottom.

The morning came quickly and rays from the sun peered through the curtains to announce the beginning of my new life. I looked over at Joshua as I lay there thinking Mom was right — everyone needs family and I was taking Joshua away from the only family he may ever have. I wanted my dad to ask me to stay even though I knew I had to leave.

Rhonda came by to see us off and helped me load the last of my stuff. All my belongings that hadn't left on the truck were now packed in my Chevette. I hugged Rhonda and promised to call when I got settled. My hands trembled as I reached to take Joshua out of my mother's arms. I hugged her while she held my son.

"I love you, Mom," I told her, unable to hold back the tears. "Thanks for everything."

"You're going to be alright," she said trying not to cry, too. "I love you, baby girl. Promise me you won't be a stranger with my grandson. Remember this is always home."

"I know," I cried. "I'm so scared of being by myself."

"You're not alone." Mom wiped my face with her hand. "God is watching over you." She began to sing Nana's favorite song, "If God's eye is on the sparrow, then I know He's watching over you." Her voice was beautiful.

My dad unexpectantly interrupted us. "Danielle, we need to have a word of prayer before you get on the road." He took my hand and motioned Rhonda to join us. "Dear Lord," my dad's voice lightened, "bless my daughter and my grandson, Joshua. Lord, guide her down the highway, dispense Your angels of mercy to go with her and place Your hedge of protection around her. Lord God, open doors for her in Columbus, place godly people in her path. Lord, I'm asking You to make her heart fertile ground." It sounded like my dad's voice quivered. "Lord, I've claimed her soul for You — my daughter will be saved."

Completely overwhelmed by him calling me his daughter and recognizing Joshua as his grandson, I hugged my dad for the first time in years and wept in the comfort of his strong arms. There was so much that needed to be said. I was grateful for the moment, and it made me smile. Nana was watching from Heaven's balcony and smiling, too.

"I love you, Daddy," I told him, not wanting him to let me go.

"I love you, too." He wiped the tears from my face with his handkerchief. "I've always loved you and I'm sorry I didn't give what you needed."

He hugged me again and then took Joshua from my mom and gave him a hug. "You be a good boy for your mom," he whispered in his grandson's ear.

I hugged everyone again before putting Joshua in the car. Driving off, I waved out the window while Joshua blew kisses. I cried until I reached the Pennsylvania Turnpike. Saying good-bye was the hardest part of leaving.

My life started over nine hours later when I arrived in Columbus. I called Denise from a gas station and we met so she could show me how to get to my apartment on Sullivant Avenue. Living on the West Side of Columbus would be a twenty-five minute commute, but Denise rationalized the rent was cheaper.

"Welcome!" Miss Emma greeted me as I walked up her steps. "Welcome to Columbus."

"Thank you," I said hugging her.

Denise introduced us. "Miss Emma, this is Danielle and Joshua Allen."

"Come on in, let me get your keys for you," Miss Emma smiled. "And I made dinner. I knew you'd be hungry."

I was more tired than hungry and just wanted to lie down. The movers wouldn't be delivering my furniture until Monday, and I still had to blow up my air mattress so we would have somewhere to sit and sleep. Miss Emma took us to the side door and showed me the apartment upstairs. It was a small two bedroom with a living room, dining room combo and a kitchen. The bathroom was inside a little dressing room. It was cute. It was my first apartment. I thanked Miss Emma as we walked back to the car to get my things. Joshua sat on the porch with her while Denise helped me unpack the car. After several trips, I thanked them both and finally took Joshua upstairs to our new home.

Joshua adjusted to the University Daycare better than I anticipated. On his first day, when I was extremely nervous, he smiled and waved bye without a second thought. When I arrived to pick him up at noon, he didn't want to leave. That was good for him, but I wished he were a little clingy and crying, at least during the first few days. My maternal instincts wanted him to need me.

During my first week in Columbus, my mornings were spent looking for a job, and my experience in Pittsburgh was an asset. I was offered two positions and took the one at the Neighborhood Youth and Family Center.

It was near the University, didn't require any weekends and offered more flexibility. My weeks would be long and the weekend would have to be divided between Joshua and studying. At least, that was the plan.

The waiting list for parking permits was ridiculously long, so I left my car at the daycare every day. Having nice legs was my motivation as I walked across campus. At the end of three weeks, I felt thinner and looked forward to wearing some of the fall favorites that hadn't been worn in two years.

I quickly acclimated to my job and realized there was a critical need for intervention in the high schools — our agency maintained a waiting list for services. Parents, school counselors, probation officers and pastors were calling on a daily basis for our assistance. Omar Powell, the program director, was ecstatic; however, the dire need for our services was a sad testament to the direction our society was moving. The gang phenomenon was spreading across the country like wildfire, killing kids, especially boys. Andrea was a high school counselor and I often consulted with her. She admitted that her office was also overwhelmed by the increasing violent nature of students, and schools were not prepared to handle the gang war.

My job was intense but my co-workers were helpful and seemed to appreciate my tenacity. I was ready to add my classes. I was also grateful that Monday was Labor Day.

Mom called Friday night to tell me she missed her bus and I almost cried because I was looking forward to her visit. Josh was sitting on the floor playing so I joined him. After dinner, I put on *The Muppet Movie* and we fell asleep on the air mattress we were now using for a couch.

My doorbell rang Saturday afternoon. I was shocked and pleasantly surprised to see my parents in the doorway.

"Let me get you a chair," I said getting my two kitchen stools.

"You need a couch," my dad smiled. "The first order of business is to get you one." His countenance was exceptionally pleasant.

I wanted to say, 'You don't have to,' except I both needed and desperately wanted one. "We would really appreciate a couch," I answered with a big smile.

"Well, it's a couch and then lunch," Dad declared.

After shopping, Mom suggested seafood, so we found a Red Lobster. It was the first time I had been in one since the last time Greg had taken me.

"How is everything going?" my dad asked as we waited for our food.

"Good," I smiled, "really good."

"What about the daycare?" It was only a matter of time before Mom asked. "Does Josh like it?"

"He loves it. You'll have to see it before you leave."

"Did all of your financial aid come through?" My dad was extremely paternal and it was weird. "Your mother and I don't want you out here hungry."

I relished the concern he was showing.

We spent most of Saturday together and I took my parents on a quick tour of the campus. My dad seemed impressed, and Mom thought it was huge. On Sunday, we attended the church down the street from my apartment and the service reminded me of St. Luke's. Over dinner, my dad repeatedly mentioned how many young people he noticed at the church and I promised to go again. After dinner, we drove through the downtown area.

It was early evening and I convinced my parents to head back to their hotel. Unable to remember the last time they went on vacation, I wanted them to spend some time together. Mom promised to stop by on Monday morning before they left.

The alarm startled me at 6:45, and I jumped up wanting to at least have coffee ready when my parents arrived. My dad was anxious to get on the road, but they came in for coffee and muffins.

"Keep in touch," he said standing at the sink, sipping the last of his coffee.

"I will," I promised, "don't worry I will."

He put two fifty-dollar bills in my hand and squeezed my hand in his. I hugged him.

"Thank you," I whispered in his ear.

Mom's eyes filled with tears as I took Joshua and hugged her before she got in the car. This time the good-bye was easier.

Joshua and I ate breakfast and then headed for the park. I was jealous of the couples playing with their children. Joshua deserved that, too. He needed a dad who would play with him in the park on sunny afternoons. My guilt about being a single parent was a major hurdle for me to get over. I wanted so much more for Josh and for me. I wanted to know the love Nana talked about. "God," I sighed out loud, "can you help me?"

While Josh napped, I studied the files of my clients. After dinner, we watched *The Muppet Movie* again, and my son fell asleep in my arms.

My classes were not as hard as I imagined — in fact, except for all the required readings, I found graduate school to be much more gratifying than undergrad. The discussions in class were intellectually stimulating, and I appreciated only having to take classes in my major.

By November, I was ready for Thanksgiving break. The two friends I had made, Denise and Elaine, were both going home for Thanksgiving to take a break before becoming obsessed with studying for finals. Having no idea of what to expect during finals, the uncertainty was overwhelming. On top of finals, I had put in more thirty-hour than twenty-five hour weeks and the thought of driving eighteen hours for a four-day break seemed self-defeating. I called Mom to let her know we would be spending Thanksgiving in Pittsburgh. This would be the last Thanksgiving with 'just us' because Alicia was getting married in June.

Seven

Josh and I arrived in Pittsburgh around noon on Thanksgiving Day. Driving past the Oakland exit on the parkway, it crossed my mind that Greg might still be in his apartment. I looked over at my son sleeping peacefully, and felt sorry for him. I had made such a horrible mistake and he would be the one to pay — it wasn't fair. I exited the parkway at Squirrel Hill and detoured down Murray to Forbes Avenue. I had to drive by Greg's apartment. If he was still in Pittsburgh, I needed his son to at least meet him.

The same faded blue curtains were in the window, but I didn't see his car. The reality that Greg went home to the wife who didn't know about Joshua or me was a bitter pill to swallow.

I cut across Morewood to Fifth Avenue and took the scenic route to Penn Avenue. The branches on the trees that lined the street were bare. During my last visit, the trees were full and green. The trees had changed and so had I.

As I pulled up in front of the house, Alicia and Dennis greeted us in the driveway.

"Look at this baby," Alicia said, taking Josh out of the car. "You are such a cutie!"

"Thank you," I said wryly. "I always knew you thought I was cute."

"Yeah, you're cute, too," Alicia smirked. "You get your stuff, I have the baby."

Alicia's fiancé, Dennis, took my bags.

"Let me guess — you must be Dani and that's Josh," he said warmly.

"And you must be Dennis," I said. We shook hands and he took my bag upstairs.

"Where's Andrea?" I asked, hugging Alicia after she sat Josh on the couch.

"She went to the store to get applesauce for Josh. Does he still like it?"

"Yeah, but he eats regular food now. She didn't have to do that."

"How was the drive?" Dennis asked, as he came back into the living room and began playing with Josh.

"Good," I said noticing how Josh instantly warmed up to him. "I made good time."

"Do you drive like Alicia?" he asked, loud enough for her to hear.

"Hey," Alicia said from the kitchen, "I heard that."

"She can't help it," Dennis teased. "She has a lead foot."

Alicia joined us and hugged him as he held Josh. "He loves this lead foot."

I was happy for Alicia because she was happy. Every time we spoke, she talked about Dennis and how much she looked forward to spending the rest of her life with him.

"How are the wedding plans coming along?" I asked feeling the need to have something to say.

"Girl, good as done. And while you're here, we can get you fitted for your dress."

Andrea came in the door with a dozen balloons. "Where's my baby?"

"Balloons," Josh said running to her. Andrea picked him up and twirled him around.

They both laughed. "How's my baby?" Andrea asked him in baby talk. "Hey baby cuz," she looked over at me. "What's doing?"

"I'm good," I smiled, "and hungry!"

"We can eat when the bird is done — maybe

around two o'clock," she said, still playing with Josh.

Andrea's boyfriend Harvey joined us for dinner. I was panicked at feeling like a third wheel, but the evening was like being with family. Dennis and Harvey treated me like we were old friends. Still, I wished I had a date. When I went upstairs to put Josh to bed, my cousins had their goodnights with their boyfriends. One day, I promised myself, someone was going to love me, too.

We reserved Friday night for our oldies party. We put on pajamas and sang along with all of our old favorites as we listened to Alicia's albums - Brenda & the Tabulations, Little Anthony & the Imperials, Isaac Hayes, The Five Stair Steps, The Emotions, The O'Jays, Tina Marie, Ashford & Simpson, The Jackson Five, and the Delfonics. Before we knew it, it was four o'clock in the morning. Just like old times, we slept on the floor in the living room.

It rained Saturday and we spent the day watching movies. I was packed to leave Sunday morning until my cousins convinced me to leave after church.

The Sanctuary was crowded and we weren't able to sit together. I saw a few familiar faces and a few I didn't recognize hugged me, commenting on how big Joshua had gotten. I assumed they were friends of Andrea and Alicia and had seen his picture at their house. Joshua played with the little boy sitting behind us. I should have made him turn around and sit quietly, but my mind was back in Columbus – if only they knew. "God," I whispered during the prayer, "please help me."

After church we ate leftovers, took pictures and hugged a lot. It was three o'clock before I left and I hoped Joshua would sleep in the car.

It started raining before I hit Wheeling. I hated driving in the rain and my windshield wipers were bad. It was hard to tell if this was a sign from Nana - perhaps she was crying with me. Things were supposed to be better. Funding for my job had been cut and my graduate assistant stipend would only leave me one hundred and fifty dollars after I paid rent and daycare. I turned on the radio for some driving music and of all songs, "Good Morning Heartache" was playing. I turned it off and listened to Josh snoring. It rained until I got to Reynoldsburg.

Although Monday morning greeted me with a dreary sky and dark clouds, I reminded myself to have a better attitude. My budget would be cut by a third after the holidays, but it would be less work, no overtime and I wouldn't have to take any work home. This would be better for Joshua; after all, he loved Spaghetti O's. I had to refocus on my finals.

The elevator was crowded and had gone by once. My plan was to sign the papers in the Student Affairs Office for my grad assistant placement and get to class in time to review my notes before the final. The second elevator was more crowded than the first, but I squeezed on anyway.

His breath was hot on my neck. He was standing so close behind me that I could smell his cologne. He smelled good. Lagerfeld. My dad wore that, too.

"I guess I shouldn't stand this close to a beautiful woman who I don't know," a voice I didn't know said. He was smiling when I got the courage to turn around.

"Elevator's crowded," was all I could think to say without blushing.

The door opened on the ground floor and he stepped in front of an elderly gentleman to get in front of me.

He extended his hand as we exited together. "Jason Singleton."

"Danielle Allen."

"Nice to meet you," he said, walking with me. "I've seen you around and you always seem like you're in a hurry." He paused. "Do you have time for coffee?"

"Actually, I was on my way to the coffee shop."

We walked to the coffee shop and I sat at a small table while he went to the counter.

"I got a lot of sugar and a lot of cream," Jason said as he handed me the cup before sitting down. "I didn't know how you like it."

"Oh, this is fine." I couldn't stop smiling. "Thank you."

He sipped his coffee. "So how do you like OSU?"

"So far, so good. What about you?"

"I like it, but this is déjà vu for me. I completed my undergrad work here."

"Did you just continue straight through?" I asked, feeling a level of comfort.

"No," he shook his head, "I graduated, moved to Atlanta, got married, got divorced and then came back for grad school."

"Wow, you've been busy."

"That's history – I'm looking forward to graduating in the spring."

"What are you studying?"

"Finishing my MBA. What about you?"

"Just starting in the School of Education." I smiled at him because he was smiling at me.

"Teacher?"

"Guidance Counselor."

A female student interrupted us. "Jason, can I talk to you?"

"Would you excuse me for a minute?" He stood to speak with her. "Oh, Danielle, this is Renee, one of my study group members - Renee, Danielle."

I waved and she spoke a hurried hello.

"Jason, I can't meet tonight — something came up at Will's job, so I don't have a sitter."

"It's okay," he told her. "I can start the presentation and we can go over it tomorrow. Can we meet after class?"

"Yeah. I'm really sorry about tonight. I know we won't get anything done if I bring the baby."

"Renee I understand. Really, it's okay," he said.

"Well, I gotta run. See you tomorrow," Renee said in a rush.

"Sorry about that," Jason apologized as he sat down. "Now that I'm free for the evening, can I take you to dinner?"

"Tonight really isn't good," I said quickly, knowing I didn't have anyone who could babysit for me.

"Is that a 'tonight' isn't good or is it that 'no night' is good?" He leaned forward on the table. "You're not married, engaged or madly in love with someone are you?"

"None of the above and it's just tonight," I couldn't stop smiling. "I'll honor a rain check."

"Promise?"

"Promise." As I got up from the table, I noticed how much he smiled. "Thanks for the coffee break."

"How will I claim my rain check?" he asked.

"You could meet me at the elevator every Monday and Wednesday at two o'clock, or you can call me," I suggested.

"I think I'll try both, but I'll need your number," he noted.

I wrote my number on a napkin and handed it to him.

The following morning, I rushed to get Josh ready. I was anxious about seeing Jason and wanted to have a few minutes to talk if our paths crossed. *I should have asked for his number, too,* I thought. I wondered how long he would wait to call me.

There was no sign of him as I walked across campus. So much for a little flirting before class.

Jason called that evening right after I put Josh to bed and we talked for two hours. Over the next week and a half, we met for coffee or lunch every day. I managed to avoid the date question because we were absorbed in studying for finals and writing papers. Denise and Elaine encouraged me to go for it. I had not dated since Greg and wasn't sure how to tell Jason about Josh. Actually, I was afraid he wouldn't want to see me anymore. I was enjoying being flirted with, even if it didn't turn out to be anything. It also felt good to flirt back.

It stormed the night before my last final, and Joshua woke up with each crack of thunder. Determined to make him sleep in his bed, I sat next to him and held his hand until he went back to sleep. By the time the sun came up I should have been exhausted, but my mind was racing as I stared out the window watching the street come alive. Mr. Brown was in his door when the paper was hurled from the station wagon. Miss Paulette and Miss Edna were in their sixties, but maintained their pace as they came around the block for their second lap. Kevin stumbled out the door to take Duke for his morning walk.

I stirred more cream into my coffee and thought about Jason. He wasn't what I imagined my Prince Charming would look like. He wasn't six foot five and he didn't have dimples, but there was something about Jason. He reminded me of Joey – always neatly dressed in khakis with loafers. He had nice eyes and he always smelled good. He made me laugh, he made me feel beautiful. Jason's presence made my heart flutter and I liked that.

Walking across campus, I wondered if I was reading too much into this chance encounter. What did I really know about him? Why was he divorced? Could he love my child? What would he think of me after finding out I had a baby by a married man? I entered the room to take my psych final, feeling like I was the one who needed a psychiatrist!

Jason was standing by the door when I came out of my class. "Let me give you a ride, it's starting to rain."

I was caught off guard because I hadn't expected him to be waiting for me. "I'm just going across campus," I said.

"No problem," he replied. He put up his umbrella and held the door. "Where do you need to go?"

He was parked in front of the building and I walked toward the car, intentionally not answering him. He opened the car door and the smell of fried chicken greeted me.

"Your dinner smells good," I said when he got in.

"There's enough to share," he offered.

"I don't want to take your dinner," I said meekly,

"but thank you."

"Where did you say you were going?"

"The University Daycare."

"Applying for a job?"

"Picking up my son."

Jason hesitated as if my words were unclear. "I didn't know you had a son," he said trying not to sound shocked. "How old is he? What's his name?"

"Twenty months, Joshua," I answered in one breath without looking at him. "I'm a single parent trying to get through grad school."

"You'll do it," he assured me. "I know you will."

We arrived at the daycare and I thanked him for the ride as I searched my purse for my keys. Jason was staring at me and I turned to face him.

"I couldn't go out to dinner with you because I didn't have a babysitter," I explained.

Jason took my hand and said, "He could have come with us."

"I have a sitter for tomorrow," I offered.

"I really don't mind if you bring him," he responded.

I reached for the door and said, "I'll be ready tomorrow at 6:30."

"I need to know where you live," he added.

"Three fifty-two Sullivant Avenue, apartment two. Thanks again for the ride."

Jason picked us up at 6:15, and we drove to Denise's to drop off Josh.

"I really don't mind if he comes along," he said again, opening the car door.

"Maybe next time," I replied as he reached for my hand to help me out of the car.

"Hi, Jason," Denise said coming down her front steps. "Let me get the baby so ya'll can get on with your date."

"Denise," I said trying to catch her eye, "we'll be back around eleven."

"Oh, y'all take your time. We're going to watch the Muppets, eat Jell-O, color, and bang on some pots. This will be the best date I've had in months!"

"Thank you Denise," I said, giving Josh to her.

"She's a nice girl Jason," Denise said in a motherly tone.

"I'll be a perfect gentleman," Jason responded and winked at her as he closed my door.

We drove off laughing and went to a jazz club. Over dinner, we laughed and talked about our dreams and goals. Our conversation was easy and Jason didn't mind sharing about himself. I liked that.

On the way back to my apartment, after we picked up Josh, my anxiety returned. I was unsure of what I would do if Jason tried to kiss me. I wanted him to, but wasn't sure if I should, especially in front of Josh. He opened my door before getting Josh from the back seat.

"I'll carry him upstairs for you."

Jason put Joshua on the couch.

"Thanks so much," I smiled at him. "I had a great time."

"What about him?" He asked, looking over at Josh sleeping.

"I think he did, too!"

"Maybe we can do this again."

"I'd like that."

As Jason walked toward the door, I forced myself to keep breathing. He hugged me and kissed me on the cheek.

It was late, but I called Denise anyway. I had to tell someone about my date.

Over the next week, I saw Jason every day for coffee or lunch, but Christmas break was coming and I wanted more time to be with him.

Elaine agreed to keep Josh so Jason and I could have another date night before Christmas break.

"What time are you leaving tomorrow?" he asked on our way to the restaurant.

"My plan is to leave by seven. I don't like driving at night. What about you?"

"I'm not sure, probably by noon. Can I call you over the holiday?" Jason asked.

"I'd like that," I replied

He pulled into the parking lot. "Do you have any plans for New Year's?"

"Just the usual — church and breakfast," I replied.

"Can I interest you in coming back early so we can bring in the New Year?" he continued.

"Sure, I guess," I agreed, knowing Mom was going to have a fit.

After dinner, Jason placed a beautifully wrapped box on the table. "Put this under your tree, and open it Christmas morning."

"Thank you. You didn't have to," I told him.

He smiled and took my hand, saying, "A special lady needs special gifts."

We held hands all the way to Elaine's house. I felt special and that was the best present of all.

After he carried Josh inside my apartment, he went back to his car and presented me with three gift-wrapped boxes.

"This one is for you, too, and these are for Josh."

"Well, we have something for you," I said, handing him his gift.

He put the gift on the couch and kissed me. "Thank you," he said still holding me. "You really didn't have to."

"I know, I wanted to." I tried to think of something that wasn't cliché, but my heart was beating too fast to supply adequate oxygen to my brain.

Mom met us in the driveway when I pulled up. Josh called out, pointing to her and she hugged him after taking him out of his car seat. I decided to wait until later to let her know I'd be leaving on the thirtieth.

Rhonda came by the next morning before we were dressed. She couldn't wait to show me her ring and I was excited to tell her about Jason. She promised to stop by on Christmas morning because she was already committed to spend the bulk of her day with Lance's family in Philly.

The church dinner was after the Christmas Eve Cantata and Mom busied herself cooking. My dad didn't get home until after we had gone to bed.

I called Noah on Christmas Eve, and he invited us to spend a few days with them. I took a rain check and promised to get to New York in the near future. Joey called to let us know he would be spending the holiday in his first house — a brownstone in Brooklyn Heights. Andrea and Alicia called later that evening, and Alicia reminded me to pick up my dress in January. I told them both about Jason, describing him as a friend.

Joshua and I joined Mom in the living room

on Christmas morning. We took rolls of pictures, and Joshua still preferred unwrapping the gifts as much as the presents themselves.

Mom read the tag on Josh's gift. "Who's Jason?"

"Just a friend at school," I replied.

"He must be a special friend," she commented. "There are two boxes with your name on them from him."

The phone rang and I jumped up to get it. I knew it was Jason. He wished me Merry Christmas and thanked me for the sweater. He told me to open his gifts and I opened the little box first. It was a gold bracelet with a charm that said '#1 Mom'. I could see my mom smiling in the hall mirror as I talked on the phone. The bracelet was beautiful. Jason also gave me an Ohio State sweatshirt and signed the tag from Josh. Time passed quickly and we talked for over an hour.

"Must be a special friend," Mom teased when I hung up the phone.

"He really is."

"Anything else I should know?" Mom was probing.

"No, not yet," I assured her. "When there is, I'll let you know!"

The doorbell rang and it was Rhonda and Lance. Mom served warm apple cider and pecan rolls, while Rhonda and I exchanged gifts. Lance was very personable and by the time they left, I felt like we were old friends. Mom approved of Lance, too.

My dad came back a little after two o'clock that afternoon, and we sat down for an early dinner. "How's school?" he asked across the table.

"Good," I answered, grateful he didn't have a paper in his face. "I think I did well on my finals."

"Are you okay for money?" he inquired.

"I'm just as well off as all the other grad students," I answered, hoping he would read between the lines. If he did, he didn't say.

My dad dominated the dinner conversation with stories about the men he visited at the prison. It never ceased to amaze me how involved he was in the lives of others. I wondered if he ever thought about being so involved in the lives of his family. He knew more about the inmates than he did his own sons.

After dinner, Josh and I took a nap. It was six o'clock when Josh got up and we went downstairs to watch television with Mom. The television was watching her sleep in the recliner.

I shook her gently to wake her.

"Dani," she said still leaning back in the chair with her eyes closed, "I want you to be happy."

"I'm getting there," I said sitting down at her feet. "I'm working on it."

"I mean really happy. I want you to do the things you want and have a good life," Mom said with a tone that was serious and solemn.

I listened but didn't say anything. I wasn't exactly sure what she was talking about.

She opened her eyes and looked down at me, saying, "I could have been a model."

"Why weren't you?" I asked.

"It would have killed your dad," she said sadly.

"Why?"

"He wanted me to be at home," she explained.

"A lot of women work," I said almost defensively.

"When you love, you give your all," she stated flatly. "People need to know they're loved. I've loved

your daddy since I was a teenager," she said before paus-
ing. "And I've proven it everyday."

Mom closed her eyes again. I assumed she was
tired because she had been up late cooking for two days.
I decided to let her sleep until we went upstairs.

I sat on the floor thinking about the conversation
Mom and I had in October. Mom was upset when I
called and said some things that seemed out of character
because she never complained and always found at least
one good thing in every situation. Mom suspected Noah
was smoking reefer and was afraid that Joey might turn
out like Uncle Matt – chasing fame and fortune and
never finding happiness. Mom said she had failed and
was sorry. She was also angry because she didn't feel that
she received an equal return for what she had put into
her marriage. When I talked to her the following day,
she seemed fine. Mom never mentioned the conversation, so I didn't either.

Curiosity made me smell her glass after I picked
it up off the coffee table. I was mortified by the smell
of wine and never knew my mother to drink. Questions flooded my mind. Did my dad know? How? Why?
Where was Mom getting liquor without everyone in
town knowing?

As I walked past my dad's study to get a throw
to put over my mother, I wanted to spit on the sign that
read 'Quiet Please, I'm conducting God's business'. I
wanted to scream at him that his wife was drunk in the
game room. Instead, I covered my mother and sat on
the couch, crying quietly while Josh watched television.
Nana could help me, but she was gone. "God," I whispered, "please help me."

I let Mom sleep in the chair hoping my dad would
come down to see why she hadn't come to bed.

Anxiety was already ruling my life, and this was one more worry to add on top of taking care of Josh and getting through school. Tums were a regular part of my diet and eating usually made me feel like I was having a heart attack. I was lying to my mom every time I told her "No" when she asked if I needed anything. I was failing as a mother because my son's diet consisted of Spaghetti O's, Dinty Moore Beef Stew and grilled cheese sandwiches. I was one step from welfare and keeping it together by a thread. I stared at the ceiling unable to go to sleep. It was the twenty-sixth and I still hadn't mentioned leaving on the thirtieth.

Mom was scrambling eggs when I came downstairs later that morning. My heart palpitated as I rehearsed in my mind how to bring up the drinking. I couldn't do it. There was already so much pain in her life, and she seemed to find joy in being with Josh and me. I couldn't tarnish the holiday.

"Good morning," she greeted me as I came in the kitchen. "Are you hungry?"

I reached for a cup from the cabinet. "Just a little."

"Eggs will be done in a minute. Is Josh up yet?"

"Not yet." I sipped my coffee and took a deep breath. "Mom, I'm going back to Columbus on the thirtieth."

"Are you meeting your friend Jason?"

"Well, sort of." I didn't want to lie and I didn't want to hurt her feelings. "I have to get ready for classes."

"And bring in the New Year with your friend Jason?"

"Yes, Mother," I said and could feel myself blushing.

She put some eggs on a plate. "What about Josh?"

"He'll be with us," I said, as I headed out of the kitchen to get him.

After we ate, I called Jason. I needed to talk. I wanted to tell him about my mother, but I didn't. I just let him flirt with me and tell me how he couldn't wait to see me.

The snowstorm hadn't come as predicted and the thirtieth was a good traveling day. The sun glistened off the snow as I traveled through the mountains and the traffic was minimal. Josh and I made the trip in eight hours exactly.

Jason came over as soon as I called to let him know we were back. He kissed me when I opened the door.

"I couldn't wait to see you," he said still holding me. "How was the drive?"

"It was okay," I answered, glad to be in his arms. "I couldn't wait to see you either."

Jason went back to his car to get a pan of lasagna to put in the oven. Then he played with Josh while I unpacked. We ate a late dinner and then sat on the couch with Josh to watch *The Great Muppet Caper.*

Jason and I watched *Raiders of the Lost Ark* after Josh went to bed. I made hot chocolate topped with marshmallows and let him taste some of Mom's sweet potato pecan pie. After the movie, Jason told me about his family, his failed marriage and his older brother.

His parents, Dr. and Mrs. Singleton, were still happily married after thirty-four years. His dad was a college professor at the University of Michigan, and his mom was a retired school nurse. Jason was very close to his sisters, Maureen and Adrienne, who he described as best friends. Maureen was getting married in April and he wasn't sure what his sisters were going to do if they couldn't see each other every day. He envied the relationship between them and wished he could have had that kind of relationship with his brother. Phillip was killed in a drunk-driving accident two weeks after getting his license.

"We were never really close though," Jason sighed. "He liked getting into trouble and I didn't."

I squeezed his hand, not knowing what else to do or what to say. He paused for a moment, and then continued telling me about his ex-wife.

"Our mothers were best friends and we were high school sweethearts." He sat up resting his elbows on his knees. "We were voted the Most Likely to Get Married and we did. She went to Michigan State and I came here to OSU, but we continued to date. There were red flags she was seeing other people, I ignored them. I was the one who played around in high school, broke her heart, and wasn't always a nice guy, but she stuck with me through some really hard times. I settled down after realizing that I loved her. She was supposed to love me back." He paused before continuing, "Do you really want to hear this?"

"Yeah," I nodded my head, "I really do."

"We got engaged at the end of our junior year in college and got married the week after she graduated. We both got jobs in Atlanta and moved there to start our life together. My job kept me on the road and after about six months, and realizing that I spent most of our marriage traveling, I decided to surprise her. Saundra wasn't expecting me until Friday night and I went home on Wednesday to an empty apartment. She came in at one-thirty the next morning with her boyfriend who kissed her goodnight in my living room. I moved out of the apartment the next day. A month later, I filed for divorce and applied to grad school. That following August, I was back at OSU."

It was five o'clock in the morning by the time we looked at a clock. Jason helped me wash the dishes before he left.

Jason cooked dinner on New Year's Eve, and we went to church with friends to bring in the New Year. Elaine was living with her boyfriend, Tyrone, and they invited us to a midnight brunch after service. By the time service ended, I asked Jason if we could just go back to my apartment. Josh was asleep and it was going to be crowded and noisy at Elaine's. I called her and we took a rain check.

I made coffee while Jason put Josh in the bed. We settled on the couch listening to Grover Washington. Jason had told me about himself and I assumed it was my turn. It was uncomfortable, but I wanted him to know me. I shared with him about keeping to myself as a kid, growing up in the Allen household and my brothers. My memories of Nana brought tears to my eyes and I told him about the wisdom seeds. We both laughed when I told him about the Allen Thanksgiving catastrophe. Then I told him about Greg.

"I loved him," I admitted feeling embarrassed. "I never felt that way about anyone before him. I believed he loved me, too. I thought we were going to get married."

Jason was staring at me and the shame I felt retelling the story made it difficult to look at him.

"I found out I was pregnant after my internship ended. When I told him, thinking he would marry me, he told me he was already married and wanted me to terminate the pregnancy." The tears wouldn't stop and Jason wiped my face with his hand. "He left me to raise this baby alone. I was a fool."

Jason pulled me into his arms. "We all make mistakes. We make mistakes, we learn from them and then we move on."

It felt good to hear him say that, and I hoped he really meant it. I told him about Rhonda, Andrea and Alicia, and how I treasured my relationships with them. In the middle of my sentence, Jason got up to change the tape. He put on "Reasons" by Earth, Wind and Fire, and pulled me to my feet to dance with him. Then he kissed me, again and again.

"Let's play that again," he suggested when the song was over. "You're a good dancer."

"You're a good kisser," I teased him, "and I don't need a song."

We sat snuggled on the couch, listening to music and watched the sun rise. That was the first sunrise we shared on January 1, 1983.

Eight

It didn't take long to appreciate being a graduate assistant, even though it was financially limiting. Jason helped by bringing dinner over, cooking at his place or taking us out to eat. Although I never told him, Jason seemed to know I was struggling financially. He offered, several times, to assist me with paying for daycare, however, my pride and fear of needing him made me decline.

My new position allowed me to spend more time with Josh. I was picking him up from the daycare at four-thirty instead of six, we were eating dinner by six-thirty and Josh was getting in bed by eight. That gave me the evening to study and to spend time with Jason. By the end of January, we were studying together every day and spending weekends with one another. Sometimes Elaine or Denise would babysit so Jason and I could have a date night.

Time seemed to move quickly and Jason began interviewing in March. It seemed that he only talked about jobs in other cities, and I was afraid he would relocate after graduation. My feelings for Jason were more intense than I was willing to admit to myself or anyone else.

Jason went home for the weekend to help his sister, Maureen, move to Detroit. It was the first Saturday we hadn't spent together since January — I really didn't mind because I didn't feel well and knew I wouldn't be good company. Elaine took Josh to a birthday party, and I went to the campus library to look up case studies on school law.

"Danielle," I heard my name called. "Hey Danielle," she repeated while hugging me. "Are you here for the conference?"

"No," I smiled trying to remember her name. "I'm a student."

"Grad school?"

"Yeah, first year," I added, finally realizing who she was.

"So how's life? I thought you'd stay in Smithtown forever," my high school classmate commented.

"Just out here trying to spread my wings and fly," I replied.

"I hear you studied a little more than books in undergrad. I still keep in touch with Kathleen – she told me you had a baby," she said all in one breath.

"His name is Joshua," I informed her

"So what about his dad?" she asked.

"We're not together. I'm in this by myself," I said, consciously trying not to sound indignant.

"Well good for you, girl!" Her tone sounded almost patronizing. "I never thought I'd see the day when you would do something so radical. Is the good Reverend still speaking to you?"

"Of course," I responded, "my parents are doing just fine."

"Well, I'm at the Holiday Inn, here's my number." She scribbled on the back of a business card. "Give me a call. We can have a drink or do dinner. I'm here until Monday."

I read the card as she closed the door of the cab – Lisa Gayle, Editor, *New York Times*. It didn't surprise me. She always had a way with words. Lisa was the smartest girl in the class, the entire class. She told everyone she would be valedictorian when we were in the eighth grade, and I'm sure she was. She always wanted to be philosophical about God and I had no answers to her many questions on things I never thought about. If Jesus is from Africa, why is he pictured with blonde hair and blue eyes? Who taught fish to swim and birds to fly? How did the writers of the Bible know God inspired them? Why did Satan get mad at God and turn against Him? Where exactly is Heaven?

Lisa was attending a writer's conference at Ohio State. I hadn't seen her since the tenth grade when her family moved to New York. I was shocked she even remembered my name.

My body ached and I was miserable by the time I got home later that afternoon. I was asleep when Elaine dropped Josh off at six — he was wide-awake and full of sugar. I curled up on the floor in the living room so Josh could play in front of the television. After he fell asleep, I took more Nyquil and hoped I would hear him if he woke up.

By Monday morning, I felt like I had been hit by a truck. After taking Josh to the daycare, I went back home to get some sleep. I set my alarm for three o'clock and wrapped myself in a blanket. The knock on the door woke me at 2:30.

"Didn't mean to intrude," Jason apologized as I opened the door. "I thought we were meeting for lunch?"

"I have the flu or something. I feel like crap," I complained.

Jason followed me into the living room and I plopped down on the couch.

"Why didn't you call me, Dani? I didn't call last night because it was late. Do you need anything?" he asked.

"Would you get Josh from daycare?"

"No problem," he said, folding his jacket over the

back of the couch. "I'll take care of him for the evening so you can get some rest."

"I can't ask you to do that," I protested.

"You don't have to ask," he said calmly.

Jason made me a cup of hot tea with honey and lemon and sent me to bed. I don't remember drinking the tea and it was nine o'clock when I woke up. Josh and Jason were asleep on the couch. There were toys everywhere.

"What are you doing?" he whispered as I was putting toys in Josh's toy box.

"I just came to check on you and Josh," I tried to smile. "I'll put him in the bed."

"He's fine," Jason said, getting up from the couch. "He's been bathed and fed. We were just spending a little time getting to know each other."

"Thank you," I mumbled, mindful not to get too close to him. "Were you able to get any work done?"

He motioned for me to sit on the couch. "Let me put him in the bed and I'll make you another cup of tea."

Jason held me and stroked my hair. At 6:20 the next morning, he was still holding me. I got up to start the coffee maker. School Law was not a class to miss and I needed to put in a few hours in the Advising Center. I jumped in the shower and tried to wash off all the Vicks I had rubbed on myself.

I was standing at the kitchen sink making coffee when Jason woke up.

"I know that was a horrible night's sleep," I said, as he stood and stretched, still in his jeans and sweatshirt from yesterday.

"It felt good to hold you," he said and hugged me. "Do you feel better?"

"Sleeping in your arms made me feel better," I

replied.

He kissed my cheek. "That doesn't have to be the last time."

I handed him a cup of coffee. "Half and half is in the fridge, sugar's in the middle container."

Jason left to get ready for the day and I woke Josh for breakfast. I didn't completely feel better, but I felt good inside.

The cold was putting up a good fight to hold off spring. It was April, but had been snowing off and on all day. We decided against going out for pizza and opted to celebrate Josh's birthday with his favorite — grilled cheese sandwiches.

We put on party hats while we sang happy birthday, but Josh was more interested in opening the brightly-wrapped gifts than eating cake. Mom sent two outfits and signed the card from her and my dad. Alicia and Andrea sent a Sesame Street comforter with matching curtains for his room. I used the JC Penney gift certificate from Rhonda to buy Josh several summer outfits. Elaine gave him two books, *A Snowy Day* and *Teddy Bear, What Will You Wear?*, and Denise gave him a container of Lego blocks. Jason bought him a Tonka truck and an Ohio State sweatshirt.

It was almost nine o'clock before Jason gave Josh a bath and put him in the bed. I cleaned up and did the dishes and was waiting for the teapot to boil while watching a car struggle to get down the street when Jason came out of Josh's room.

"Snow is pretty, but I'm afraid to drive in it," I explained.

"What else are you afraid of?" he asked, turning off the television and sitting on the kitchen stool.

"Sometimes I'm afraid of us," I said, mindful to keep my voice down because Josh wasn't asleep yet.

"What exactly are you afraid of?" he asked, genuinely concerned.

I turned off the tea kettle and intentionally sat on the couch instead of sitting on the stool next to him. "Us. This. Sometimes I feel like we're playing family. Josh is getting attached to you. I heard him call you daddy. I have to think about him," I said seriously.

"Is this about Josh or is it about you?" He sat next to me on the couch and took my hand.

I didn't answer.

"I'm not playing, Dani. For me, this feels right. It's time to move forward."

"What do you mean when you say move forward?"

"Me, you, Josh — us, we," he paused. "What were you thinking when I said move forward?"

"I want to make sure I don't get hurt again."

"Life gives no guarantees." He turned my face toward him. "I don't ever plan to hurt you or Josh."

I smiled and he kissed me. When he tried to pull back, I kissed him because I didn't know how else to respond.

"My sister is getting married in two weeks," he said playing with my fingers, "and I'd like you and Josh to come home with me."

My throat went dry. What would his parents think of me? The more I thought about meeting his family, the more my stomach knotted.

"Jason, I'm afraid," I repeated, getting up from the couch, not wanting to look at him. I turned the teakettle back on.

His tone changed. "What do you mean afraid?"

"I don't think that's a good idea," I said, still afraid to look at him. "I'm sorry."

"Sorry?" His voice was agitated.

Numb, and angry with myself, I had no words. I was staring out the kitchen window and Jason was standing behind me.

"It's been three months and you still change the subject when I want to talk about us. Are you still in love with Greg?"

"No," I whimpered, "it's not that at all."

"Well, what is it? You don't seem to mind portraying us as a happy family."

I wanted to answer, but I didn't know what to say.

"I've told my family I want them to meet someone very special. I thought that was you. Is it?"

"Jason, it's complicated," I said, finally looking at him.

"What's more complicated than me loving you and you keeping me at a distance? You think you're the only one who's been hurt? My heart's been broken before Dani — it wasn't you who was unfaithful to me. You happen to be the one I want to start over with. You and Joshua. But you have to decide."

I had never seen him angry before.

"Are you waiting for Greg to come back riding on a white horse to sweep you off your feet and carry you off to his castle? Will you be waiting if he does?" he asked in rapid succession.

His eyebrows met and his words were cutting. I should have refuted his allegations. I stood motionless, fighting back tears and wishing he would stop staring at me waiting for a response. No words would come. My mind raced and searched for something to say. He was right. He loved me and I was pushing him away. The room became hot and the air seemed to thin out.

"I'll tell you what," he finally said walking away from me, "let me know when you stop waiting."

He got his coat and went into Josh's room. He kissed him and told him goodbye. He never said goodbye to him – it was always goodnight or I'll see you later. He came out of the room and walked out the door. I wanted to run after him and beg him not to leave. Unable to speak or move, I listened as he walked down each step outside my door. The teapot was whistling and I didn't realize I was crying until Joshua hugged me around my legs.

"Don't cry, Mommy," he said smiling at me, "don't cry."

I put Josh back to bed and called Denise. She volunteered to come over before I asked.

"What is wrong with you?" Denise stated as she pushed past me when I opened the door. "You get a man, a good one at that, and you just let him walk away. You're crazy, you need help!"

"This is not why I called you," I interrupted her.

"I know why you called," she continued. "You called because you just can't believe how stupid that was. Girl he loves you, he loves your son, he's educated, his nails are clean, his shoes are polished, and he knows how to buy a suit! And did I mention that he loves you?"

"Okay, okay I'm stupid!" The tears came and I slumped to the floor. "What's wrong with me?"

Denise's voice was calmer as she sat down next to me. "Dani, Greg is not coming back for you and he doesn't care about Josh. He's probably drowning himself in a bottle somewhere hoping you never show up with this baby."

I buried my face in my hands and tried to keep from hyperventilating. Her words were like salt in an open wound.

Denise put her arm around me. "Girl, you gotta move on. I know you love Jason. Stop fighting it." She paused. "Tell me you don't love him."

"He makes me laugh. He's comfortable to be with, and Josh really likes him."

"Do you love him?" Denise was persistent. "I think you love him."

"I think I do too," I confessed. "But I think I blew it."

"So what are you going to do?" Denise took the dishtowel out of my hand and stood to finish drying the dishes.

"I don't know. Any suggestions?"

She smiled. "You could start by calling him and admitting it was temporary insanity."

"Do you think he'd come to dinner? I could make smothered pork chops, his favorite."

"Girl, if you act right, it won't matter what you make for dinner!"

After Denise left it took almost an hour to find the box of stationary Mom gave me for Christmas. I wrote a formal dinner invitation so I could mail it in the morning.

You are cordially invited
to be the honored guest of Danielle Allen
who requests the opportunity to apologize
and have dinner.
Your favorite meal is being served
Saturday evening at 6:30.

Denise had plans for Saturday evening, so Elaine

and Tyrone agreed to babysit. I dropped Josh off at three o'clock and went home to start cooking. By five o'clock, I convinced myself Jason wouldn't come. He avoided me on campus and hadn't called all week.

The doorbell rang at five minutes after six. I closed my eyes, paused and took a deep breath before opening the door.

"I'm sorry," I announced. "I've been foolish, well actually stupid."

He wouldn't look at me. "Can I come in or do I have to stand out here?"

"Of course you can. You're the guest of honor."

"Where's Josh?" He walked past me looking for the usual sign of toys.

"Elaine and Tyrone are babysitting."

He put his coat over the back of the couch.

I picked it up and hung it in the closet.

"I need to talk to you."

"I've missed Josh. I was looking forward to seeing him." He was ignoring me.

I went into the kitchen.

"He's missed you, too. And so have I."

"Have you really?" He joined me in the kitchen.

I turned off the green beans and looked him in the eyes. "Yes, I really have."

"How much?"

I kissed him lightly on his lips.

Jason pulled me toward him and held me tight and close, like our bodies would mesh.

"Girl, I love you. Really love you — not just using the L word for pretense, from my soul I love you."

"I love you, Jason. I'm sorry I hurt you," I apologized.

"How long will you punish yourself?" he asked,

still holding me.

"I'm so afraid," I confessed. "It's so good what we have. I'm afraid someone with no baggage will come along and take you away from me."

"I love you and Josh," he exclaimed. He lifted my chin so our eyes met. "I know what I want. You ready to take this leap with me?"

Dr. and Mrs. Singleton left a note for us to meet them at the church and a stuffed teddy bear for Josh on their kitchen table. When we arrived at the church, Mrs. Singleton wanted Josh to sit with her during the wedding rehearsal and other members of Jason's family took turns playing with him. Maureen was busy with last minute details, but took time to welcome me. Adrienne made a point to let me know that Jason told her all about me.

The conversation after the rehearsal dinner was on Jason's plans and his antics as a child. Mrs. Singleton wanted to know about me and we had the chance to talk while I helped her put food away. It was overwhelming. Jason loved me and his family was accepting. What more could I ask for?

Maureen's wedding was beautiful. The train on her dress was trimmed in pearls and sequins that glimmered in the sunlight. The wedding party wore tangerine and the church was decorated with tangerine- and ivory-colored bows. When the preacher asked who was giving her away, Dr. Singleton, Mrs. Singleton, Adrienne and Jason all said, "We do." Jason kept turning around and winking at me during the ceremony. When Maureen kissed Ellis, Jason blew a kiss to me.

We left the reception right after Maureen and Ellis. It was almost one-thirty in the morning when we arrived back in Columbus and Jason drove to his house.

"I thought you had a lot of work to do?" I asked as he took Josh out of his car seat. "I don't want to get in your way."

"I can study later."

I stood in the doorway of his bedroom and watched Jason undress Josh. He laid him in the middle of his bed. "Are you keeping him tonight?"

"No," he whispered, "we both can. I was hoping you would stay."

"Spend the night?"

"I just want to hold you, like I promised I would."

Jason gave me a tee shirt and a pair of shorts. We sat on the couch and he held me while we attempted to watch a movie. I only remember Jason waking me to get in the bed. We left Josh in the middle, I slept against the wall and Jason slept on the other side of him. When I realized we were all in the bed, I smiled. This was family.

I was preparing for finals and trying to find a summer job. Jason was studying for finals, interviewing and preparing for graduation. He had been offered a very good job at Morgan Stanley in New York, but had not yet accepted. I had only talked to Jason twice that week and assumed he was afraid to tell me he would be leaving. I couldn't blame him, even though I wanted him to love me enough to stay. He came by the night before graduation.

"Hey stranger," I greeted him as Josh ran to him.

Jason smiled and kissed me on the cheek. "Hey stranger yourself."

He sat on the floor and began playing with Josh. "I didn't take the job in New York," he announced stacking blocks for Josh to knock down.

"I know you really wanted that job." I sat down next to him on the floor.

"What I really want is you," he said and put Josh on his lap, "and this little guy here. I took the Business Manager position with the school district. I start in June."

Dr. and Mrs. Singleton, Maureen, Ellis, Adrienne and her fiancé, Scott, came to Jason's graduation. We went to dinner afterward and Jason told them of the job he had taken. Mrs. Singleton smiled and no one questioned why he turned down the job in New York. Maureen's husband, Ellis, played with Josh during dinner and talked about looking forward to having a playmate for Josh at future family gatherings.

It was a good evening and I was happy to be part of it. Maureen and Ellis invited us to Detroit for the Fourth of July — the family cookout was at their house. By the end of the evening, I felt like family. I exchanged numbers with his sisters and promised to keep in touch.

June was busy and my two classes sometimes seemed like a full load. Jason came with me to Pittsburgh for Alicia's wedding. My parents were unable to attend, which meant they would have to wait until October, when Rhonda was getting married, to meet Jason. I tried to get up the nerve to wink at him during the ceremony, but couldn't do it. As we walked down the aisle after the ceremony, Jason caught my eye and winked at me.

We arrived back in Columbus early Sunday afternoon. The sky was clear and the sun was shining. I felt guilty about having to study because it was a beautiful day to go to the park. Jason volunteered to take Josh while I went to the library.

Jason insisted we go out to dinner the night before we went to Detroit. I should have suspected something, because Denise called me and offered to babysit.

After we ate, Jason handed me a huge gift bag. "This is just because I love you. Open it," he said, beaming from ear to ear. "I think you'll really like it."

It was a huge red velvet pillow wrapped in layers of white tissue paper. "Do you like it?" he asked anxiously. I was hesitant to answer because I didn't want to offend him.

Jason took the pillow from me and put it on the floor. Kneeling on the pillow, he took a ring box out of his jacket pocket.

"It's only been six months but I know we're supposed to be together. I want to love you and Josh for the rest of my life. Will you marry me?"

I was speechless and had to remind myself to breathe. It was as if time stood still and I couldn't say yes fast enough. Jason kissed me and everyone in the restaurant applauded.

By the time I got home, it was almost midnight, but I called my mother anyway. She was sleeping and asked me to repeat myself. Then she congratulated me through her tears and said she couldn't wait to meet her future son-in-law. Jason announced our engagement to his family at the cookout, which really wasn't too much of a surprise. Mrs. Singleton obviously knew and had asked to see my ring when we arrived.

Mrs. Singleton hugged me. "Now you can call me Mom and Josh can call me Grandma," she smiled. "He's my first grandchild."

Again, I was overwhelmed and overjoyed to be

welcomed into the Singleton family with open arms. It was another good weekend and I had the chance to meet Jason's aunts, uncles, cousins and his high school friends.

We arrived in Pittsburgh a few weeks later, and Andrea cooked dinner to celebrate my engagement. On Saturday, Andrea arranged for two of her undergraduate sorority sisters to keep Josh so we could go to Kennywood Park. Harvey talked us into riding the Racers, but I hate roller coasters, so I held onto Jason and screamed during the ride. We ate funnel cakes and Potato Patch fries, and stood in lines for hours. It was one of the best times of my life.

October didn't come soon enough and I was anxious to introduce Jason to my parents. We arrived in Smithtown for Rhonda's wedding just before the last of the leaves fell to the ground. Smithtown was always beautiful in the fall.

"Oh, Danielle!" Mom hugged me. "I'm so happy for you! Congratulations to you, too," she said hugging Jason.

Mom took Josh out of his car seat and kissed him repeatedly. She put him down and he played in the leaves piled in the yard.

I was upstairs changing my clothes when I heard Mom introduce Jason to my dad.

"David, this is Jason. Dani's fiancé."

"Well I guess congratulations are in order," was his stoic reply. "This seems rather sudden. When's the wedding?"

"Next year sir," Jason said shaking his hand. "We're looking at May or June after Dani graduates."

"Hey Dad," I said coming down the steps. "I'm

getting married!"

He turned and smiled at me. "So I hear, so I hear. Will I get the honors of performing the ceremony?"

"Don't you want to walk me down the aisle?"

"We can talk about that later," Mom interrupted. "The three of you better get going over to the church. Josh and I have cookies to bake."

Rhonda's wedding was everything she always talked about, including the designer dress from Saks. The bridesmaids wore lime-colored Lois Lane suits with matching pillbox hats, gloves and shoes. Her cousin, Karen, and I wore the same suits in lemon. The changing leaves provided a breathtaking backdrop for pictures after the ceremony. Rhonda deserved every moment, and I hoped her happiness would last forever.

Before going back to my parent's house, Jason and I drove to Atlantic City. We talked about the kind of wedding we wanted as we strolled along the boardwalk. The night was clear, the stars were shining and I was in love.

Unintentionally, we dressed in coordinating outfits for church the next morning. I wore the navy pinstripe coatdress Jason bought for my birthday. As Rhonda so often reminded me, I added a red silk scarf for color. Joshua had on navy pants with a white cotton sweater trimmed in navy and red. When Jason came down to the kitchen, we laughed because he was wearing a navy pinstripe suit with a white shirt. His tie was shades of blue with two red pinstripes. Mom took our picture on the front porch. It was our first family photograph.

I should have warned Jason, but I hoped my dad wouldn't do it. However, just as I expected, before the benediction, my dad announced from the pulpit that I was getting married. He had Jason stand and introduced him to the congregation. After the service, some people wanted to congratulate us and some only wanted to see my ring. The pretentiousness made me laugh — some things in Smithtown would never change!

Time was moving quickly and planning a wedding was much more detailed than I anticipated. Elaine agreed to be my wedding coordinator and Denise agreed to sing. Josh would be our ring bearer, my nieces would be junior bridesmaids and my nephews would be junior groomsmen. Andrea, Alicia, Rhonda, Adrienne and Maureen were happy to be bridesmaids. My excitement about getting married made focusing on my first semester difficult.

My final semester was spent at a middle school where I completed my internship. My former boss, Omar Powell, was the guidance counselor and supervised me. He continued to be encouraging and permitted me to implement the self-esteem model that I developed in my Group Therapy class. By the end of April, I fulfilled my required hours, and Omar gave me an outstanding evaluation along with an employment recommendation. I submitted my application to the district for the upcoming school year. Omar and I worked well together, and I welcomed the opportunity to work with him again.

My mom and Mrs. Singleton surprised me with a bridal shower the Sunday after graduation. Everyone who had become special in my life was there — only Nana was missing. Hard as I tried not to, I cried through my shower.

Jason and I were married on July 21, 1984 at

St. Luke's Baptist Church. In spite of the storm during our wedding rehearsal, the morning was beautiful. The flowers glistened from their fresh watering and someone placed white bows on the hedges lining the front walk of my parent's house. This was the day my dreams would come true.

As much as my dad wanted to do the service, he said it meant more to him to give me away. He was presenting me to Jason, and I would be someone's wife, not just his daughter with a baby. One of his closest friends, Reverend Welch, performed the ceremony.

Standing at the back of the church with my dad, I smiled at the wedding party. Joshua wore a white tuxedo, just like Jason's, and he held my hand as we waited for the bridal march to begin. The groomsmen wore black tuxedos with peach colored vests. My brothers were groomsmen and Noah surprised me by getting a haircut. My nephews looked like a pair of little Noahs, and took turns waving at their mother.

Our bridesmaids wore peach gowns that scalloped off their shoulders. Rhonda, my matron of honor, carried a bouquet of ivory-colored carnations, and the bridesmaids carried bouquets of peach-colored carnations. My nieces wore ivory, tea-length dresses made of taffeta and lace. Elaine made them small baskets, which were filled with peach-colored rose petals.

I felt like a princess as I descended the aisle. My ivory Victorian lace gown was scalloped off my shoulders and flared at my waist. The front of my gown touched the floor and my train flowed from the bow on the back of my dress. I carried a mixed bouquet of peach- and ivory-colored roses.

Jason's eyes followed me down the aisle and he mouthed 'you're beautiful'. In an attempt to stop the tears, I bit my quivering bottom lip. As we took our place at the altar, my dad wiped my tears with his handkerchief. Jason took my hand and kissed it after my dad took his seat.

My parents invited the congregation to the wedding and a repast in the church fellowship hall. Our dinner guests joined us at the Crystal Palace Ballroom, which Elaine decorated with white lilies and white taffeta bows. Everything was perfect, from the rehearsal to the ceremony. Our wedding day was more than I ever imagined. Only Nana was missing.

NiNe

Joshua stayed with my parents while Jason and I honeymooned in Bermuda. Neither of us had been to the Islands, and we were awestruck by their beauty. The clear blue water allowed us to see our feet no matter how far out we went. The sand was pink and warm, the sun was hot and the people were friendly. We spent hours on the beach — sitting, talking and napping, and once we tried to build a sandcastle. We rented motorbikes, went to the crystal caves, toured on a glass bottom boat and played with the dolphins at the aquarium.

On our last day, we watched the sun rise and set and let the changing tide bury our feet in the sand. The wisdom seeds had finally taken root and were growing. My life with Jason would be perfect and the seeds would bloom into beautiful flowers, just like Nana said they would.

The joy I felt when we arrived in Smithtown ended the next morning after I went downstairs to have coffee with my parents. My intention was to thank them for all they had done.

"Nice tan," Mom said as I sat down. "Want some juice?" She poured the glass before I answered. "Is Rhonda bringing Josh or are you going to get him?"

"We'll get him," I said sitting down next to my dad. "Bermuda is beautiful!" I pulled the paper down from in front of his face. "Dad, you and Mom should go for your anniversary."

He put the paper down on the table. "I can't just take off for a week," he protested.

"Sure you can," I stated matter-of-factly. "Even the pastor needs a vacation, and the pastor's wife deserves some time with her husband." I was out on a limb and didn't care. "Mom, wouldn't you like to go?"

"I guess it would be nice," she replied hesitantly. "David, we haven't been away in a long time," she said looking at my dad. "I think we should."

He sipped his coffee and mumbled, "Something to think about."

"Good morning." Jason hugged my mom as he came into the kitchen. He kissed me on the cheek and sat down between my dad and me. Mom handed him a cup of coffee.

"Good morning, Jason." My dad finished the last of his toast and sipped his coffee. "I'm glad you're up. We have some things to discuss."

"We do?" I almost choked on my apple juice because my dad's comment caught me off guard.

"Yes, we do," he answered still looking at Jason. "What about Joshua? Have you thought about that?"

"What do you mean?" I replied, unsure of what my dad was implying. "Thought about what?"

"David," Mom interrupted, "it's their life."

"What will you do about Joshua's last name?" My dad finally looked at me. "Now that you're a Singleton, will he remain an Allen?" He turned to look at Jason.

"I'm adopting him." Jason answered, maintaining eye contact with my dad. "I am his father and he will be a Singleton."

"Is that it?" My dad's tone was patronizing. "What will you tell the boy about his father? Doesn't he deserve to know the truth?"

"David, don't do this!" Mom's tone was sharp, even though her eyes filled with tears.

"Dad!" My voice level escalated as I turned to face him and maintain eye contact. "Jason is the only father he has ever known and you know that. Greg made a choice three years ago not to have anything to do with him. Jason is his father."

"So you're going to lie to him? You think you can create a skeleton that will stay in the closet forever?"

"I mean no disrespect, sir," Jason said, while holding my hand as he addressed my dad. "We will do what is best for Joshua. I am his father and he will bear my name. Whatever we choose to tell him when he gets older is our decision."

"Don't make him live a lie because you can't deal with your sin," my dad's tone was condescending as his eyes remained fixed on me.

Anger, pain and disappointment consumed me and I ran upstairs refusing to let my dad see me cry. Jason followed me and pulled me into his arms at the top of the steps.

Jason was in the shower and I was sitting on the bed folding Josh's clothes when Mom came into the room. She sat next to me and I put my head on her shoulder.

"Why does he always mess everything up? Life doesn't come in perfect little packages."

"I wish you didn't have to leave so quickly. I was going to make lunch," her voice was almost pleading.

"Mom, I can't take him. I have to go. I already told Rhonda we were on our way to get Josh. We'll eat later."

Her eyes were sad — just like I had seen them many times before. I hated having to leave, but my dad had tainted Jason's welcome to the family.

We stopped in Breezewood for lunch and then

Joshua fell asleep in the car.

"What was that all about with your dad?" Jason asked.

"He's hated me since I was pregnant," I stated sarcastically, being mindful to keep my voice down. "I was his third child who failed him."

"Time moves on, people grow – you've changed." Jason's tone was reassuring. He held my hand.

"Everything changes. My dad is the only one stuck somewhere in the past." My tone was flippant. "He may choose not to move on, but I have."

Jason wiped the tears from my face with his hand. I looked over at him and he smiled that same smile from the day we met on the elevator.

"I'm sorry," I said, breaking the silence. "My dad was wrong to do that."

"He's old school, I think his intentions are good."

"You don't have to defend him," I protested.

Jason took my hand, "But you have to forgive him. We all have to move on from here."

Later that week, during a phone call with my mother, my dad took the phone and apologized for his comments at breakfast. He agreed to respect our decisions as a family and promised to continue praying for us. Before asking to speak with Jason, he told me he loved me. I was still angry and didn't say it back.

In September of 1985, we purchased a house on Felix Drive in the Southfield section of Columbus. It was a small multi-ethnic neighborhood not far from the former Rickenbacker Air Force Base. Many ex-military and government workers from the Defense Construction

Supply Center also settled into the community with their young families. Jason and I agreed it would be a good place for Joshua to grow up. Like most of the families in the community, we attended Southfield Baptist Church, and Josh participated in the Sunday school activities.

Our picture perfect life began to fade and I assumed God was punishing me when I couldn't get pregnant. After trying for more than a year, I went to a fertility specialist. I was temporarily relieved when my test came back okay, yet unnerved because Dr. Fisher wanted to run a series of tests on Jason. A few weeks later, we sat nervously waiting to get the results that confirmed we would not be having any more children – Jason was sterile.

"I know you don't want Josh to be an only child," he said as we sat on the back porch one evening. "I'm sorry."

"Jason, don't blame yourself," I said.

"I want your life to be perfect," he countered.

"It already is," I said as I held his hand against my cheek, "you make it perfect."

We spent Thanksgiving in Ann Arbor with the Singleton's. Scott, Adrienne's fiancé, announced that he completed his dissertation and we celebrated with sparkling cider and cheesecake after dinner. Maureen and Ellis' news that they were expecting their first baby was overshadowed by Jason's news that he was sterile. I felt helpless.

We arrived back in Columbus on Sunday and the first message on the answering machine was from Alicia and Dennis. Ashley Sharon Hines was born the day after Thanksgiving. I called to congratulate them and we mailed a layette package from Sears.

We decided to spend Christmas at home to begin creating our own traditions. We decorated the tree with gold ornaments, and Jason held Josh up so he could put the star on top. Then we had hot chocolate after we lit the tree for the first time. On Christmas morning, one minute after midnight, Jason and I exchanged one gift.

In spite of everything, life was good and I was happy. I often wished Nana was alive to see that I finally got it right. I was beginning to understand this game called life instead of being whipped by it.

Jason legally gave Josh his name when the adoption was finalized in February of 1986. That spring, Ellis, Jr. was born to Maureen and Ellis. We drove to Detroit for Easter to celebrate Josh's birthday and welcome the new addition to the family. We were back in Pittsburgh in May for Andrea and Harvey's wedding.

Yearly vacations were added to our family traditions, and our first one was a week in New Orleans at the end of July. I was happily married with a beautiful son and doing the things I had longed for all of my life. We started every morning eating beignets in the French Quarter. We spent an afternoon listening to the jazz players on the street, we let Josh taste jambalaya and crawfish, and we took pictures on Bourbon Street. We were making memories. I began to understand the love Nana shared with Grandpa Booker. Her wisdom seeds were blooming and my life with Jason was beyond anything I ever imagined. He loved me and Josh was our son.

Adrienne married Scott Nelson in August and we shared another memorable family weekend in Ann Arbor. We spent Labor Day in Cleveland at the Singleton family reunion. Alicia and Dennis moved to Raleigh in October.

Dennis was from Florida and they wanted to be in the middle of their families. And, Alicia admitted she hated winter. Rhonda and Lance welcomed Angela Michelle on New Year's Day of 1987. We spent our family vacation at Disney World in July and in September Josh started first grade. He was growing up so fast.

In 1988, Corey Allen was born to Andrea and Harvey, and Maureen and Ellis had the twins, Maurice Jay and Elise Jai. Christmas brought two more babies — Chase Jackson was born to Adrienne and Scott on December 23rd and Cynthia Cherelle was born to Rhonda and Lance on December 26th. Dennis, Jr. was born to Alicia and Dennis in 1989.

In 1990, Monique Amirah was born to Maureen and Ellis and my niece Maisha had Aisha during her junior year in college in 1991. Rhonda and Lance's final attempt to have a boy in 1992 resulted in the twins, Victoria Lanelle and Veronica Janelle, and that spring, Tiffany Marie was born to Adrienne and Scott. It seemed like every year someone was having a baby and I could see the pain of failure in Jason's eyes each time we congratulated them. We talked about adopting — Jason felt it wasn't the same. My efforts to console him continued to be in vain. In Jason's eyes, our picture-perfect lives were incomplete.

Our family vacation memories were growing, and now included New York, San Francisco, Busch Gardens, Dallas, Baltimore and Martha's Vineyard. For our tenth anniversary, we cruised to Jamaica. My mother, the Singleton's, Maureen and Adrienne and their families joined us in 1995 when we cruised to Puerto Rico. Life was good.

It was the summer of 1996 when our lives changed forever. We returned from our family vacation in Virginia Beach and Jason was offered a job in Milwaukee. We contemplated moving and spent a week looking at houses and schools. It was the end of July when we found out Jason had colon cancer.

Damon, his best friend, flew to Columbus to be with us after we got the news. Colon cancer. Saying it was devastating. Damon urged us to rely on Jesus. He said that no matter what happened, we would never get through this without Him. He suggested we join a support group for cancer patients. I didn't want to join a support group for dying people even though Damon insisted it would help both of us.

My in-laws were supportive in spite of their pain and Mrs. Singleton cried whenever we spoke on the phone. Mom cried every time I spoke with her on the phone, too. Both of them agreed we should seek comfort in the Lord. Our parents had tried, several times over the past twelve years, to get us to do more than just attend church regularly by submitting our lives to Jesus. It always seemed like something we would get to later.

Rhonda prayed with me over the phone and gave me scriptures to read. She and Lance had been Christians for almost five years and she encouraged me to get into a Bible study. Alicia and Andrea both volunteered to drop everything and do whatever I needed. I didn't know what I needed. I was numb.

The sermon on the fourth Sunday in August was titled, "Take Your Burdens to the Lord and Leave Them There." The pastor concluded with the reading of Matthew 11:28-30:

> *"Come to Me, all you who labor and are heavy laden, and I will give you rest. Take My yoke upon you and learn from Me, for I am gentle and lowly in heart, and you will find rest for*

your souls. For My yoke is easy and My burden is light."

The words resonated in my head. Reverend Compton opened the doors of the church and Jason grabbed my hand.

"I need to do this," he said as he stood to his feet.

I didn't know what to say.

"We need to do this," Jason whispered as he gently pulled me to my feet.

Before I knew it, we were standing at the altar. Jason, determined to find a miracle, was willing to give Jesus a try. I went with him because I couldn't imagine my life without him. I needed to believe God would help Jason. I cried uncontrollably as Jason held me at the altar.

"Lord God, please help him," I whimpered. "I don't know what to do."

People were gathering around us praying and thanking God that we had come. They didn't know we came selfishly because we needed a miracle. I heard Josh whisper in my ear, "Mom, please don't cry."

We were emotionally drained after morning service. I retreated to my room and Jason sought refuge in his recliner. It was five-thirty that evening when Josh woke me.

"Mom, get up." He was almost pleading. "I made dinner."

I sat up and tried to smile. I could tell my eyes were still swollen. "Thank you," was all I managed to say.

"Come on." Josh pulled me by the hand. "Dad's already downstairs."

Jason was setting the table when I walked into the

dining room. I went over and hugged him. Josh came in behind me and we all hugged.

"I love you, Dad," Josh said without looking at him. "I don't ever want you to die."

"Always know that I love you," Jason told him lifting his face as he had done so many times before. "And remember – remember everything."

We hugged and cried in the dining room.

Two weeks later, after completing the new members classes, we were baptized at Southfield Baptist Church. I called my mother and asked her to pray for me. My father got on the phone and began to share scriptures that felt like trite biblical quotes. As the calls from family and friends continued through the evening, everyone was careful not to make promises, but diligent in reminding me that God would see us through the worst storms of life. I wanted a miracle. I wanted Jason to be cured and I wanted us to see Josh graduate from high school and college, to see him married, to play with our grandchildren and grow old together. No one was promising a miracle – only strength. I needed faith. The flowers that had begun to bloom from my wisdom seeds were choking on the weeds of my distress. Love, kindness, goodness and peace – the petals of those flowers were turning brown.

Josh began his sophomore year looking forward to basketball season. He anticipated starting and let conditioning dominate his free time. He pretended to be able to handle everything, but I would hear him crying at night and was unable to comfort him. I had not yet found a way to comfort myself.

I was having a pity party one Saturday afternoon

when Miss Mary, a mother of the church, came by with a pound cake.

"I don't mean to intrude," she said as I welcomed her in. "I wanted to bring this cake and to pray with you."

I didn't know what to ask for. The cancer was progressing rapidly and the love of my life was dying before my eyes. His suffering crippled me. Miss Mary prayed Nana's words – she said tears were for growing and then the sun always smiled down after each rain. Her words were almost poetic, but my life was hurting and I found no comfort in them. Jason had taken a turn for the worse and we were coping poorly with more cancer, more treatment, more doctors and shattered hope.

By December 1996, Jason was spending more time in the hospital than out. I was emotionally shattered trying to deal with the cancer that had blind-sided us and turned our lives upside down. We were sending people to the moon, yet there were no cures.

The chemotherapy rendered Jason helpless and he was unable to help us decorate the tree. Josh and I decorated it while he slept.

The Jordan jersey was the last gift I wrapped. My intention was to wake Jason at midnight so we could exchange gifts – I fell asleep in the game room before the news came on.

"Hey lady," he said shaking me, "it's midnight."

"Are you okay?" I was startled and I sat straight up. "Is something the matter?"

"I'm fine," he said smiling and sitting next to me. "I have something for you." Jason handed me a little box with a huge bow. "This is for you."

"And this is for you," I said and handed him the

box on the end table. "It's your turn to go first."

Jason opened the box and his trembling hands attempted to hold the jersey up in front of his tee shirt.

"Baby, you shouldn't have."

Guilt made me buy it. When Jason first talked about buying it, I fussed that no shirt was worth that kind of money, no matter whose name was on it.

"You should have the things you want," I said fighting back tears.

He kissed me. His closeness still made my heart flutter.

"Now your turn," he said as he put the jersey on. "Open the box."

It was an eighteen-karat gold Hershey's kiss. We went to Hershey Park the year after we were married and I faked being sick and stayed in the hotel room. A month later, I admitted being afraid of seeing Greg. Jason was angry that I had not been honest with him. It was the only fight we ever had during our marriage.

"I'm sorry," he said wiping my tears with his hand. "It was a dumb thing to be angry about. I should have understood. Can you forgive me?"

I slept in his arms on the couch under the twinkling of the Christmas tree lights.

We made our usual calls on Christmas morning and everyone was relieved to hear that Jason was feeling better. He had several good days and we went to see Josh play in a Christmas tournament. Josh was named MVP and gave the trophy to Jason. We celebrated by going to dinner and then to see *The Preacher's Wife*. I cried when Whitney Houston sang "I Believe in You and Me" — it was our wedding song.

By the end of February, Jason had lost twenty-five

pounds and getting out of bed was difficult. On March third, he was admitted to the hospital again.

Jason was heavily sedated for over seventy-two hours. His body trembled from the pain as he went in and out of consciousness. Dr. Whitlock told me Jason's prognosis was poor and he probably wouldn't live through the week. I never left him alone. I made sure Joshua, one of his parents or one of his sisters was with him, even if I only went to the bathroom. I rationalized that Jason would hold on as long as he was not alone. I liked Dr. Whitlock, but I hated his words. My mind told me he was doing his best to prepare the family for the inevitable; my heart told me he had already given up.

I awoke to Jason moaning at 6:17 on the morning of March seventh.

"I'm here baby, I'm right here." I held his hand and ran my finger across his brow. "I'll get the doctor," I whispered, reaching for the buzzer.

"No," he groaned, "open the curtains."

I obeyed and drew the curtains back to reveal the black sky. He heaved through his pain as he motioned for me to sit on the bed. I knew I wasn't supposed to. The nurses had reminded me several times to stay off the bed. Jason tried to hug me and I snuggled against his heaving chest. His trembling hand played in my hair. I wanted to breathe life into his body. He was dying, and we both knew it.

"I love you," he whispered, "very much."

"I love you more," I sobbed because I could feel him trying to hold me tighter than the pain was holding him.

"Time?" He asked as tears flowed freely from his eyes.

"6:29," I said, looking at the big clock on the wall.

When Jason was admitted, the ticking got on my nerves, but grief and anxiety now made me oblivious to it.

"Sunrise," he whispered, "our sunrise."

"A new beginning, a brand new day," I began to recite our vows, "the beginning of a lifetime of love." We spoke these words every year as we watched the sun rise. Twelve years had passed so quickly.

"Thank you for your love and for a son," he whispered as his breathing became more labored.

"Jason, let me get the nurse," I pleaded, but he shook his head.

"I'm going to meet Nana," he said weakly. "I'll be watching now, too."

"Jason, don't leave me," I said clinging to his trembling body. "I love you." I kissed his dry, cracked lips and wiped the tears from his eyes.

"Love you, love Josh," I heard him whisper. "Jesus loves you, too."

We had watched the sunrise on our honeymoon and every anniversary. It was over. Jason died before the sunrise on March 7, 1997.

Jason touched many lives — his co-workers, the high school kids he mentored, the Boy Scout troop he started when Josh was six, his family, his friends, Josh's and mine. We celebrated his life at Southfield Baptist Church with a host of family and friends. The beautiful songs, the loving sentiments, the words of comfort were all endearing — but Jason was gone. When all the people went home, it was Josh and I alone in the house with our pain and the void of Jason's absence.

I was lying on the couch wearing one of Jason's tee shirts and his sweat pants. I had been there all weekend. Josh sat in Jason's favorite chair, the recliner. We watched *Raiders of the Lost Ark*. It was Jason's favorite movie.

"Mom are you going to work tomorrow?" Josh asked breaking the silence.

"Not sure, why?"

"If you go to work, I'll go to school," he said without looking at me. "We've been home for a week."

I had a few tranquilizers left, but couldn't even go upstairs to get them. I stayed numb with or without them. The thought of leaving the house was still unbearable.

"He loved you very much Josh," I said sitting up.

"Why did God let my dad die?" Joshua asked.

His eyes filled with tears and I motioned for him to come to me. I held him and we grieved together. He was trying so hard to be strong for me and had not cried at the funeral. I held him tight and close.

"I don't know," I said softly.

We went to Smithtown for Easter. Joey was bringing his fiancé to introduce to the family and I looked forward to seeing Stormy, she had just turned twenty-three. Where had the time gone?

We arrived on Good Friday in time to attend the evening service. My dad spoke from Matthew 28:5-6:

> "But the angel answered and said to the women, 'Do not be afraid, for I know that you seek Jesus who was crucified. He is not here; for He is risen, as He said. Come, see the place where the Lord lay.'"

The title of his message was "What Did They Expect to Find at the Tomb?", the same question I was asking myself. I wanted to put fresh flowers on Jason's grave, but was mentally unable to handle replaying the funeral. What did I expect to find at the tomb?

It was my intention to avoid people and we left immediately after the benediction.

Josh was downstairs watching TV when I heard the car door close. I was in bed.

"Dani," Mom peeked her head in the room, "are you okay?"

I tried not to sound too pitiful and said, "I'm just tired."

"I know you're hurting," she said, sitting on the bed. "You really loved Jason."

I heard his footsteps and then my dad was standing in the doorway, "Jason was a good man. He loved you and he loved Josh."

Fighting tears, tired of crying, I bit my lip and kept my face in the pillow.

"Tell me what I can do," Mom said, her voice consoling.

"Just hold me," I whimpered, and put my head in her lap and cried.

The aroma of coffee greeted me the next morning and I almost stepped on Josh who was sleeping on the floor.

"Josh!" I said just missing him. "What's the matter?"

"I wanted to make sure you were okay."

"I'm okay."

"I heard you crying last night." He paused and then sat up. "I hate when you cry."

"Are you hungry?" I asked, changing the subject and helping him up from the floor. "Breakfast is done, I can smell it."

"What's this?" He picked up the basket of neatly folded letters at the bottom of the bed.

"Love letters," I smiled. "Your dad and I wrote them."

"When you were dating?"

"Every Valentine's Day and every anniversary."

I took the basket from him.

"You'll understand one day when you fall in love."

"I'm in love with Nicki."

"Real love," I clarified for him. "Two months from now the two of you might not even remember each other's names."

"Mom!" He tried to sound offended.

"Boy, let's go eat."

As soon as Josh left the room, I took out the last letter Jason wrote. On top of everything else, it was a skeleton that needed to stay in the closet.

My dad spent most of Saturday at the church, and Mom busied herself cooking all day. Our family hadn't gathered in fifteen years, and she was really looking forward to Sunday. Josh volunteered to peel apples and potatoes, and I chopped onions and green peppers. Not much was said, and I was okay with that. Not all the tears were from the onions.

When Mom wasn't cooking, she was sleeping in that old recliner. I tried to imagine my parents with no company, no children or grandchildren visiting. My dad in his office and my mom in the recliner with the TV watching her. It was too much to think about, so I decided to take a nap. I felt lethargic.

Rhonda was spending Easter with Lance's family, but she stopped by Saturday evening with the girls. Even though they hadn't seen Josh in over a year, he loved them like sisters and time was no barrier. Lance and Rhonda often reminded Josh that he was the only son they'd ever have. Rhonda and I talked about old times and life lessons. She shared several scriptures with me and told me her church was praying for me. We had planned to spend a week in Acapulco over the summer. Now that Jason was gone, I didn't want to go.

Noah called around ten o'clock that evening to send his regrets for Sunday dinner. He and Tashika were both working and were only off on Good Friday. They were settling into their first house in the Bronx and said they were doing well. Noah invited Josh and I to visit over the summer. I promised I would try to get there.

Sunday service at St. Luke's was a major highlight of the Easter weekend in Smithtown. Shawn Campbell, a childhood friend, was now the associate minister and he was preaching the morning sermon. This was the first time I remembered my dad relinquishing the pulpit on a holiday.

Joey, Stormy and Stephanie arrived around nine o'clock Sunday morning and met us at the church. Joey was playing for the morning service and Stormy and Stephanie were singing. My brother had been a Christian for two years and was directing a young adult male choir. I was happy for him. He seemed to be in love with Stephanie, like I loved Jason.

St. Luke's almost looked like Southfield Baptist Church. People were standing up, clapping their hands and shouting. For the moment, I felt comforted, and I thanked God for getting me through the past month. Then I thanked Him for giving me Josh.

After the benediction, I graciously accepted each sentiment of sorrow from the members of the congregation. Although I had agreed to stand with my parents at the back door, I was inadequately prepared. Each expression of sympathy was merely a reminder that Jason died three weeks ago. I managed to smile, hug and agree with each one of them that the Lord would be my strength. They felt sorry for me; I could see it in their eyes. I felt sorry for me, too. I thought about the pills Dr. White gave me for the headaches. My head didn't hurt as much as my life did.

Joey wasn't able to stay for dinner. He was playing for a community concert choir that evening in Brooklyn, which only left me a ten-minute meeting with Stephanie. I wanted to like her because Joey loved her. Stephanie seemed to have a good relationship with Stormy and that was important. We exchanged numbers with promises to call. Stormy was only in for the weekend and had a flight to catch to Ann Arbor where she was a grad student at the University of Michigan. I gave her the number to the Singleton's and made her promise to call and introduce herself. My niece had grown into a beautiful young lady.

My old bedroom was a temporary sanctuary. Coping with losing Jason was unfathomable. I didn't know how I would ever get beyond the pain, and I decided it was a good time to take a tranquilizer. It was my hope that by the time I woke up, everyone would be sleeping and no one would want to talk.

I woke up Monday morning at five. Staring at the ceiling, I remembered the night we came home from our honeymoon. We laughed and giggled under the covers and practically held our breath to keep quiet. The bed was squeaky and we had to be very still. I heard my dad clear his throat on the steps. Jason was so loud!

"Mom, are you awake?" Josh startled me as he

came into the room.

"Yeah, what's the matter?" I asked, sitting up and realizing I had been daydreaming.

"I'm worried about you," he said and sat on the bed facing me. "You've been asleep since yesterday. I tried to wake you up twice last night and you didn't answer."

"I was really tired."

"Mom, let's talk to someone," Joshua suggested.

"Like who?" I asked.

"A, um a, a counselor like Ms. Butler," he stammered.

"A counselor?" I said, a bit surprised.

"I talked to Ms. Butler every day last week. She told me death can be traumatizing and can make you feel depressed."

"I'm not depressed," I stated in my defense.

"Mom, she said there are counselors for you too," he continued, "and we can both go. I'll go with you."

I cried and my son held me.

"Don't cry, Mom, you still got me," he said, trying to comfort me. "Please don't cry."

On the flight back to Columbus, I admitted to myself that I didn't want to stay there. It was the home I made with Jason and it would never be the same again. Josh was finishing his sophomore year and would not be happy about moving and changing schools. He wouldn't understand, but he would have to adjust. Starting over would be good for him, too.

Getting through to the end of the school year was the difficult part. Josh was distant and moody. He didn't care about school and it showed — his grades dropped. Three months had passed since Jason died, and I was even more determined to relocate.

Josh thought we were just going to visit Andrea the week after school ended. I didn't tell him about my job interviews just in case nothing came of them. Alicia called from Raleigh to let me know she agreed that we should move closer to family.

We arrived in Pittsburgh at 10:30 Sunday morning and went straight to The Sanctuary. Harvey and Corey met us at the front door.

"Boy, you missed my Sunday school lesson," Harvey teased Josh. "I bring the Word to life."

"Well, good morning," I interrupted, "we'll make it next time." I didn't want Josh to feel on the spot about missing Sunday School.

Attending church was not optional while staying with Andrea and Harvey. Their lives were entrenched in their faith. They both served as Sunday School teachers and had family Bible study every Thursday. Harvey was involved in the Salvation Soldiers, which taught boys how to do things around the house like clean the gutters, mow the grass, and fix leaky sinks. Andrea was leading the women's ministry, and started My Sister's Keeper, which helped young single mothers achieve self-sufficiency through education and employment. Corey was in the youth choir, the mime ministry and, of course, a Salvation Soldier.

Although we were members of Southfield Baptist Church, we had not gone regularly since Jason's death. I wanted God to be happy that Josh and I were still attending church. After all, He hadn't answered our prayers and those wisdom seeds were now just anecdotal stories that my Nana told.

My interviews on Monday went well. I was hoping to be hired full time, but indicated on my applications that I would accept a long-term substitute counselor position. Monday was tolerable for Josh because he spent the day at Kennywood Park with the Salvation Soldiers. By Tuesday evening, however, Josh was bored. I could only empathize with him; after all, he didn't know anyone and was being entertained by his nine-year old cousin. Although Josh was like a big brother to Corey, hanging out with him was no substitute for his own friends. After three days, Josh was ready to go back to Columbus.

"Mom, I don't want to move to Pittsburgh," Josh stated flatly on our drive back to Columbus. "I like where we live."

"I used to like it," I admitted. "It's not the same without Jason."

"So you just want to forget all about him and leave?"

"I'll never forget him and you know that!"

We rode in silence for about thirty minutes.

"Josh, I know this is hard for you because it's hard for me. Jason was the love of my life. Can you understand that?"

"Yeah."

"Sometimes in order to move on you have to physically move to another place."

"Can't we move after I graduate? I promised Nicki I would take her to the prom."

"I'd be willing to consider you coming back to Columbus to take her to the prom," I said, trying not to smile. I didn't have the heart to tell him there would be many more Nickis.

"What about me playing ball?"

"What do you mean?"

"I can't just walk on to a team, Mom," he said with a serious tone. "I'm trying to get a basketball scholarship."

"Oh really?" I responded.

"Yeah, that way I can take care of you."

"Josh, you don't have to take care of me. I want you to take care of yourself. Do you trust me?" I asked, looking over at him.

"Of course I do, Mom. Love and trust, Dad always said those are the roots of our family."

"Trust me to know that this would be a good move for us."

Josh didn't respond.

"If I don't get a job in Pittsburgh, we can stay until you graduate," I conceded.

The job offer came three weeks later with a public school that was being privatized. It would be controversial, but challenging. I accepted knowing Josh was praying the offer would never come. The news went over a little better because of the argument he and Nicki had that afternoon. The next day after they made up, however, he wanted to know if I was sure that I really wanted to move. His tone was somber and his eyebrows met. Jason's mannerisms were becoming prominent in Joshua's expressions. That made me happy because I would always have Jason's expressions to look at on Josh's face.

I put my house on the market and within a week, a young family relocating from Cleveland placed a bid on it. They had three small children and fell in love with the house and the neighborhood. It felt good to know that someone else was going to make wonderful memories in our house.

Ten

We arrived in Pittsburgh on August fourth, and temporarily settled into Andrea's game room. Keith Jackson, a friend of Harvey's, showed me several of his apartments, and I selected the one he was just finishing. It would be ready for us to move into on September first.

Our new apartment was located in the Highland Park section of Pittsburgh. It was the second and third floor of an old Victorian house with two large bedrooms. Ian Sumpter was my first floor neighbor. He introduced himself as we were moving in and offered his assistance. He was attending graduate school at Carnegie Mellon University, and assured me he was not a party animal. While they were bringing in the dining room table, I heard Harvey inviting him to The Sanctuary on Sunday.

"I never miss a chance to witness," Harvey smiled at me as we passed on the steps.

On our first night in the apartment, I watched the sun set from the living room's bay window.

This was the first time Josh could remember living in an apartment. He never said he didn't like it, but he talked about how much he missed the house, especially his basketball hoop in the driveway. It was an adjustment, and his anxiety was heightened at the thought of going to a new school. I selected a parochial high school, which did not make him happy. This would also be the first time he attended an all-male school. The thought of no girls did not sit well with him, and the excellent reputation of the school meant nothing to him.

Harvey took Josh to a Salvation Soldiers meeting and introduced him to young men his age. John, a Salvation Soldier, lived two blocks away from us and they became fast friends. Josh even mentioned joining the youth choir and participating in some other activities at the church. I encouraged him to participate, and we began attending The Sanctuary regularly.

Church services at The Sanctuary were focused on worship. I began feeling guilty about being angry with God, and hoped to move beyond that point in my life. Andrea invited me to join the women's ministry and I began attending in October. Each meeting was opened with prayer concerns, and the group prayed for all of them. Testimonies of God's goodness, grace and mercy were shared, and after the lesson, one of the members would conclude by playing an instrument, singing or presenting an interpretive dance. The women were like sisters. Everyone had overcome something and their motto, "Comfort others with the comfort you yourself have received." was lived by each member.

The fourth Sunday in October was the first time Josh sang with the youth choir. He sang about the joy I wanted to have and I hoped, with everything in me, that he was finding that joy, too. I felt reassured that moving to Pittsburgh was the right thing to do.

Working at Turner School turned out to be more political than I anticipated, but still exciting and challenging. This, however, was a different arena. Although the school's administrative team implemented an innovative concept to improve student outcomes, they were met with hostility by the teacher's union and administrators from the remaining schools in the district. Instead of the adults working together for the benefit of the children, two camps emerged. The divisiveness overshadowed the success of the children - politics has no place in education.

My parents came to visit for Thanksgiving and, as usual, stayed in a hotel. Mom said my dad didn't think we had enough room. It wasn't a problem and my dad knew that, but for the sake of having a nice holiday, I let it ride. Every time I thought it was getting better between us, he seemed to pull away. There was no need starting the holiday with anyone being angry. I met my parents at the airport and drove them to the Hilton.

Andrea and Harvey hosted dinner at two o'clock. This was my first Thanksgiving without Jason, and I was holding on by a thread to get through the day. Additional stress was not needed or welcome. Before leaving to get my parents from the hotel I prayed that the day would be a positive one to remember.

When Josh came out of the hotel, laughing with my parents, I noticed how he walked like Jason and had his smile. He liked the preppie look and was now able to wear Jason's sweaters. Josh had also kept Jason's Kangol and wore it with pride.

"Well, good afternoon," I greeted them as they got in the car. "How was your evening?"

"Just fine," Mom began to say before my dad cut her off.

"The baby in the room next to us cried until after eleven o'clock!"

"I would have turned the TV up," Josh added.

My dad shook his head. "I did and the baby cried louder."

"It's just a baby, honey," Mom said, still trying to make things better.

Josh told my parents about the Salvation Soldiers and the youth group, while I quietly drove to Point

Breeze. Harvey greeted us at the door and introduced himself.

"Reverend Allen," he said extending his hand, "it's nice to finally meet you. And Mrs. Allen, it is my pleasure to make your acquaintance."

I couldn't tell if he was being sincere or patronizing but it sounded good and my parents seemed impressed.

"Uncle D, it's been such a long time," Andrea said, greeting my dad with a hug. "How are you?"

"Just fine, just fine." My dad was his usual stoic self. "How are you? How's your father?"

"He's finally taking it easy," she said, giving Mom a kiss on the cheek. "How are you Aunt Judy? You're looking well. Still beautiful, just like I remember."

Mom handed her coat to Harvey and hugged Andrea.

"My dad had triple by-pass surgery last year." Andrea continued her response to my dad. "You know how you Allen men are, work-a-holics!"

"Is he doing better?" Mom asked because my dad didn't.

"Well, he doesn't have a choice. He'll either take it easy or it won't matter."

Corey came up the steps, and he and Josh began acting like they were boxing.

"Who is this handsome young man?" Mom asked.

"This is your great-nephew Corey Allen Terrell," Andrea said.

"How are you?" Corey extended his right hand after taking one last jab at Josh.

"I'm doing just fine," Dad said, shaking his hand. Mom hugged him.

"Stop kissing up!" Josh teased him, and they both

laughed.

The conversation after dinner was pleasant, but my stomach knotted each time Andrea mentioned her father. Thankfully, my dad managed to refrain from any sarcastic comments. Harvey was his usual jovial self, and entertained us with his wit and impersonations.

By 5:30 it was apparent that Josh was ready to leave because he kept looking at his watch and asking to use the phone. The afternoon had been memorable and I was grateful. I thanked them for dinner, dropped Josh off at John's house and then took my parents back to the Hilton.

My dad insisted on taking a cab to my house for lunch on Friday. We were settled at the table when my dad shifted the conversation from questions about my job to Josh.

"So, who's the lucky girl?" my dad asked Josh as we were eating.

Josh blushed and answered, "We're all just friends."

"You don't change your shirt three times to go out with just friends," Dad noted.

"Her name is Sydney," Josh finally replied.

"Sydney," my dad repeated. "That's a very unique name. Is she pretty?"

"Very," Josh said smiling.

"You're the new kid on the block," my dad whispered to him. "Use that to your advantage."

They laughed as Mom and I watched from across the table.

My mind's eye tried to visualize Sydney, but I

didn't know the names of the kids. It never crossed my mind that Josh was getting involved in the youth ministry because he liked a girl in the group. My grief was still consuming me, but it was clearly time to refocus on the realities of life, especially Joshua's.

We drove my parents to the airport Saturday afternoon and had lunch before they boarded their plane. I promised my mother we would have many more visits. I also told her that Joey asked Josh to be in his wedding in the spring. Josh and I hugged my parents and waved good-bye as they disappeared down the walkway.

"So who is Sydney?" I asked Josh when we got back in the car.

"She's just a friend, Mom. She sings in the choir," he answered, trying to sound nonchalant.

"What do you like about her?" I inquired.

"She's nice and she's funny," but I noticed he couldn't stop smiling.

"And she's pretty," I added because he left that out.

He replied with a sheepish grin, "Yeah, she's pretty."

"What else do you know about her?" I asked.

"She wants to be an actress so she can pay for medical school. She has a little sister and she lives with her mom." He rattled off the information like he had memorized her bio.

"I'd like to meet her," I said and caught his eye, "and her mother."

"She doesn't even know I like her," he complained.

"Well, when are you going to tell her?" I pressed him.

"I don't know," he said turning up the radio and then singing along with Lauryn Hill. He was trying to avoid the conversation, so I let him.

My emotions vacillated as December approached. I kept the ornaments from our family tree, but it would be difficult decorating without Jason. I was determined that Josh and I would continue our tradition of having cookies and hot chocolate after lighting the tree. Jason and I always exchanged one gift at midnight and I had no idea what I would do at twelve o'clock.

The youth department presented an annual cantata the week before Christmas, and Josh was excited about being in *It's Not Your Birthday* with his friends. Andrea met me in the vestibule and we sat together for the performance. Harvey and Corey were both in the play, too. It was a well performed hip-hop musical about remembering Jesus at Christmas. After the cantata, I found Josh in the Fellowship Hall.

"Mom, this is Sydney," Josh said, introducing me to the young lady who brought people to their feet when she sang, "Some Day At Christmas".

He was right, she was very pretty. "Nice to meet you," I said, shaking her hand.

"Hi, Miss Andrea," she said smiling.

"How's it going, Sydney?" Andrea asked. "You did a really good job tonight."

"Thank you," she answered as she turned when she heard her name.

"Hey Sheila," Andrea spoke to the woman who called Sydney. "How are you? We've missed you at the women's ministry meetings."

"I know and that's where I need to be. I'm coming back," Sheila replied.

"Sheila, this is my cousin, Danielle," Andrea introduced us.

"Mom this is Josh's mom," Sydney interrupted.

"Dani," I said extending my hand, "it's nice to meet you."

"You too," she said shaking my hand. "We need to talk about the Snow Ball, it's right after Christmas."

"Snow Ball?"

"Oh yeah Mom," Josh spoke up, "I told Sydney I would take her to the Snow Ball."

"We'll have to talk," I said to Sheila. "This is the first I've heard of it."

"And this is Shae, my youngest daughter," Sheila pointed to the young lady standing behind her with her arms folded.

"Hello Shae," I extended my hand, "it's nice to meet you."

"Nice to meet you, too." She smiled and shook my hand.

Sheila looked more like their sister than their mother. Her houndstooth pants suit and black patent Ferragamo's were classic. She reminded me of my mother. She was beautiful, too.

The Salvation Soldiers hosted Christmas breakfast for the homeless and Harvey was picking up Josh at eight-thirty. I set the clock for seven-thirty so we could share at least one gift before he left. This was our first Christmas without Jason. Josh had left a beautifully-wrapped package in front of the coffee maker, but I was waiting for him until opening it. I heard him in the shower when my alarm clock rang, but at 7:50 he still hadn't come downstairs.

I called him from the kitchen. "Josh, you're going to be late."

No answer and no sounds.

"Josh," I yelled a little louder on my way up the steps, "let's go."

"Merry Christmas," he shouted, sitting on the side of his bed tying his shoe when I opened his door. "I know you and Dad exchanged gifts at midnight, so I left one for you in front of the coffee maker. Did you get it?"

"Yes, thank you very much," my tone softening as he got up from his bed to hug me.

"I want to make it special for you," he said as we walked down the steps.

Christmas was going to be okay. Josh was going to be okay. And I was going to be okay, too.

While I drank my second cup of coffee, I called everyone to wish them Merry Christmas. My parents were planning a quiet evening after delivering gifts to the hospital and serving an early dinner at the senior center. Mom and Pop Singleton wanted to know when we would be visiting. I assured them that we had no intention of excluding them as we tried to rebuild our lives. Joey reminded me that his wedding was Memorial Day weekend and Josh would need a tux. He was equally excited for Stormy who got engaged for Christmas. She and José were planning to get married after she graduated and then move to Puerto Rico — at least for a few years.

Noah enrolled in community college to pursue his associate degree in communications. Tashika was planning to enroll in a nursing assistant program. Taisha eloped over the summer and was happily married, living in Atlanta and working on her dissertation. She was also pregnant with twins. Maisha finally came to the realization that Bobby's future didn't include her or their daughter. She was moving to Atlanta to start over.

Raheem remained unsure of what he wanted to do after he graduated from Fordham, and Rakeem was contemplating relocating to Virginia because he couldn't find a job he liked in New York. Rhonda and Lance were considering adding kindergarten to their preschool centers and their girls were doing fine. Adrienne and Maureen were also remembering Jason, and hoping Josh and I would have a Merry Christmas. I promised them that Josh and I would not be strangers and told them we were planning to attend their family reunion in Charlotte, North Carolina over Labor Day weekend.

Elaine was leaving Tyrone, but decided she would wait until after Christmas because he gave nice gifts. Denise was finishing her first gospel CD and was disappointed that it wasn't released in time for Christmas. Alicia was trying to plan a reunion for the summer. In spite of my grief, I felt blessed to have these people in my life.

Andrea, Harvey and Corey joined us at our house for Christmas dinner that afternoon. Sheila and the girls arrived in time for dessert and we exchanged gifts that evening. Christmas turned out to be wonderful.

We sang in the New Year at The Sanctuary and I looked forward to 1998. It was time for the wisdom seeds to bud. Love, kindness, goodness and peace were on my resolution list and I wanted them back.

The Snow Ball was a first for Josh and me. My excitement was slightly tempered because Jason wasn't there to share the moment.

"You look good," I said as he admired himself in

the mirror. Josh was a little over six feet tall, and the tux looked like it had been made for him.

"I don't like the shoes," he replied, looking down.

"You look wonderful and handsome. Let's go so you're not late. It's already 5:30," I urged him.

"Uncle Harvey isn't picking us up until 6:15," he said looking at his watch.

"We need picture time," I smiled.

After a quick lesson in placing a corsage on Sydney's wrist, we left for Sheila's.

Sydney descended the stairs into the living room like a princess. She and Josh blushed as they tried to inconspicuously stare at each other.

"You know you like him," Shae blurted out, as only a little sister could, in the middle of picture taking.

"Mom," Sydney sighed, "get your daughter."

"Mom, she really does like Josh," Shae stated in her defense. "She's just afraid to tell him."

Josh ignored Shae's comments. "My uncle's here," he said, trying to rescue the moment.

"Let's go!" Sydney grabbed her coat and walked toward the door.

"One more picture," I said motioning them to pose.

"Mom," Josh said through clenched teeth, "just one more."

I took five pictures, including one of them walking down Sheila's front steps. "Want coffee?" Sheila asked, as we stood in the doorway watching the car drive down the street.

"Yeah, that sounds good."

"It sounds real good," Shae added.

"Does that mean you'd like hot chocolate?" Sheila

asked.

Shae nodded.

"And how come you didn't go to the Snow Ball?" I asked the giggling thirteen-year-old.

She responded with a straight face, "Mom wouldn't let me."

"Oh, and why not?" I asked.

"She said I'm too young."

"Well, maybe next year," I consoled her.

"This is Sydney's second one. Last year she went with TJ."

"Shae," Sheila interrupted her, "TMI."

Shae immediately stopped talking and excused herself to her room.

"TMI?" I whispered to Sheila.

"Too much information," she whispered trying not to laugh. "That's our cue when she's talking too much."

Sheila poured coffee and we talked until midnight. She told me she met her ex-husband at the University of Pennsylvania and married him during her senior year.

"I don't know if Sylvester ever really loved me," she said trying to smile like it didn't matter. "I guess I always thought if you did all the right things, God wouldn't let bad things happen to you. I had a fairy-tale wedding and I wanted to be like Claire Huxtable. All I wanted was for my husband to love me forever."

I told her about Jason, the love of my life. Consciously, I omitted ever meeting Greg and I intentionally told her that Jason was Josh's father. Actually, I told my usual lie that Josh came first and we waited until after graduate school to get married.

Sheila and I were raising our kids alone, both of our parents held positions in church and we were still searching to define our relationship with Jesus. For just meeting her, I discovered we had a lot in common.

Sheila began attending the women's ministry with me in February. The plain-language Bible Alicia gave me for Christmas was helpful as we studied the Word of God together. I was working on not being angry with God and was able to sincerely thank Him for giving me Jason and allowing me to experience love, kindness, goodness and peace. I was working at trusting Him, and believing He could get me through this thing called life. I was also working on eradicating the weeds that were choking my wisdom seeds.

The women's ministry challenge was to pray every day for thirty minutes. I often thought of Jason during my prayer time and found it difficult to concentrate for the entire half-hour. I wondered if Jason was happy with my decision to sell the house and move to Pittsburgh. I wondered if he thought I was in search of Greg or if he knew I was trying to start over. I hoped he had met Nana and they were both watching me.

The smell of frying bacon greeted me when I came into the kitchen on the morning of March seventh.

"Morning Mom," Joshua said.

"Good morning," I said hugging Joshua. "To what do I owe this surprise?"

He handed me a cup but didn't respond.

I poured my coffee and exhaled, "I still miss him."

"Me, too." Josh removed the bacon from the pan. He turned to face me. "We don't talk about Dad anymore."

I had no words. He was right. A year had passed since my life stood in limbo as I watched Jason's life slip away. We hadn't talked about him since Christmas.

"I'm sorry," I said as I turned his face toward me. "We should always talk about him. I think about him all the time. I just want you to be able to move on and not live in the past."

"So you were listening when we went to see that counselor?" He smiled and poured two glasses of orange juice. "I'm moving on, but I don't ever want to forget."

"I could never forget Jason," I said as I let my tears flow freely as my mind reminisced. "He was the love of my life and he will always have a piece of my heart."

While Josh fixed our plates, I put *Stevie Wonder's Greatest Hits* in the cassette player. Jason loved Stevie Wonder and had given Josh the tapes on his last Christmas. We ate Jason's favorite breakfast while Stevie serenaded us.

Sheila and I joined the singles ministry when it started the second Saturday in March. We were initially reluctant because we didn't want to participate in a dating service. However, the focus of the singles ministry was fellowship and fun, not matchmaking. Although I was the only widow, there were others who had been deserted and betrayed, others who were hurting. We were a group of adults getting together to grow stronger in Christ and to study God's Word on being single and living holy.

The singles ministry was co-facilitated by Jennifer, and she shared her testimony at our first meeting. Two weeks before her wedding, her fiancé decided he didn't want to get married. Six months later, he eloped with her cousin.

"Forgiveness is the key to your freedom from the hurt and anger," she spoke confidently. "You choose to let it go or continue to carry it."

Jennifer walked across the front of the room with her arms extended and her fists clenched.

"You have to be available for God's blessings," she said, opening her hands and lifting her arms. "Let it go. Don't let the cloud of pain and disappointment block your view of the S.O.N. He who the Son sets free is free indeed."

Forgiveness. That was the hardest for me. It was easy to believe in a loving God who sent His only Son as the perfect sacrifice for my sins so I could be a joint heir and have eternal life. It was easy to believe I could go to Heaven, sit at the feet of Jesus, walk the streets of gold, and see Jason and Nana. It was even easy to believe I could live forever in glory with no fears and no heart-aches. But forgiveness was easier to receive than give. I was thankful for God's forgiveness, yet having much difficulty forgiving others. I was angry with my dad for loving the church more than he loved his family. I was angry that Jason and Nana left me when I needed them, and some place down in me, I hated Greg.

After the meeting, I looked up Bible verses pertaining to forgiveness. I had yet to learn that my ability to forgive others would help me forgive myself, too.

Josh and I joined Sheila and Shae for the opening night performance of *The Wiz*. Sydney was playing Glenda, the good witch.

"She is awesome," I said to Sheila after the curtain calls. "Her dad is really missing out if he doesn't come see this."

"He always promises to come," Sheila started to say before being interrupted by Shae.

"Then he makes an excuse and just sends flowers."

"Shae!" Sheila's irritation was apparent in her tone.

"He never sent me any flowers," Shae whined.

I walked away so they could talk privately.

Sheila and Shae joined me for dinner the following Monday evening.

"Hey," I said after opening the door.

Sheila didn't answer, but looked at Shae standing beside her with hands in her pockets and downcast eyes.

"Dinner's almost ready," I said as they were taking off their coats.

"Can I play Josh's video game?" Shae solemnly asked.

I nodded my head.

"Just the game," Sheila added, "don't get into Josh's things!"

I waited for Shae to disappear up the steps. Sheila followed me to the kitchen and leaned against the counter.

"Girl, what's going on?" I asked.

"Shae was suspended from school."

"What happened?" I inquired, turning the chicken in the frying pan.

"The principal said she got into an argument with a girl named Yvette before school started this morning. When they went to lunch, the argument resumed and ended up in a fight."

Sheila helped herself to the iced tea in the refrigerator before taking a seat at the dining room table. I took the last of the chicken out of the frying pan and sat next to her.

"What were they fighting about?"

"Shae's story is that the girl was telling kids on the school bus that she's gay because she's a good basketball player. When the girl kept repeating it, Shae slapped her."

"Have you ever seen her angry and lashing out before?"

Sheila was silent for a moment and then admitted, "It's jealousy."

"Jealousy?"

"It's been brewing for a while. She doesn't feel like Sylvester loves her and she doesn't know how to deal with Syd getting flowers all the time."

"What do you mean?"

Sheila spoke slowly.

"Every time Sylvester sends Sydney flowers or calls and talks longer to Syd than he does to her, it's a problem. Shae is so angry about his refusal to be involved with her like he is with Sydney and the acting out has progressed to this. Shae's been called gay before, and usually responds by telling the person that everyone should be happy. She was angry because Sylvester called this morning and told Syd he was sending flowers. Sylvester's never seen Shae dance or play basketball. And, he's never sent her flowers."

"Have you guys talked to anyone about it?"

"No, I've never told anyone. It's embarrassing," she said as her tears rolled down her face and dripped from her chin. "I don't know what I'm doing wrong."

I gave her a napkin to wipe her face and hugged her. "Girl, it's not your fault. Do you want me to talk to

Shae?"

"I'm not sure. I don't know how she'll respond."

"I can get her one day this week and we'll talk."

My heart ached for Sheila. As a neophyte at helping adults cope with pain, I wasn't sure of what to say.

Sheila proceeded to tell me that her marriage to Sylvester was complicated from the start. She stayed with him in spite of the rumors until she found love notes and receipts from a cruise when Sydney was fifteen months old. They separated for a year and after he swore he wanted his family, as Sheila put it, they reconciled to make Shae. When she told him she was pregnant, he said he hadn't been back that long and wasn't sure the baby was his. Sheila left Philly the next day and moved back to her parent's house in Washington, PA.

"Sylvester's involvement with the girls has never been more than minimal, but it was always more with Sydney than with Shae." She patted her eyes with the napkin, trying to preserve her mascara.

"Do you really think he doubts Shae is his?"

"I don't know what he thinks, but I know it's easier to send flowers with a note than to have a relationship with your children. Syd relishes even the slightest attention from him; anything he does becomes enough even though she wishes for more. Shae is more demanding and wants him to spend time with her, but he doesn't know how to do that."

We talked until 8:30 and never ate dinner. I wrapped some chicken in foil and gave Sheila a warm washcloth to wipe her face before I called Shae to come downstairs. Sheila's red, puffy eyes were evidence she had been crying, but Shae never mentioned it.

"Call me when you get settled. See you later Shae." I waved as they were leaving.

Josh came around the corner as they were getting in the car.

"Bye, Miss Dani," Shae waved and smiled. "Bye, Loser," she yelled at Josh.

"Brat," he yelled at her. "See ya, Miss Sheila."

Josh kissed me on the cheek as he came in the door and walked to the kitchen.

"Wash your hands!" I reminded him.

"I'm just looking," he responded.

The phone rang and Josh made a mad dash for it. Answering it was out of my domain once he came home. He broke his neck to get it before the first ring stopped. I assumed it was Sydney.

I was drowning my chicken wing in hot sauce when Josh came into the dining room.

"Is Miss Sheila okay?"

He was so direct, just like Jason.

"She'll be fine. The potato salad is in the green bowl." I changed the subject, hoping he wouldn't ask any more questions.

He took his plate, a mason jar filled with iced tea and his trigonometry textbook to his favorite spot on the couch in front of the television.

Sheila called me at work to let me know she and the girls talked until almost three o'clock and were at home. She said everyone felt better and thanked me for being a listening ear.

"That's what friends are for," I replied, feeling good about finally being able to say that since it had been said to me so many times before.

"I appreciate you," she said, "and I want you to know that."

"Two are better than one," I told her. "That's an

African proverb."

We made plans to go to the grand opening of Jennifer's hair salon the following Saturday and then to see Sydney's final performance. Sheila said Shae planned to give roses to Sydney after the show. I thought that was a good sign.

Eleven

Spring break came before the weather got warm and I planned to spend the week doing nothing. My job was in the process of expanding to include the ninth grade, which meant an additional 150 students in the fall. I was bringing work home at least three days a week, but promised myself I wouldn't look at any of it during the break.

My parents said they had plans and declined my invitation to visit. Andrea was going to Raleigh to visit Alicia, and Josh was going on the Black College Tour over the Easter break. I would be alone for the first time since Jason died.

We joined Sheila's family for an early Easter dinner on Saturday. Her brother, Raymond, Jr., and his family were also visiting for the weekend. Sheila's nephew and Josh spent the afternoon talking about basketball. Later that evening Josh went to the movies, with John and Danny. After dropping him off, I went to a gospel concert at Rodman Street Baptist Church — its choir was directed by one of the teachers at the school.

I waited until the bus drove off for the college tour and didn't get home until after one in the morning. When my alarm clock rang at 6:15 I jumped up thinking I had to go to work. After pressing the snooze button for the third time, I realized school was closed.

Sheila invited me to lunch at her house on Monday afternoon — I declined so Shae could have her mom to herself. I spent my afternoon with Mrs. Crosby, a real estate agent, looking for the perfect house. I concluded the day watching *Beaches* and eating pizza.

Sheila and Shae joined me for an early dinner on

Tuesday, and then we went to the mall. On Wednesday, we went to Bible study and on Thursday Sheila came with me to look at three houses. The second house I saw on Monday was still my favorite, and I convinced Mrs. Crosby to take us there so Sheila could see it. The house was on Sonny Street, a quiet, one-block, tree-lined street with brick houses. It was completely residential and most of the original homeowners still occupied the homes.

The three-bedroom ranch had a finished basement and an integral garage. It was big enough for me and Josh, and small enough that it wouldn't be too big when Josh left for college. The owner, Mrs. Adams, was recently widowed and was going to live with her daughter in Tulsa. She was trying to have the house sold by July. I was ready to make an offer on the house until Sheila suggested I look at a few more. Reluctantly, I agreed.

On Friday, I thought about the house on Sonny Street all day.

All the kids were sleepy when they got off the bus Saturday morning. Josh said he had a good time, even though the trip was very structured. Between doing his schoolwork, the evening Bible study, and visiting the schools, there really wasn't much down time. I took Josh home before heading to the church for the women's ministry meeting.

"He went straight to bed, didn't he?" Sheila asked as we met at the door. "So did Syd."

"What school did she talk about?"

"Tennessee," Sheila replied.

"Josh is torn between Tennessee and Hampton," I said, holding the vestibule door.

"I want Syd to go to Spellman," Sheila sighed. "I've been buying her Spellman paraphernalia since she was born."

"She also said you've been buying her red since she's been born!"

"Subliminal messages are the best."

"Yeah, but she loves pink."

"Someone brainwashed my child," Sheila stated with a distressed Southern drawl.

We found two seats in the second row just as the meeting opened with prayer. The guest speaker was a young woman who had been doing ministry since she was fourteen. She talked about God preparing us for specific ministries and the blessings that follow when we are obedient. She spoke on how Ruth had been united with Naomi and then stayed with her even after the death of her husband. God was preparing Ruth for a place of prominence even though she couldn't see it while she gleaned in the fields. Ruth was blessed because she was obedient.

One day I hoped to have a testimony to share. My life was not as traumatic as some of the women I had come to know, but like them, I was learning the meaning of salvation. My hunger to grow spiritually was fresh and new. I was beginning to understand the significance of the wisdom seeds, and now knew they were more than just stories. I wanted to be like Ruth and trust God to get me through, even when I wasn't sure where the road would end. Heading home after the meeting, I decided to read the book of Ruth. I finished chapter two before Josh came downstairs.

"Were you partying all night?" I asked, hoping the answer was no.

"They had a party for us at Tennessee," he said pouring orange juice.

"Is that why you want to go there?"

"Mom," he responded, pretending to be insulted, "of course not!"

"Tell me about the other schools," I pressed, even though I could tell he didn't feel like talking.

"Most of them were nice. I liked Tennessee and Hampton the best."

"Didn't you like Morehouse?"

"Since you're making me go to school with all boys now, I want to make sure there are plenty of girls when I go to college," he said and winked at me.

"Ever think about Ohio State?"

"Nope," he stated emphatically, "too cold!"

"I thought you loved Columbus?" I asked.

"I want to go to school where it's warm."

"Have you given any more thought to what you'd like to major in?"

"Nope!"

"Do you want to look at any other schools?"

"Maybe one or two."

"Which ones?" I kept pressing for information.

"Georgetown and Michigan."

"Isn't Sydney considering Georgetown and Michigan?"

"A lot of people are considering them," he said, taking a mixing bowl from the cabinet.

"Still planning a trip to Columbus to go to the prom?"

He filled the mixing bowl with cereal and just smiled.

After church on Sunday, I detoured so Josh could see the house I was claiming as mine. Despite the lack of his enthusiasm, I decided to place a bid, and left a message for the real estate agent to call me.

"Syd made the paper," Josh yelled from his room. "She's nominated for best supporting actress."

Sydney's play received wonderful reviews and she was nominated for an Adam Wade Award. The Cultural Foundation established the award in Mr. Wade's honor to recognize the exceptional talent of high school youth. The program was similar to the Academy Awards.

"I always dreamed of being nominated and now it's real," Sydney confessed when she called to let us know she had several copies of the paper. "I hope my dad comes."

Monday greeted me with a full agenda. We were preparing for state assessments and the entire staff was on edge. Test scores for the previous year indicated that ninety-five percent of the students performed at a two-year deficit and their attendance was a dismal fifty-six percent. The expectation of the students testing at grade level after one year was ridiculous. Our program had done well, academically and socially. Based on our own assessment, student outcomes increased by at least one grade level in reading and math. Student behavior significantly improved and our attendance increased to eighty-nine percent. By the end of the day, I was glad to be heading home.

"Hey Mom," Josh said as I came in the door. "Mrs. Crosby called about the house. She said she'd be in her office until 5:30."

My excitement was short-lived. Mrs. Adams had accepted someone else's bid on the house. I retreated to my room and called Sheila.

"It must not have been for you," Sheila said, trying to console me on the phone.

"I wanted that house," I pouted.

"You'll find a house. God has one for you."

Faith was the topic in Bible study and I assumed this had to be a test.

Memorial Day weekend turned out to be busier than I anticipated with the Adam Wade Awards on Thursday night and Joey's wedding in New Jersey on Saturday.

After sitting through the entire award show with intense anticipation, the next to the last awards were for supporting actor and actress.

"Sydney Daneen Henderson," the announcer stated as the audience rose to their feet. If the opportunity ever presented itself, I planned to let Sylvester know what he missed just in the time I had known his girls. I made a mental note to practice saying it without malice. He was choosing to miss the moments with his girls that Jason so desperately wanted to have with Josh.

Through her smile and tears, Sydney's eyes revealed the pain of disappointment. Her dad didn't come. True to form, he sent a note of congratulations and a dozen red roses.

Harvey picked us up in the rented minivan at 7:00 on Friday for our trip to New Jersey. Harvey and Corey were meeting most of the family for the first time.

"He should know his cousins," Andrea said referring to Corey. "I wouldn't want him to grow up and start dating a family member he never met."

We arrived at 1:00 and went to pick up Josh's tux after checking into our hotel.

Our family were all staying in the same hotel.

After hearing my nephew's music from the elevator, I was glad we weren't on the same floor. I mentioned to Tashika how loud the music was, and she nonchalantly stated, "They like loud music."

Taisha was now a Christian, a wife and a mother of twin boys. Her husband, Donald, and the twins, Donte and Donovan, were with her. Taisha was completing her dissertation and anticipated receiving her doctorate in December. Maisha was teaching in Stone Mountain, Georgia and writing her first novel. Her daughter, Aisha, was already in the second grade. Noah was still employed at the phone company, and Tashika was a nursing assistant. They were looking forward to having the house to themselves once Raheem graduated from college. I had never thought of living alone. That's what I would be when Josh left - alone.

As we were leaving for the church, I thought about my eclectic family and smiled. We spanned the extremes from my stoic dad in his tailor-made suit to my nephew in braids to my sister-in-law in a skirt too short and too tight. We were the Allen family.

When we returned to the hotel, I called Sheila to tell her about the wedding. She had big news, too. She met a man named Doug at the singles ministry bowling party.

"I started not to go since you weren't here," she said trying to hide her excitement. "Then I figured it was better than sitting in the house."

"Did the girls convince you to go?"

She laughed and said, "Well, sort of."

Doug was a friend of Isaac's. He was new to the city and was a music professor at Duquesne University. He and Sheila did more talking than bowling and ended up exchanging numbers when the night was over. Sheila was indecisive about telling the girls she met someone. I had no advice to give. I made a mental note to ask Josh how he would feel about me dating — if and when the time came.

The Allen family met at Corinthian Baptist Church for Sunday service before going to Bob Evans for brunch. We talked about planning a family reunion, and Andrea said she would work on her father attending. Even though our last family gathering at Thanksgiving hadn't turned out as planned, I hoped my grandparents would be able to attend.

The trip back to Pittsburgh was spent filling in the blanks for Andrea from all the stories shared at the reception. We tried to engage the boys in conversation about the weekend, but Corey was more interested in his Game Boy and Josh preferred listening to his Walkman.

"We're going to see Alicia this summer. You guys should come with us," Andrea stated.

"Sounds like a good idea," I said and nudged Josh, "doesn't it?"

"We'll drive down and stay for about a week."

"Just tell me when," I said.

"Don't forget about basketball camp," Josh interrupted. "It's the third week in June."

"I wanna go!" Corey stated with excitement.

"Sorry cuz," Josh patted him on the head. "It's a high school thing!"

"We're planning for the fourth," Andrea said, looking at Harvey for confirmation.

"Yeah, I requested the week off," Harvey said, drumming his fingers to the beat of the Winans. "I'll know for sure when we get back."

I could hardly wait to tell Andrea that Sheila met someone. I didn't want to say it in front of the boys, so I waited until we stopped on the turnpike.

"Girl, guess what?" I said as she came out of the bathroom stall.

"What?"

"Sheila met someone at the single's fellowship on Saturday," I informed her as we washed our hands.

Andrea handed me a paper towel and asked, "Who is it?"

"His name is Doug."

"Is he new?" she asked as we headed for the vending machines. "I don't recall anyone named Doug."

"Sheila said he's a friend of Isaac's."

"Who's a friend of Isaac's?" Harvey interrupted us. I looked at Andrea.

"A guy Sheila met at the singles fellowship," she told him. "She hasn't told the girls."

Harvey nodded his head. "So in other words, don't talk about it in the car."

"You're such a good man!" Andrea said.

The boys were in line buying pizza, and we signaled them to meet us at the car.

"Want me to check him out?" Harvey asked, as we sat in the car waiting for Josh and Corey.

"Of course," I stated emphatically. "Make sure the FBI doesn't know who he is!"

"I know that's right!" Andrea gave me a high five.

There was a message on my answering machine to call Mrs. Crosby immediately. I was hesitant because it was Sunday night, but I called anyway. To my surprise, the potential buyer was unable to get financing. I reiterated my offer on the house.

"Josh," I called up the steps, "come here."

He came down the steps two at a time.

"What's the matter, Mom?" he asked.

"I just bid on the house on Sonny Street." I informed him.

"How? I thought someone else was buying it?"

"They couldn't get a mortgage so I made an offer," I explained.

"When will we know?"

"Maybe by Friday," I replied.

Sheila was my next call.

"I bid on the house!" I blurted out after she said hello.

"Which house?"

"The house on Sonny Street. The house I wanted!"

"What happened to the couple who bid on it?" she asked.

"They couldn't get a mortgage. I called Mrs. Crosby and made an offer right before I called you."

"Congratulations girl, the house must be for you!"

"Now share your good news. Tell me about your friend Doug," I asked excitedly.

"We met at church this morning."

"So you told the girls?"

"I told them I had a friend I wanted them to meet," Sheila explained.

"How'd they take it?"

"Syd was very excited. She's been trying to get me to date forever. Shae hasn't said much."

"How was she when they met?"

"She gave him a cool hello, but Syd was very cordial."

"So when do I get to meet the mystery man?" I asked.

"Well actually," she hesitated, "Isaac suggested we go to the movies and to dinner next weekend."

"We, who?"

"You and Isaac, me and Doug, a double date night!"

"Me and Isaac?"

"Girl, I told you he liked you a long time ago. You've just been acting like de-queen-of-de-nial!"

Isaac was my friend. It had only been a little over a year since Jason died. "Okay," I nervously agreed. "I guess that's okay."

Guilt interrupted my thoughts. How could I think of going out with anyone?

"Dani," Sheila's voice was raised.

"Yeah."

"It's okay," her tone softened. "We're going out to have a good time. I'm not asking you to marry him."

"What time next Saturday?"

"6:00. Put that on your calendar!"

I went upstairs and told Josh about my plans to go out with Isaac. He listened as I reassured him repeatedly that we were friends going out to have a nice time.

"I like Mr. Isaac," he finally said, "he's cool."

"What do you mean?"

"He came with the Salvation Soldiers when we went rock climbing, and he plays ball with us."

"Oh really?"

"Yeah, he can be funny, too. I like him."

"We're just friends," I repeated again. "Friends going out to have a nice time."

"I want you to have a nice time, Mom." He turned over on his bed and resumed his video game.

Isaac picked me up promptly at 6:30. We met Sheila and Doug at the movie theatre in Monroeville and ate dessert at Friday's afterward.

"I had a nice time," I told Isaac as he walked me to my door.

"Can we do this again?"

"I don't know," I said facing him. "I enjoyed myself. I just don't think I'm ready for any kind of relationship."

"I'm not talking relationship," He explained while still smiling. "We had a nice time and I'd like to do this again." He hesitated and asked, "You did have a nice time, didn't you?"

"Yeah," I could feel myself blushing, "I. . ."

"Don't want to lead me on," he finished the sentence for me.

"I want us to stay friends."

"Does that mean we can't go out and have a nice time?" Isaac asked.

"No, I guess not."

He grabbed my hand and squeezed it gently, "No strings, just a nice time."

He smiled and turned to walk away.

I watched his Explorer drive down Jackson Street before going inside.

"It's after midnight young lady!" Josh startled me from behind the couch.

"What are you still doing up?"

"Waiting on my mom," he said sarcastically.

"I had a really nice time," I said locking the door. "We all did." Before he could ask another question, I disappeared upstairs.

In spite of his initial disdain for having to transfer

as a junior, Josh's school year ended positively. He raised his grade point average and seemed to be acclimating to his new school. His sophomore grades consisted of Cs and Ds and his interest in completing high school had diminished. I wasn't sure if those grades were solely the result of Jason dying or a reflection of Joshua's motivation. At any rate, I was thankful for the change and the As and Bs on his eleventh grade final report card.

While I enjoyed the privatized school concept, it was a lot of work. Not only had I functioned as the guidance counselor, but I also became the queen of assessments. I completed more hours than I cared to remember on the new state assessments and felt confident to give the training myself. I welcomed summer and looked forward to having a few weeks off.

Josh was looking forward to spending two weeks at John Cheney's basketball camp at Temple University. He was meeting Danny and John there for the first session. Sheila and the girls drove with us to Philadelphia.

"Wasn't Syd born here?" Shae asked as we were leaving Temple's Ambler campus.

Sheila bit her bottom lip and replied, "Yes."

"Where does my dad live?"

"He lives outside of Philly," Sydney interrupted. "The flowers always come from Germantown."

Sheila put her head back and closed her eyes. She appeared to be praying that Shae didn't have any more questions. Syd began singing songs from *The Wiz* and Shae joined in. They had natural harmony. I let Sheila enjoy the temporary mental solitude as we headed to Smithtown to spend the night with my mom. My dad was out of town at a convention and Mom welcomed our company — even if just for one night.

I tried to persuade her to come back to Pittsburgh for a few days as we were leaving on Sunday.

"Your dad will be home on Tuesday," Mom explained.

She tried to smile as we were getting in the car. I knew that look. It was the mask to hide the sadness her heart was really feeling.

The drive from my parent's house to the turnpike was filled with memories. I remembered driving back to Columbus to bring in the New Year with Jason.

"Why did your husband die, Miss Dani?" Shae asked, interrupting my thoughts as we pulled onto the turnpike.

I answered without looking at her, "He had colon cancer."

"Is that like breast cancer?" Her questions were sincere and she sat up between the seats.

"Cancer is cancer," Sydney replied flippantly and then rolled her eyes and frowned her face.

"I didn't know, that's why I asked," Shae retaliated.

"Girls!" Sheila's voice was authoritative. "Don't start."

"But, Ma," Shae continued.

"Shae! No buts," Sheila interrupted her.

We rode in silence for a few minutes.

Shae whispered, "Did you cry?"

Sydney sighed out loud and Sheila shook her head.

"Yes baby, I did," I answered her. "I was very sad and I still miss Jason."

That seemed to satisfy her query, at least for the present.

Shae went to sleep, Sydney read *The Bluest Eye*

and Sheila and I talked about my new house. I was excited about moving and glad to have the entire summer to get settled.

When Josh came home two weeks later, I surprised him with the keys to our new house. Moving in would have to wait because we were leaving the following week to visit Alicia in Raleigh. Shae and Sydney were coming with us to give Sheila some down time.

Alicia's daughter, Ashley, and Shae were the same age and became fast friends. Most of their time was spent out back at the pool or playing jokes on DJ, Alicia's nine-year old. While in Raleigh, we visited North Carolina State, Duke and UNC at Chapel Hill. Dennis took Josh and Syd to Charlotte to visit his alma mater, Johnson C. Smith. Josh decided that he wanted to attend Johnson C. Smith or NC State. Syd really liked Duke and NC State, although she was still considering Tennessee.

Four days passed quickly and the visit was bittersweet. I missed my cousins and our girl talks. As I lay in bed on our last night in Raleigh, I thanked God for that first summer with my cousins.

Before we drove off, Alicia made us promise not to let too much time pass before we returned. Andrea and I agreed that the kids needed to see each other more often and we needed a ladies trip one weekend just to go shopping.

After returning home, I spent two weeks preparing to move. I was pleasantly surprised when the single's ministry showed up with the movers on Saturday morning. I made a pot of spaghetti and we concluded the evening with a few rounds of Bible Trivia. Before everyone left, we had prayer to bless my house. I smiled, thinking Jason and Nana were happy for me, too.

Isaac and I continued to date over the summer, and we frequently doubled with Sheila and Doug. Although we had been out several times, Isaac never tried to kiss me. I wasn't sure that I wanted him to and was equally unsure about the absence of his attempt.

Josh was working at The Sanctuary's summer camp, and a few mornings I let him drive my car. I spent my days putting the house together and promised myself I would unpack every box before going back to work.

The youth ministry's yearly fundraiser for the food pantry was a musical. The play, *Cindy*, was an adaptation of Cinderella and had been written by one of the youth ministry advisors. Josh would be playing "The Royal Son formerly known as Prince who changed his name to Charles."

My parents came in to see the house and, of course, the play. My dad's appearance startled me when I met my parents at the airport. His hair was almost completely gray and his eyes looked weary. His body seemed too small for his suit. Mom did not look any of her sixty-five years. She was still meticulous and the colors in her outfit were coordinated and matched her shoes exactly. I hugged them and was alarmed at how heavy my dad was breathing. Not wanting to spoil the moment, or the weekend, I decided to ask questions later. Isaac was joining us at the house for dinner and I only had the car ride home to inform my parents and answer their questions.

My dad was silent as he sat next to me in the passenger seat.

"Well how long have you been seeing him?" Mom

asked, and I could see her grinning in the rear view mirror.

"I'm not really seeing him. We're just friends," I responded.

"Is it serious?" Mom pressed the issue.

"I wouldn't call it serious. We're friends and we have a nice time when we go out," I explained.

"I'm sure he's a nice person."

Isaac was sitting in front of the house when we pulled up, and I introduced him to my parents. My dad's response was minimal, as I expected, but Mom gave him a hug. Isaac told my dad he would get their bags while I showed them to their room. After a quick house tour, I told them to get comfortable on the enclosure while Isaac helped me with dinner.

"Dani, the house is lovely," Mom told me as I set the table. "I could stay out here all day."

"I knew when I saw it that this was my house," I enthusiastically explained.

"You've done very well, Danielle," my dad beamed as he complimented me. "I'm proud of you."

A hug would have made the moment perfect, but I was grateful for the sentiment. Unable to respond, I nodded and grinned.

Josh joined us after his rehearsal. He hugged my parents and greeted Isaac with their usual 'Fresh Prince' handshake.

"And how long have you been acting?" my dad teased Josh. "Do your plans include New York or Hollywood?"

"I'll check with my agent." Josh replied, sitting next to his grandfather. "Maybe you should wait until after you see me tomorrow."

Our dinner conversation was superficial and comfortable. Neither of my parents grilled Isaac, and he seemed to flow along with whatever was being discussed. Isaac left around 8:30 that evening, and my anxiety decreased ten notches. I reminded myself to enjoy the weekend with my parents.

"Have you thought about college, Joshua?" Mom asked while she helped me clear the dishes.

"Yeah, I'm thinking about NC State or Johnson C. Smith."

"Is that where your girlfriend is going?" my dad inquired.

"She's not my girlfriend," Josh blushed. "We're friends."

"Are you seeing someone else?"

Josh shook his head no.

"Is she seeing someone else?"

Josh smiled, shaking his head no. "Not any more."

"So you're really dating each other just not calling it dating?" my dad asked and winked at me.

I was glad Isaac had left.

Josh took the dishes into the house. As Mom sat down, my dad took her by the hand.

"Did your mother tell you we're going to Jamaica?"

Mom blushed and my dad gently moved her hair away from her face. They smiled at each other and I saw a glimpse of the love Nana talked about. I couldn't remember ever seeing any affection between my parents and it was refreshing. I was happy for my mother.

The performance was held in the auditorium at the high school down the street from the church. We arrived thirty minutes early and sat in the fourth row in the center section. Isaac joined us and sat next to me. Doug, Sheila and her parents sat with us, and Andrea's family sat behind us. I was nervous for Josh. He had never done anything like this before and I wanted him to be great.

My concerns were premature and unnecessary. Josh was a natural comedian and had an amazing voice – melodic, smooth runs and a nice range for a tenor. Guilt tapped me on the shoulder. How had I missed that in him?

For the finale, Harvey and his frat brothers digressed to their college days on the yard and barked while the kids were stepping.

Driving my parents back to the airport, I intentionally avoided asking about my dad's health. I rationalized the avoidance was worth it. We had a good time and my parents seemed to enjoy the weekend. If it had been anything serious, Mom would have mentioned it. They were leaving for their ten-day cruise in August. I assumed my dad needed a long overdue vacation and a lot of rest.

Leaving the airport, I smiled to myself. The sun was shining and I felt like those old wisdom seeds were finally beginning to bud again.

"Love, kindness, goodness and peace," I looked up to the clouds and whispered to Nana, "thank you. I remember everything."

Twelve

A week after the school year started, we were on our way to the Singleton family reunion in Columbia, South Carolina. The previous year was the first Labor Day we didn't attended the reunion. In spite of my best intentions, our relationship with the Singleton's had diminished to phone calls, cards and an exchange of pictures. Josh needed his family and they needed to be a part of his life. Jason would have wanted it that way, and I knew I would have to do better at making sure it happened.

We arrived at Maureen's house in Detroit on Thursday evening. Mr. and Mrs. Singleton arrived from Ann Arbor earlier that morning and greeted us as we drove up.

Maureen reminded me several times that Detroit was not that far from Pittsburgh. Ellis was a Lion's fan and planned to come to Pittsburgh when they played the Steelers. Maureen agreed to come, only if we could spend the weekend doing anything except watching football. Then she called Adrienne in Los Angeles and we talked for over an hour. Mrs. Singleton reminded us that we would all be together on Friday evening. Adrienne and her family were flying to Columbia in the morning. Our bus was leaving at midnight.

We arrived in Columbia at 5:00 Friday evening and rushed after checking in at the hotel because the dinner started at 6:30.

"Are you nervous?" Josh asked, sitting on the bed when he should have been in the shower.

"Not really," I lied. "We're here with family."

"I'm sort of nervous," he admitted. "I don't want

people to keep asking if I'm alright."

"Are you okay?" I asked, to clarify for myself.

"I'm trying to be," Josh said, clenching his teeth. He had Jason's expressions. "I miss my dad so much," he continued. "I'm not angry any more that he died. I just wish he was still alive."

I sat next to him. "I know, me too. No one will ever take his place in my life."

"Not even Mr. Isaac?"

"Not even Isaac," I assured him. "If I ever fall in love again, it will be different. I can't replace Jason."

"Would I have to call Mr. Isaac 'Dad' if you married him?" Josh asked.

"I don't have any plans to marry him," I smiled. "We're just friends. If I ever plan to get married again, we can talk about what you call my husband at that time. Right now, it's not an issue." Getting up from the bed, I took a deep breath and said, "And no matter who I marry, Jason is always going to be your father. Nothing will ever change that."

Josh stood and hugged me, "I love you, Mom."

"Show me how much and take a ten-minute shower."

While Josh was in the shower, I cried. Being with the Singleton's triggered memories, and at the moment, I missed Jason more than I could describe.

Most of Jason's relatives had a favorite story they felt compelled to share with us and it was endearing. As I walked across the room to the buffet table, I noticed Jason's cousin, Alexis. We weren't close enough to speak and that was good because I was still angry about her comment at Jason's funeral. She told several people that it was nice of the Singletons to remain involved in Josh's life.

Dinner conversation at our table was spent catching up. Maureen and Ellis added a deck onto their house. At twelve, EJ was becoming quite a basketball phenomenon and was claiming MVP for the year. Ten-year-old Elise was an honors student and was planning to be an actress and a doctor. Her twin, Maurice, was taking guitar lessons and playing the drums, and eight-year-old Monique was starting piano lessons because she wanted to write her own songs. Adrienne and Scott were looking at houses in San Diego because they wanted to get out of LA. Tiffany was six and starting ballet and tap dancing lessons. Although only ten, Chase had already decided that he wanted to be President of the United States.

I promised Maureen and Adrienne that I would maintain better contact and suggested we plan to visit at least yearly. They wanted to stay connected and invited Josh to visit them. Maureen was planning a trip to Los Angeles for New Year's and suggested we come along.

On Sunday morning, during church service, I thanked God for the Singleton family. After church, we went to the mall while the kids went to the movies.

"So how are you really doing?" Maureen asked at the jewelry counter.

I felt put on the spot, but said, "I'm okay."

"Are you dating?" Adrienne passed a pair of earrings to me. "It's been over a year and you're still young."

"Josh will be leaving soon," Maureen added. "You don't want to end up by yourself."

"I'm not dating," I said handing the earrings back to the sales clerk, "but I do have a friend that I go out with sometimes." I intentionally avoided making eye contact.

"Oh yeah?" Adrienne asked. "Just how friendly

are you?"

"Have-a-nice-time friendly," I told her. "It's nothing serious."

"Well what's Mr. Nice Time Friendly's name?" Maureen inquired.

"Isaac. Isaac Turner."

Adrienne wanted more and asked, "When will we meet him?"

"When it gets serious." I could feel myself blushing.

We purchased matching ankle bracelets and took pictures at the photo booth. Our last stop was the Gourmet Pretzel store. Garlic for Adrienne, cinnamon raisin for Maureen and a pizza pretzel for me. We were quite a combination in the taxi going back to the hotel.

I was the first to cry at the airport later that night. Before Adrienne boarded the plane, she made me promise to come to LA to bring in the New Year. I made her promise to send pictures of the kids. Adrienne and Maureen hugged as if they weren't sure if they would see each other again. The love between them was a bond that miles could never shatter. They still talked daily, as if they lived around the corner from each other.

When I got back to the hotel, there was a note from Josh on top of his suitcase so I could see that he was packed. He was in the game room with his cousins, and Isaac had called. Isaac wasn't home so I left a message that I would call Monday night.

The bus ride back to Detroit didn't seem like fifteen hours. Pretending to be asleep, I was conflicted by the memories triggered by the weekend and thoughts of Isaac. I liked him more than I was comfortable admitting, and it would be difficult telling him I wouldn't be around for New Year's.

We arrived in Detroit a little after nine o'clock on Monday night. I was thankful for Maureen's offer to stay and leave the next morning. Mrs. Singleton was glad we were staying, too. I had already taken a personal day on Tuesday and Josh didn't mind missing a day of school. I called Isaac to let him know we wouldn't be back until Tuesday. Then I called Sheila, but she wasn't home either.

Mom Singleton made breakfast and we ate at 7:30 before Ellis went to work. I helped Maureen get the kids ready for school, and then we sat down for a cup of coffee with Mom Singleton. Pop Singleton showed Josh how to go over a car before getting on the highway. Then they took it to the gas station and filled the tank. That's what Jason used to do before we took a road trip. We departed at 10:15 after many hugs, kisses, tears and promises.

We were finally settled into our house, Josh began his senior year and I contemplated going back to school to get my principal certification. There were so many things I wanted to do at the school that were out of my current authority, and I needed to be running my own building to make the changes I felt necessary. Andrea and I had also participated in several think tanks about the charter school movement, and we found the idea of operating a college preparatory charter school intriguing.

"I know what I want to do," Josh announced one Sunday on our way to church.

"Do about what?" I asked.

"College. I know where I want to go."

"NC State?" I guessed.

"Johnson C. Smith," Josh stated. "I liked Charlotte."

"Is that for school, or for basketball tickets?" I teased.

"For both," he replied matter-of-factly.

"And because Syd will be at NC State?" I couldn't help myself.

He was smiling, but replied, "No, not really."

"Oh really? What about majors?"

"I don't know what I want to do yet," Josh said impatiently.

"Josh you need to think seriously about picking a college."

"I want to go to Johnson C. Smith. John's going to check it out, too," he definitively stated, ending our conversation.

We pulled into the church parking lot and all I could do was shake my head. It was seventeen-year-old rationale, and I didn't understand it.

Isaac was standing in the lot talking to Doug. Josh walked over and greeted him with their usual handshake and it made me smile. Intentionally, I took my time walking over to his car so he would meet me half way. He always hugged me when we met and I liked that. This time, after he hugged me, he kissed me on the cheek. I blushed.

Sheila came in after Sunday School started and sat in the back. I caught up to her on our way to the Worship Center.

"Late night?"

"No, not really." She batted her eyes. "Just a great time."

The school year was off to a good start for both

of us and, after much discussion, Josh applied to Johnson C. Smith, the University of Michigan, the University of Pittsburgh and Hampton. He wasn't able to give reasons for his choices, but he understood that it would be a four-year commitment. We were looking forward to spending Thanksgiving in Smithtown with my parents. Isaac planned to join us, so I started praying early that we would have a nice time. When I called Rhonda about our visit, she was excited, especially about meeting Isaac. While I was making plans, I called Maureen to coordinate our trip to California for New Year's. I was able to get a flight that landed forty-five minutes after hers which would keep Adrienne from having to make two trips to the airport.

October was a collage of earth tones as the leaves descended from the trees. It was beautiful, but I hated raking leaves. I made a mental note to remind Josh to rake and bag the leaves after church. As I was leisurely reading my *Essence* magazine, Josh came in from playing basketball in time to answer the phone. As usual, he raced to get it before the first ring ended. My stomach knotted when the tone of his voice confirmed that something was wrong.

My dad was dead of a heart attack. Shawn Campbell found him slumped over his desk.

Josh and I arrived in Smithtown on Thursday morning while Joey, Stephanie and my mom were at Ozrell & Sons Funeral Parlor making arrangements. Thursday afternoon was exhausting and we gratefully retreated to the house after finalizing the program. Mom sat in her recliner, unable to greet guests and numb to the sentiments of consolation. Josh sat at her feet. I sat in the dining room and cried. Stephanie made dinner, but no one ate. There was little conversation.

I jumped up from the table when the doorbell rang. It was Lance and Rhonda. "We gotta stop meeting like this," she said hugging me.

Rhonda and Lance joined us in the dining room and initiated small talk, which everyone seemed to appreciate. Rhonda reminisced about the things she remembered as a little girl at St. Luke's. It made Mom smile.

"He kept putting off going to the doctor," Mom suddenly shifted the conversation. "He knew he was sick. He kept saying he had so much to do. It was difficult for him to breathe and he was tired all the time. I begged him to see Dr. Baird."

We sat motionless, allowing her to talk. "He left at 8:30 and said he would be back by noon. We were going to have lunch."

I moved my chair closer to Mom so I could put my arm around her. My grief over Jason returned. There were no words that comforted me, and I was unsure of how to comfort my mother.

"Shawn called about noon and I told him David was at the church." Mom stared blankly as she was wringing the end of the tablecloth. "When he didn't come home for lunch I assumed he got caught up in his work." She paused. "Shawn came to get me and we went straight to the emergency room. He was already gone when I got there."

Mom buried her face in her hands and there wasn't a dry eye around the table. "I loved him," she repeated over and over again.

"Everyone in Smithtown loved him," Rhonda said and gave me one of those 'you say something' looks.

"We all loved him," was my weak attempt to comfort my mother. Although I remembered saying I love you to my dad, at that moment, I couldn't remember if I ever told him how much.

"I loved Grandpa." Josh hugged his grandmother.

"He loved you, too," Mom said and wiped her eyes with the yellow monogrammed handkerchief. "He really loved you, Joshua."

I wanted Joey to join our sentiments. He sat across the table, holding Stephanie's hand, studying the marble pattern on the dining room floor tiles. Although he avoided eye contact, I knew Joey was unsure of my dad's love. I also knew Joey hoped my dad knew, deep down, that he really loved him, that he was sorry there had been so many schisms between them, and that he was angry my dad died before they had the chance to get it all straight. Had I been stronger, I would have been able to comfort him, too. I wasn't and I couldn't.

The stillness of the moment was interrupted by the knock on the door. I knew it was Noah because he never rang the bell. Before I could get up, Joey was already in the foyer. Josh began to clear the table. Rhonda and Lance hugged my mom.

"I don't know what to say," Grandma Rita said, slowly walking over to hug Mom and me.

"Just sad," Grandpa Tim added, shaking his head as Joey wheeled him into the dining room.

Noah hugged Mom intensely. Tashika went around the room and hugged everyone. Rhonda and Lance had to leave to pick up their kids so I walked them to the door. We hugged and cried some more. If no one else understood my pain, Rhonda knew the history of my dad and me.

People were still waiting to get their last view of Reverend Allen when we arrived at the church on Saturday. Mr. Ozrell, the funeral director, had been instructed to close the casket before we entered the sanctuary. We said our good-byes after the viewing on Friday. Having to watch them close the casket would have been too much for everyone, even Noah.

My uncles were standing by the vestibule door – they hadn't come to the house or to the viewing. My grandparents had not been together with their sons in a long time and the moment was awkward. Grandma Rita cried, and I was unsure if her tears were from sorrow or happiness. Grandpa Tim was more difficult to read. I wanted to believe he was grieving over his son even though there were many unresolved issues. Uncle Matt hugged my mom, Uncle Paul hugged Andrea, and Corey shook hands with the grandfather he hadn't seen in years. Andrea began to cry and Uncle Paul held her.

Uncle Matt was the thinnest of the brothers and looked the most like Grandpa Tim. Like my dad, he dressed impeccably and appeared solemn. He could have easily been on the cover of *GQ Magazine*. The diamond in the ring on his index finger was bigger than any diamond I had ever seen. Uncle Matt never spoke above a whisper and avoided eye contact.

Uncle Paul had aged since I saw him at Andrea's wedding. He was a lot grayer and had gained a few pounds. At six foot five, he was the tallest of the brothers and his stature was that of an officer. The olive colored double-breasted suit was a precise fit, like a uniform, and his shoes had that military shine. His deep voice was commanding. His eyes were sad. He and my dad had Grandma Rita's eyes.

As we lined up in the vestibule, Miss Beth, the head nurse at the church, came to get Joey. Stormy was crying uncontrollably at the casket. She missed the viewing and became inconsolable as the casket was being closed. I could hear her moaning when they opened the main door to the sanctuary. Stormy was my dad's favorite grandchild.

I sat next to Grandpa Tim. History was repeating itself. He buried his son fifty-seven years after burying his father. He was estranged from both of them, and their last words had not been kind. Grandpa Tim's heart had to be heavy.

Grandma Rita cried throughout the service. She also was emotionally estranged from her children, and now one was gone. The other two, although they sat behind her, appeared nervous and distant, unsure of how or if they should try to console their mother.

The service was long and drawn out. Joey played for Stormy and she struggled through "Going Up Yonder", the song my dad taught her. Uncle Matt played "Precious Lord" – it was true, he could make the piano talk. Although the program read like a mini-concert, the songs were welcomed diversions. Twelve preachers, the mayor, the congressman, the postmaster and about seven people I didn't recognize wanted to have five minutes to say something profound that no one would remember.

Shawn Campbell concluded the eulogy with 1 Corinthians 15:58:

> "Therefore, my beloved brethren, be steadfast, immoveable, always abounding in the work of the Lord, knowing that your labor is not in vain in the Lord."

He opened the doors to the church, stating that my dad's eternal wish was for his entire family to be saved. Uncle Paul began to cry.

Two hours later, we were standing in the cemetery. Isaac put his hand on my shoulder to let me know he was there, and I tried to smile at him. Sheila and Doug were on the other side of the casket, and I saw Josh wave to them with his hand that wasn't holding mine. José was standing behind Stormy, and she stood between Joey and me. Noah and his crew stood on the other side of Stephanie. Uncle Matt, Uncle Paul, Andrea, Corey and Harvey stood on the other side of Josh. Mom and my grandparents were seated in front of us. It was too soon to be doing this again.

Josh drove back to Pittsburgh with Isaac on Sunday, and I reluctantly gave in to his request to stay at the house by himself for three days. Isaac reminded me that Josh would be leaving for college and was old enough, and responsible enough, to stay at the house alone. I made Isaac and Harvey promise to check on him. Sheila and Andrea were my back-ups to keep the fellas on task and make sure they called and went by.

Noah's girls left Sunday night, and Noah used my dad's car to take them to the airport in Philly. Stormy and José left Monday morning. Noah, Tashika, their boys and my grandparents left Monday afternoon. Joey, Stephanie and I stayed with Mom until Wednesday.

Mom agreed to spend Thanksgiving with us in Pittsburgh. Joey and Stephanie promised to spend Christmas in Smithtown. Noah and Tashika promised to come home, too. I refused to feel guilty about going to California.

It was almost 2:00 in the afternoon before I left Smithtown. There was no traffic on the Pennsylvania Turnpike and construction was minimal. I was alone with my thoughts for five hours and before I knew it, I was at exit six.

Josh left me a note that he would be at John's until eleven. I returned Isaac's call and left him a message. I called Andrea to let her know I was home and to thank her. Uncle Paul was visiting until the following Saturday, and then they were driving down to Raleigh for Thanksgiving. Uncle Paul was returning to France the first of December. When I called Sheila, she came over.

"Hey, girl," Sheila said as I opened the door. "I made your favorite — vegetable lasagna." She put the dish on the counter.

I lifted the foil off the Pyrex dish. "Girl, I'm not going to say you didn't have to."

"How's your mom?" she asked, taking a seat in the dining room.

"I don't know," I sighed and sat across from her. "I'm not sure how she's going to be now that everyone is gone."

"How are you?" Sheila asked.

"Tired."

"Okay, but really, how are you doing?"

I put my head down on the table and began to cry. Life was hurting again and I didn't like the feeling. My biggest fear was that if Mom was still drinking, it would get worse. I had never told anyone and was co-dependent with her. My thoughts and fears were overwhelming.

Sheila placed her hand on my shoulder and began to pray before the doorbell startled me.

"Go wash you face," Sheila said in a motherly tone. "I'll get the door."

After letting the cold washcloth lay on my face for a minute, I looked in the mirror. I had my mother's eyes.

Isaac was standing at the bottom of the steps

when I came down. "Hey," he said embracing me, "are you okay?"

I had been strong for everyone while I was in Smithtown and there was no one to be strong for me. It felt good to cry in Isaac's arms and we sat on the couch while he held me. His words were not important and my feeble attempts to talk with Isaac were defeated by my need for sleep. The sound of Isaac snoring woke me. It was almost 2:00 AM.

"Where's Josh?" I sat up, feeling disoriented.

"He's upstairs sleeping." Isaac pulled me back into his arms.

"What time did Josh get home?"

"Around eleven," Isaac whispered.

Sleeping in Isaac's arms was comforting. He woke me at 5:30 when he was leaving. He kissed me on the cheek and let himself out through the garage.

"Hey Mom," Josh stated on his way to the kitchen, "how are you feeling?"

"Glad to see you," I said, sitting up on the couch.

"You must have been tired," he said, but I knew something was troubling him.

"What's the matter?" I asked.

He took a seat at the kitchen counter and looked through the mail. I got up from the couch and sat next to him at the counter. "We can't deal with it if you don't tell me."

He took a deep breath and loudly exhaled before responding, "It was different seeing you in Mr. Isaac's arms last night. You used to sleep in Dad's arms when we watched movies." Josh paused. "It was weird seeing you with Mr. Isaac like that."

"Josh," I interrupted him, refusing to cry, "you

know I loved your dad more than anything, don't you?"

"Yeah."

"If I had died, do you think your dad would never date anyone else?" I continued.

"I don't know. I guess he would," he replied, still refusing to make eye contact.

"I would have wanted him to. I would have wanted him to fall in love again, and I would have wanted the two of you to be very happy." I turned Josh's face to mine. "And I think that's what Jason would want. He wants us to be happy."

"I miss him, especially at Christmas."

"He's always right here," I reminded him and pointed to his heart with my index finger.

Mom came to Pittsburgh and we went to Sheila's for Thanksgiving dinner. I made the ham, macaroni and cheese, yams and greens. Sheila made everything else and this was the first Thanksgiving that our mothers did not have to cook. The moms — hers and mine — spent the afternoon engaged in conversation about children and grandchildren. It felt good to see my mother laughing.

On Friday morning, we went to Josh's basketball game, and then we spent the afternoon sightseeing. We rode the incline to show Mom the view of Pittsburgh from Mt. Washington. Then we went to the Point, and also on a historic tour through the Hill District, Oakland, East Liberty and Homewood. Our last stop was Josh's favorite ice cream store in Squirrel Hill.

The youth choir was in concert on Saturday and Joshua surprised us when he came forward to sing a solo. He caught his grandmother's eye and winked at her. On Sunday, Isaac took us to the Southern Platter for dinner after church.

On our drive to the train station on Monday morning, I asked Mom if she wanted to move to Pittsburgh. Just as I thought, she said no.

It was 9:40 when I arrived at work to find a stack of messages. Sheila's was the first one I returned.

"Hey girl," I said, glad to talk to her, "what's doing? How was the rest of your weekend?"

"My parents love Doug," she said excitedly.

"How was Cleveland on Saturday?" I asked.

"I'm a hit!" Sheila's voice was bubbly and I could tell she was ecstatic. "Even the girls had a nice time," she continued.

"What are you doing after work today?" I asked, hoping she didn't have any plans.

"Coming to your house so we can catch up."

"Good! I can use some girl talk time."

"I won't get home until 6:30. I have to get Shae after basketball practice and then drop off Syd at the church."

"I probably won't get home until then myself. My Pearls group is meeting after school today to finish our Christmas project. I told Josh he could use the car tonight, so he can get Syd on his way to the church."

My thoughts drifted throughout the day. Mom was going to need me, or at least I wanted her to. In a few months, Josh would be leaving for school, and I wasn't sure how I would cope with his absence. And then there was Isaac — I was really starting to like him, and questioned whether it was too soon to be falling in love again.

Sheila pulled up in front of the house as I was

turning into my driveway. I could hear her singing even though her windows were up.

"I thought you had to get Shae?" I asked as she was getting out of her car.

"Doug said he would get her," Sheila continued to sing as she walked down the driveway and in the door.

I took her coat. "That sounds like a song from the heart!"

Sheila stopped singing. "Girl, it's been years. It better be." We laughed and headed for the living room.

"So you had a nice time in Cleveland?" I asked, kicking off my shoes as we settled on the couch.

"I didn't get to see much of Cleveland, but the Bryant family really liked me!" she declared.

Sheila told me about meeting the rest of Doug's family. His mother was disappointed they missed Thanksgiving so the family reconvened for dinner on Saturday.

"So, what's the deal with Isaac?" she asked, changing the subject from her to me.

I admitted really liking him and not being ready to deal with those feelings. I told her about Josh's reaction to seeing Isaac hold me, which let me know he wasn't ready for me to be in another relationship. Before Sheila could respond, I changed the subject. I told her about my mom not wanting to move to Pittsburgh and the guilt I felt about not knowing how to help her get through her grief. I wanted to tell her about my mom's drinking but after keeping it as a secret for so long, I didn't know how.

"Syd's trying out for the witch in *Into The Woods*," Sheila said, breaking the silence.

"Into what?"

"*Into The Woods*. It combines a bunch of fairy tales into one story," Sheila explained.

"Why does she want to be the witch?"

"It's a singing part," Sheila added, stirring her coffee.

As usual, we bragged about our children. Josh was starting on the basketball team and his first quarter grades were all As. Shae was selected to play with the high school all stars, which was an honor for a freshman. She was also thinking about trying out for the spring musical because she wanted to be in a play with Sydney.

"You know we're really blessed," Sheila said, taking a cookie from my plate. "We have great kids."

Sheila hosted Christmas dinner at her house to introduce her parents to Doug's parents. Andrea spent Christmas with Harvey's family. Isaac joined Josh and me for dinner. He was going to be in Atlanta on business during the first week of January, and Josh and I were bringing in the New Year in LA.

Just as he had done the year before, Josh left my present by the coffee maker on Christmas morning. I let him sleep and opened the gift after making coffee. It was a beautiful gold cross, and I put it on before calling my mother.

"Merry Christmas," I said, holding the phone on my shoulder as I poured coffee into my cup.

"Merry Christmas, darling!"

I could hear Mahalia Jackson singing in the background. "Are you going to church this morning?"

"Well, of course I am. Joey is playing and Stephanie is singing. You're really going to miss it," Mom said in one breath.

Mom sounded happy and that made me smile.

"I'm sure it's going to be nice. Send me a tape."

"I'll have Deacon Wendell get that off to you after the holiday. Where's my Joshua?" she asked, changing the subject.

"He's still sleeping."

"Kiss him for me and wish him Merry Christmas."

"Did you get our packages?" I asked.

"Yes and I put them under the tree. I won't let Joey open anything until after church today." No gifts were ever opened until after church.

The Singleton's were next on my call list, then Alicia, Rhonda, Denise, Elaine and Maureen. Adrienne would be my first call after church. It was only 5:00 in the morning in Los Angeles.

"Merry Christmas, best mother in the whole wide world," Josh said, kissing me on the forehead as I hung up the phone with Maureen. "Thanks so much."

"You're supposed to say 'You didn't have to' so I can take it back," I explained with a straight face.

"No way," he said, holding up the Shaquille O'Neal jersey.

"You deserve it," I said hugging him. "I love you, Josh."

"I love you too, Mom. Merry Christmas." He paused midway up the steps. "Can I still take the car?"

"And how will I get to church?" I asked.

"Mr. Isaac said he was coming to get you."

"Oh really?" I said with mock surprise.

Josh smiled and continued up the steps singing, "Have Yourself a Merry Christmas."

Thirteen

Josh and I arrived at LAX on December 27 at noon. Jason and I had celebrated our second anniversary in California, and Jason wanted to bring Josh when he was old enough to appreciate it. We kept putting it off.

"Yoo hoo," Maureen's infamous call interrupted my thoughts, and I noticed them at the end of the ramp as we exited the plane.

"Hey girl," I said hugging Maureen as Adrienne hugged Josh. "We made it, we're really here!"

Adrienne hugged me. "How was the flight?"

"She slept the whole way," Josh interjected.

"Where's your crew?" I asked Maureen, looking around for Ellis and the kids.

"Scott took them back to the house and we hung around here waiting for you guys," she explained.

The kids greeted us at the door, and Chase couldn't wait to show Josh his new Game Boy. Scott prepared brunch, but we decided to open presents before eating. Mom Singleton called to make sure we arrived safely, which reminded me to call my mom, Isaac, Andrea and Sheila.

Our first two days were spent at Universal Studios, and we spent the third day sightseeing. On the other days, Josh hung out with Scott and Ellis playing basketball and watching sports. Maureen, Adrienne and I spent most of our leisure time in the kitchen talking.

We brought in the New Year at the Jerusalem Baptist Church. After service, we grilled fish and sat on the deck to watch the sun rise. Love, kindness, goodness and peace were still written on slips of paper in my Bible. All of them had come and gone. I wanted all of them permanently. I was tired of feeling like circumstances arbitrarily snatched them away from me.

Six days was not enough time. We reaffirmed our promise to keep in touch and I invited everyone to Josh's graduation. We all cried at the airport. As the plane took off, I thanked Jason for leaving me with a wonderful family.

Andrea met us at the airport along with snow. The storm was just beginning, and I hoped it would develop into a snow day.

"I'm not going to ask if you had a nice time because I know you did," Andrea said as we inched along the parkway. "Did your in-laws go, too?"

"My grandmother doesn't like to fly but I had a good time," Josh answered before I could respond. "I could live without snow. Maybe I'll move to California." He looked at me anticipating a response. "Maybe I'll go to UCLA or USC."

"That would be nice," I turned to look at him. "Maybe you should see if there's still time to apply."

"You know you don't want me to go that far," he said and nudged my shoulder.

"I didn't say I wouldn't miss you." I winked at Andrea.

"That's a long way," Andrea told him. "You would only be able to come home once a year."

Josh was silent for a moment. Determined to have the last word he stated, "I could handle that."

Andrea filled me in on the details of her Christmas with Harvey's family. They were home for the New Year and Corey was at Seven Springs Ski Resort with his basketball team for the weekend.

Josh made tracks by dragging his feet and his suitcase in the accumulating snow on the front walk. After thanking Andrea, I stood in the doorway and watched her slowly pull out of my driveway. Josh retreated to his room with the chemistry book that never left his suitcase. I settled on the couch in my robe with the telephone. There were two messages on the machine, Isaac and Sheila. I called Sheila first.

"Hey girl," I said happy to hear her voice. "What's doing?"

"I'm glad you're back. Thanks for bringing the snow!"

"Why are you and Andrea trying to blame me for the snow?" I pretended to be offended.

"Well, the weather was in the 40s until today," Sheila said in her maternal, matter-of-fact tone.

We talked for over an hour catching up on the past week. In spite of Sheila's reservations, the family gathering was great. The girls and Doug's kids were glad to finally meet and the parents signed "Grandma and Granddad" on the gift tags of the presents to all the kids.

"So when's the wedding?" I asked.

"You sound like my mother," Sheila sighed. "My heart would marry him tomorrow, but it's only been six months. I need to be really sure. . ."

"He makes you happy," I cut her off.

"I can't take another heartache," Sheila almost whispered. "I know I can't take that."

"Remember when we joined the single's ministry?" I reminded her. "Let it go. Stop holding on to the pain and disappointment of the past."

My own inhibitions made me a hypocrite in my attempt to encourage her. Sheila had taken the risk to fall in love with Doug, a risk I was dodging with Isaac. My own heartaches left me doubting if it was worth entering into another relationship — the possibility of it ending in failure, or by death, made me question if I wanted to take the chance on love again.

Isaac was the next person I called. He didn't answer the hotel phone so I left him a message. It was a little after 3:00 AM when the buzz of the television woke me. My body rebelled at the thought of going upstairs and I gave in to sleeping on the couch.

The principal, Dr. Fleming, circled the article about the governor's position on charter schools and left it on my desk. Andrea called while I was reading it and suggested we attend the conference on writing proposals for charter schools. Isaac called hoping to catch me before I got busy and the secretary, Ms. White, slipped me a note about meeting with Dr. Fleming at 10:00. I had only been in the building for twenty minutes. Just as I predicted, the start of my day indicated how the rest of the day was going to go. By 4:30 I was glad to be going home. I was mentally exhausted.

Josh was excited about driving my new Jeep to the Snow Ball, and I hoped it wouldn't snow again, at least not until after the dance. He had ordered a corsage for Sydney and registered to re-take his SAT exam without any prompting from me.

"He's really graduating," I said out loud as I stirred the spaghetti sauce. I remembered dreading having to tell my mother I was pregnant.

The ringing phone interrupted my thoughts. It was Isaac. His flight would be in at 6:40 Friday evening. On Saturday, his parents were having a Dr. King celebration at their church and his dad was one of the speakers.

"So what does Saturday look like?" he asked.

"Good," I said slowly. "I'm not sure if Josh is free."

"If I have to settle for just one, I'm okay with it being you." He knew what to say to make me smile.

"So what have you told your parents about me?" I asked cautiously.

"Just that you are their future daughter-in-law," he answered.

"What?" I shouted.

"I'm kidding, just kidding," he tried to reassure me. "I told them you were a good friend."

Isaac's parents were pleasant. They didn't make me feel on the spot or like I was being inspected. The King Memorial program was impactful and I wished Josh had come. Isaac's dad marched with Dr. King and was able to tell firsthand about the events of that day. It was a moving historical account of a time when African Americans were bound together by the hopes and dreams of a brighter future. It made me more aware of making sure Josh appreciated the privileges that we enjoy because of those who paved the way and to be cognizant of the struggle that remained.

"I imagine I'll be seeing you again," Mrs. Turner said as she hugged me.

"Thank you so much for dinner," I hugged her back, ignoring her comment. "Very nice meeting you," I said hugging Mr. Turner.

Isaac and I rode in silence for about ten minutes. "That wasn't so bad," he finally said.

"No," I agreed with him, "it actually wasn't and I had a nice time."

He took my hand. "I wanted you to have a nice

time."

"And to meet your parents," I stated sarcastically. "I knew they'd like you."

As we drove back to my house, Isaac told me about Nia, the girlfriend he lived with for eight years. They moved in together after graduating from Wilberforce University, and rationalized they could save money by sharing expenses. After about a year, they talked about getting married, but never made definitive plans. Three years into the arrangement, Nia had an abortion because she didn't want to have a baby before getting married.

Two years later, she was pregnant again and they planned a Christmas wedding after the baby was born. Isaiah was born June 24, 1988 at 5:03 a.m. He lived for seven weeks and died of SIDS. Six months later, Isaac came home to a note from Nia stating that she needed a change. Isaac regretted never marrying her. He said he really loved her and believed they could have worked through the pain of losing the baby.

Isaac was living in New Kensington when he started working at Mellon Bank and met Harvey. Heartbroken and very angry after his break up with Nia, he was going to the bar after work to drown his sorrow. After Harvey referred him to the Employee Assistance Program, he invited him to the men's Bible study. Eight years had passed since Isaac started working at Mellon Bank, moved to Pittsburgh and joined The Sanctuary. He admitted that giving his life to Christ literally saved him.

Isaac hadn't seen Nia since the day she left him. Last Thanksgiving, however, he saw her cousin, who told him that Nia was married and living in New Orleans. Up until that point, he wanted to find her to apologize and he also wanted closure. He admitted that he intentionally dated casually over the past few years while he completed his MBA and worked through some issues that he felt had finally been resolved.

I felt compelled to share something about my past with Isaac, but I kept it brief. Jason and I went to graduate school together, fell in love and married after I graduated. We shared a wonderful marriage and I only moved to Pittsburgh because Columbus didn't feel like home anymore. I also admitted feeling guilty about going out with him because it had only been two years since Jason died.

"How long do you think you should be the grieving widow?" Isaac asked.

"I don't know," I responded.

"Do you think Jason would have wanted you to be alone for the rest of your life?"

"No," I answered honestly, "he loved me too much for that."

"I can see why." Isaac put his fingers between mine, and we held hands the rest of the way home.

I thought about Nana and her wisdom seeds. Love, kindness, goodness and peace — I had experienced all of them, but still felt like life kept snatching them away from me. The guest soloist on Sunday sang "I Won't Complain," and it brought tears to my eyes because that was my song. I had had some weary days and sleepless nights, but when I thought about it, really thought about it, all of my good days truly outweighed the bad ones. I needed to stop viewing the seeds as seasonal. Love, kindness, goodness and peace were mine in spite of the rain, snow or drought.

The Snow Ball was on the Gateway Clipper and, in spite of the cold, Josh said it was better than the first one. He was serving on the yearbook committee and looking forward to having his photographs included in the yearbook — or published, as he called it. Josh was accepted at all the schools he applied to and made the decision to attend Johnson C. Smith. His basketball team was in first place in their division, and Josh was excited about the Senior Recognition Day game.

Andrea, Sheila and I sat in front of the Salvation Soldiers and made them promise to cheer along with us. Josh's team was playing to keep their title and the game was intense from the jump ball. At the start of the third quarter, Josh went up for a rebound and came down crooked. He fell hard to the floor and Isaac held my arm to keep me from running onto the court. I could feel my heart beating as the coach sauntered over to Josh and then motioned for the referee. Mr. Frazier, the assistant coach, motioned for me to come down on the floor. He suspected Josh's ankle was fractured and paramedics were taking him to the hospital.

The team made the playoffs and Josh finished the season as a spectator. He watched his first and last high school championship game from the bench wearing his warm-up.

Sydney was selected to play the witch in *Into The Woods* and she was ecstatic. She was hoping to add another Adam Wade Award, this time for Best Actress in a Lead Role. Sylvester promised to attend the opening night performance but sent roses and a note of apology for his absence.

Shae received the MVP Award in the high school All-Star Tournament, and was featured on the front cover of the February *Community Digest*. Shae was only in the ninth grade and colleges were already interested. The girls high team reigned as state champs for the third consecutive year, and Shae was the only starter who wasn't graduating. This was her shining moment. Sheila mailed a copy of the magazine to Sylvester hoping he would, at least, send flowers. He sent carnations. Doug gave her roses.

On March seventh, I thought of Jason and hoped he knew I still missed him. I liked Isaac but still felt guilty – it had only been two years. I prayed and asked God to help me.

The singles ministry went bowling on the last Saturday in March, and Isaac was noticeably quiet.

"What's the matter?" I asked as we were driving back to my house.

He wouldn't look at me. "It's complicated."

"What's complicated?" I hated that word. It always indicated a problem.

"They offered me the VP position at the bank," he said without smiling.

"Well, that's great!"

"The position is in Atlanta," he quickly added.

"Atlanta?"

He replied without looking at me, "Yeah, Atlanta."

I wanted to tell him I was happy for him, but the words wouldn't come. We rode in silence until he turned onto Sonny Street and pulled into my driveway.

"It's an opportunity of a lifetime. I wish it would have come six months ago, then this wouldn't be so hard."

He took my hand but I couldn't look at him. I had that suffocating feeling again. There was no air and

I couldn't move to open the door. He turned my face towards his. "Please say something."

"I'm happy for you," I managed to say before the tears began to flow. "I know this is something you've wanted."

We sat in the car for what seemed like an hour, and I listened to him talk. I searched my mind to remember some of the wisdom seeds, but drew blanks. One thing was for sure, my heart was breaking – again.

Two weeks later, I hosted a going away party for Isaac at my house and I was fine until after everyone left. Isaac was in the living room with Josh, and I was putting the last of the dishes away when the reality of him leaving the next day hit. Had I brought this on myself? Would he have stayed if I had been honest about my feelings? "God," I sighed out loud, "does life ever get easy?"

Isaac came in the kitchen and stood behind me. "Thank you," he said.

"It's the least I could do," I said sadly.

"I've avoided talking about us over this past week," he said and took the dishtowel from me. "I was never sure of the possibilities. I know you need time, what I don't know is how much."

"I don't either," I added.

Isaac pulled me into his arms and hugged me. Hard as I tried not to cry, the tears came. I had no words.

Monday morning was hard, and I forced myself to get out of bed and go to work. Staying at home would have been counter-productive and I was tired of crying. It was a little late to be thinking about admitting my feelings — Isaac was gone.

Andrea's advice was to depend on God, grow spiritually, focus on myself and my own spiritual development. It sounded good, but my heart wasn't listening. Sheila's advice was to keep hope alive.

"It's not over till the fat lady sings," was her favorite cliché.

Josh and I spent Easter with the Singletons. We arrived in Ann Arbor Saturday afternoon and I was pleasantly surprised that Adrienne, Maureen and their families were also there. It was good seeing everyone, and I was glad no one asked about Isaac. I suspected Josh had already told them.

The first message on my answering machine when we returned home Sunday night was from Isaac. I called him before taking off my coat. He was settled in his apartment and invited me to visit him. I agreed to come the following weekend.

"You miss him, don't you?" Josh asked after I told him about my trip.

"Yeah, I do."

"I want you to be happy, Mom," he said going upstairs. "Have a nice time in Atlanta."

"You're the best son in the world," I yelled behind him as he went up the steps.

Isaac was at the gate and hugged me when I got off the plane. "I've missed you."

"I've missed you, too," I said, glad to be in his arms again.

We spent Saturday sightseeing. I was anticipating

and dreading going back to his apartment to talk about us that evening. The inevitable came after dinner.

"I've been thinking about you," he commented as he put on a Luther Vandross CD before joining me on the couch.

"Well, that's good," I said. "I've thought a lot about you, too."

"I was hoping we could stay friends and keep in touch." He kissed me and pulled me into his arms. "I was also wondering where we can go from here?"

"I don't know. I really don't know," I said honestly.

We talked about seeing each other monthly. He told me to think about opportunities in Atlanta, and I reminded him that I just purchased a house. The evening was filled with a myriad of emotions. We finally admitted to each other, and ourselves, that Atlanta was a long way from Pittsburgh. Neither of us wanted to commit to a long distance relationship. He kissed me again, as if to leave a lasting impression. I knew it would, and somewhere deep inside of me I wished we could have another chance.

On Sunday, we went to breakfast and then to the 8:00 church service. My plane was departing at 2:00 and I was leaving Atlanta and Isaac. We would be friends and all the maybes would remain unknown. The memories were all good and would temporarily suffice to sustain me.

Sheila met me at the airport and had a million questions about my visit. I cried and admitted that whatever had started was over. We stopped at Baskin Robbins for banana splits and went to Sheila's to watch *Waiting To Exhale*.

I began praying that God would help me understand His will for my life. Andrea gave me a book by Max Lucado, *When God Doesn't Seem to Make Sense*, and I became engrossed in it.

"Life is a spiritual journey," Andrea reminded me. "God will bring you to the point of trusting Him. How you get there is determined by the road you choose. It can be the long way or the short way."

"Well of course, I want to go the most direct route," I told her, trying not to sound cynical.

"Then trust Him. Be confident in His ability to take care of you and provide for you."

Andrea seemed so wise. If only I had developed half of her faith!

Joshua and Sydney went to each other's proms just as they planned. Sydney wore lilac to her prom and the red dress she wore to the Adam Wade Awards to Josh's prom. It was an intense two weeks between the two of them, which culminated with their graduation. As I watched Josh receive his diploma, I smiled, knowing Jason was watching, too. He would have been proud and I hoped Josh knew that.

The week after the kids graduated, Sheila and I hosted a celebratory picnic in Schenley Park. Between the two families, we were expecting eighty people. My mom, the Singletons and Isaac came in for graduation and stayed for the party. Joey's family, Noah's family, Maureen's family, Adrienne's family, Rhonda's family, Denise and Elaine joined us for the party. Sheila's parents, grandparents, her brother's family, Doug, his parents and his kids were there, too. Sylvester promised to come but did his usual no show and sent flowers.

I hated having to spoil a great weekend by talking with Mom about selling the house, but it was a necessary discussion before she left Pittsburgh. On Monday morning, I brought it up while we had coffee.

"Mom, we need to talk about you being in the house by yourself."

"I'm going to sell the house," she said pouring her second cup.

"Are you coming to live with me?" I asked.

"No baby, it gets too cold. I'm old. I need warm weather all year long. Your father and I talked about moving to Florida one day," Mom gently said.

"Oh," I said, "I didn't know that. So what are you going to do?"

"Joseph and Stephanie invited me to come with them to Virginia. It's closer to Florida than Smithtown." She smiled and took my hand. "It's not that I don't want to live with you, and I appreciate the offer, but I told Joseph I would come there after the house sold."

My feelings were hurt. Selfishly, I wanted my mother to live with me. Jason was gone, Isaac was gone and Josh was leaving.

"That's great, Mom," I lied, pretending to be happy for her. I busied myself with my banana nut muffin and was relieved when Josh came into the dining room.

I was apprehensive about Josh leaving at the end of August, and the summer went faster than I wanted it to. Josh and Syd worked at the church summer camp as head counselors; Shae went to basketball camp and won her second MVP in the summer tournament at the Y;

my mother was going to Hampton to live with Joey and Stephanie; and I was missing Jason – this was supposed to be our time. I also spent too much time thinking about Isaac and the what ifs.

Josh was looking forward to going to college, but I cried myself to sleep the night before we drove to Charlotte. The morning greeted me with a clear blue sky, bright sunshine, a headache and my son whistling as he stuffed every tee shirt he owned into his suitcase. Isaac called while we were loading the car to tell Josh good-bye and to ask, again, if I wanted him to drive back with me. He asked repeatedly, and I repeatedly thanked him and declined. Our calls were now weekly and more routine than anything else. I wasn't sure if, like me, he was trying to move on or if he had met someone.

Most of my reservations about leaving Josh at school were resolved before we left Pittsburgh. Although he wasn't sure what he wanted to do, he knew he wanted to work with computers. When I asked about Syd, his reply was the same as it had been for the past two years, "we're just really good friends." Every time I pressed and asked if he liked her more than that, he would merely smile and state, "I think so."

Before I was satisfied with the set up of Josh's room, he was telling me to get on the road to Raleigh. "I'll be okay, Mom," he said walking me to my car. "You need to get on the road. It's getting late."

"It's a straight shot," I assured him. "I'll be fine."

"Mom, thanks for everything." He hugged me and kissed me on the cheek. "I love you."

"I love you, too," I said hugging him, not wanting to let go. "Jason would be so proud." I turned his face to mine. "He's watching," and I pointed to the sky.

I stayed at Alicia's for three days. Going for a swim before breakfast was addictive and I didn't want to leave. Dennis was right, part of me wanted to stay close to Josh, but it was the going home part that I dreaded. I was going home alone.

Fourteen

Loneliness engulfed me the first few weeks after Joshua left. For my own self-therapy and to help me shed the empty-nest syndrome, I began keeping a journal in September of 1999. I prayed more often too, and started getting up a half-hour earlier. There was something about talking to God in the quiet of the morning that comforted me.

While the weather was still warm, I enjoyed my prayer time and coffee on the enclosure. After finishing the book Andrea gave me, I began studying Joseph. His journey did not seem to make sense. He didn't deserve being sold by his brothers, lied on by Potiphar's wife or going to prison. While suffering, Joseph had no idea that God was setting him up for a position of authority. Although he couldn't see the end, he remained faithful to God and never doubted Him. I needed to be more like Joseph. I couldn't see the end, and I often felt victimized by my circumstances. I needed greater faith to trust that God was preparing me for something beyond what I could imagine. I began to pray for faith.

Andrea and I finalized our proposal outline for a charter school and received overwhelming support from members of the church. With much encouragement from Sheila, I applied to the Principal Certification Program at Indiana University of Pennsylvania. In submitting my application, I promised myself I wouldn't back out if accepted.

During each weekly phone call, Josh reported that he was doing well and looking forward to basketball season. I made plans for Thanksgiving and reminded Josh that we would be in Ann Arbor with the Singleton's.

As usual, the autumn leaves carpeted my lawn. October was my favorite month, but with Josh being away, there was no one to rake the leaves. The following week, Sheila went to New York on business and I agreed to keep Shae. I welcomed the company and, as promised, attended both of her exhibition games. The Youth & Young Adult Gospel Explosion at the Rodman Street Baptist Church concluded our week's adventure on Friday night.

As I pulled in Sheila's driveway after the concert, I noticed the Escalade parked in front of her house.

Shae's tone immediately changed from bubbly to indifferent. "That's my dad's car."

"How do you know?" I asked.

"See the Smurf in the back window? He collects them." Shae was hesitant and waited for me to get out of the car. We walked to the door in silence.

Sheila's voice was shrill as we came in the front door. "You can't just stop by when you're in town and expect everyone to be happy to see you!"

"You're still angry that the marriage didn't work." The man's voice was strangely familiar.

"Don't fool yourself! I'm ecstatic that you left and grateful you left me with two wonderful girls and not AIDS. You're just a whore with MD behind your name," Sheila shouted, her voice quivering.

"Mom," Shae interrupted them, peeking her head into the kitchen.

I stood in the hallway, not wanting to interfere, but knowing Sheila would need to talk when this was over.

"Hey baby girl."

I knew that voice.

"Hi, Dad," Shae's voice was solemn and just above a whisper.

"Do I at least get a hug?"

It couldn't be. My mind began to race. Sheila is from Washington, PA. She used to live in Philly, not Harrisburg. Henderson is such a common name. Her ex-husband's name is Sylvester. I walked into the kitchen to let Sheila know I'd be at home if she needed me. Before he even turned around, I knew it was him. I managed to say his name with the last of the air in my lungs. My mind went blank and the air was suddenly sucked out of the room just as it had been nineteen years ago.

"You know him?" Sheila's eyes got big and her head snapped to the side.

I couldn't answer. The sight of him triggered memories of that day in his living room.

Sheila walked toward me. "Dani, are you okay?"

"I gotta go, call me," was all I could say as I ran out the door.

I drove home in complete shock. Those old skeletons were coming out of hibernation and taunting me. My dad was right and I could still hear his words, "skeletons only hide in the closet − they never go away and they always get tired of hiding."

Forty-five minutes later Sheila was at my door. I dreaded having to tell her. Part of me wished Greg already had.

"Girl, what's going on?" she asked as I opened the door.

I silently walked to the couch and sat down.

"How do you know Sylvester?" she asked following me to the couch and taking a seat. Her question was more rhetorical than inquisitive.

"I never knew his name was Sylvester. He introduced himself as Greg," I said through tears that rolled freely down my face.

"Sylvester Gregory Henderson, the Casanova Liar," Sheila stated flatly. "How do you know him?"

"He's Josh's father," I blurted out, interrupting her.

"He's what?" Sheila was dumbfounded.

"I was an intern at Western Psych when he was a resident. We had a summer relationship, or I thought it was a relationship."

"You had a what?" Sheila attempted to interrupt me, but I continued talking.

"He told me he loved me and wanted to marry me. When I got pregnant, he told me he was married and wanted me to have an abortion." I was rambling, but I needed to say it all. "When I married Jason, he adopted Josh."

Sheila sat back on the couch, moving her hands, but unable to speak.

"It's the secret I've been keeping for years." My shame wouldn't let me look at her.

Sheila sat motionless.

"Don't hate me," I pleaded.

We sat in silence.

"Sylvester is Josh's father," Sheila repeated.

"Yeah."

"So it was you," Sheila stated as she got up and walked toward the window. "He's the son they were whispering about."

"Sheila, I'm. . ."

"Let me finish," she cut me off with a scolding tone. "When I loved him I hated the wench who stole his heart away from me. But now I don't love him, but

I'm angry and I'm hurt that you've been lying." She was almost yelling. "Were you even married?"

Her words were threaded with anger.

"Yes," I replied as I finally found the courage to look at her. "Seems like I've been lying my whole life."

"And Josh doesn't know and Sylvester has never seen Josh?"

My heart felt like it was going to explode in my chest and I shook my head no.

Sheila stared out the window with her back to me.

"How's Shae?" I asked needing to talk about something other than me.

"I took her to Amber's."

"Sheila, I'm sorry."

"Well, this truth sets you free," Sheila turned to face me with folded arms and continued. "This web includes more than us," her tone softening. "Let me show you the letter Syd sent me two weeks ago."

She took the letter from her purse and read part of it, "I really like Josh more than I ever told anyone. I can't keep pretending that all I want is to be his friend. When he comes for homecoming, I'm going to tell him how I really feel."

Sheila looked at me over the top of the letter. "I've got to call her tonight. Josh will be arriving at Alicia's in the morning."

Sheila sat back down on the couch and took a tissue from the box on the coffee table. She wiped the tears rolling down her cheeks and then folded the tissue into a tiny square.

"Honesty is so important to me. So many lies in my past. Can we just be honest with each other?"

"I promise," I said, wiping my face with the back of my hand. "No more lies, no more secrets."

I hugged her and we cried together – for ourselves, each other and our children. Before she left, we said a prayer and asked God to help us get through this.

After Sheila drove off, I called Andrea. It was almost 11:30.

"Can I come over?" I tried to disguise the panic in my voice. "I need to talk to you."

"Right now?" Andrea was taken aback. "Are you okay? What's the matter?"

"Please Annie, can I just come over?"

When Andrea opened the door I began to cry.

"Dani, what happened? Is Josh okay?"

I couldn't get a word out.

"Dani!" Andrea was shaking me by the arms.

"I saw Greg."

"Where? When? Did he come to your house?" Andrea asked.

"He was at Sheila's. He's her ex-husband. His real name is Sylvester."

Andrea quickly put the pieces together. "You've got to call Josh," she said, trying to sound calm.

"I know. I just don't know what to say." I felt even more pathetic than I sounded.

"You have to tell him the truth." Andrea was always the voice of reason. "He may be a little angry at first, but he loves you and he's a little more mature – you'll work it out."

"It just never goes away, Annie, it won't go away." The ringing phone interrupted my pity party.

"Hey Sheila," I heard Andrea saying. "Yeah, that's fine. Come on."

"Sheila's on her way over," she said hanging up. "She talked to Sydney."

Andrea disappeared into the kitchen. Harvey came downstairs and I could hear them talking.

"It's going to be okay," Harvey said and hugged me after he put the teacups on the table. "We don't always understand the whys — just remember that God is still in control."

Andrea gave me a warm washcloth to wipe my face. "You can't fall apart, Dani." She sat next to me. "You'll deal with this. Harvey and I are here for you and Josh. You have Sheila and most importantly, your son loves you very much."

The doorbell rang and as bad as I wanted to know about her conversation, I didn't want to know how much my secret hurt Syd.

"First, we need to pray," Andrea said, leading Sheila into the living room. I stood to join their hands.

"Lord, we're calling on you. We need Your divine guidance. Help us get through this storm. Touch everyone involved. Lord, give them what they need. Use me as Your vessel. Help me to help them. Amen."

"She was devastated," Shelia said before we sat down. "Nothing I said mattered."

"I'm sorry. This is my fault."

"Have you called Josh yet?" Shelia asked, looking directly at me and over-accentuating the 'you'.

"There was no answer," I paused and bit my lip, "I'll call back in the morning."

"Sydney promised she wouldn't call him."

We talked until after midnight and I drove home the long way. I was suffocating in my own deceit. Sheila was numb. Sydney was hurt. Josh was going to hate me.

It was almost 7:00 and I jumped up, realizing

the need to speak with Alicia before I talked to Josh. Dennis answered the phone. Alicia was in the shower and Dennis said he would have her call me. When she called, I blurted everything out. Alicia never said a word.

"Sydney already knows, so I have to talk to him before he talks to her," I said breaking the silence.

"I'll have him call you," was all Alicia said before hanging up.

While the coffee dripped, I tried to think of what to say. The pot seemed to fill slowly and I paced in the kitchen. I poured the coffee into my biggest mug before realizing there was only a teaspoon of coffee cream. I left the cup on the counter and sat on the couch with my head back and my eyes closed. It was 9:47 when the phone rang.

"Hello," I reluctantly answered the phone.

"Hey, Mom," Josh's voice was cheerful. "You tracked me down!"

I had no words.

"Mom?" His tone changed to concern. "Are you alright?"

"Oh, uh, hey baby." The air was getting thin. "How are you?"

"I'm fine Mom, what's the matter?"

"Josh, I uh, we need to talk."

"Mom, what's the matter?" He spoke quickly.

"Josh sit down."

"Is Nana okay?"

"Yes, Josh. This is about me and you."

"Mom, what are you talking about? Don't tell me you're going to Atlanta to be with Mr. Isaac."

"Josh, please just listen."

"Okay Mom, what's going on?"

"Josh, you know how much I love you?"

"Of course. What's going on?" He was agitated.

"Josh when I graduated from college, I had an internship at Pitt. My boyfriend's name was Greg. He told me he loved me. When I told him I was pregnant, he told me he was already married. He wanted me to have an abortion. I couldn't do it." I rambled without taking a breath.

"Do I have a brother or sister that you gave up for adoption?" He was trying to process the information.

I took a deep breath and closed my eyes. "No, Josh, the baby was you and Greg's real name is Sylvester Gregory Henderson and he's Sheila's ex-husband."

"What? Miss Sheila's ex-husband?"

"I met Jason in grad school when you were one and he adopted you after we got married."

He interrupted me, "Syd is not my sister!"

"Yes, Josh, she is."

"You let me fall in love with my sister. You've been lying to me my whole life. Mom, how could you do that? What about love and trust and all that stuff?"

"Josh, I didn't know any of this until yesterday!" I heard the phone hit the floor and Alicia picked it up. She was crying.

"Dani, he ran out of the house. Dennis went after him."

"Oh, Alicia, what have I done?" The weight of it all crushed me, and I crumbled to the floor, desperately trying to take a breath.

The hardwood floor was cold. My body shivered. Why did Jason die? If he were here, we would be living in Columbus. Why did Isaac leave me? I needed somebody. "God, where are you?" I whimpered. "I'm trying to have faith. What am I supposed to do now?"

The phone rang, but I couldn't move. It was Sheila; I heard her voice on the answering machine. She was calling to check on me. No more lies, I wasn't okay. My son hated me. There was nothing to talk about. I failed. Andrea called. Alicia called. Sheila called again. From the corner of my eye, I watched the puddle of tears grow larger. I wanted to jump in and drown.

Sheila and Andrea were kneeling beside me.

"Are you okay?" Sheila's hand was on my forehead. "Did you fall?"

The pain in my head was paralyzing. I mouthed no as tears rolled across my face.

Sheila helped me onto the couch.

Andrea was in the kitchen filling the tea kettle with water.

I tried to smile, but my head felt like I had been hit with a hammer. The sound of the spoon clanging on the cup in the kitchen echoed in my ears, and I closed my eyes.

"Girl, don't do this." Sheila was sitting beside me. It sounded like she was crying. "You gotta pull it together. We'll make it through. All of us. I promise."

Unable to verbally acknowledge her, I put my head on her shoulder and held her hand.

It was after 2:00 when I woke up. There was a pot of chicken noodle soup on the stove and a note on the refrigerator instructing me to call Andrea's cell phone as soon as I read the note.

"Hey, Annie." I spoke slightly above a whisper because my headache was lingering.

"You're scaring me and I don't know how to help you." I could hear the anxiety in her voice. "I'm waiting for Corey to come out of the dentist office. Harvey should be home by six and then I'll be back."

"You don't have to. I'll be okay."

She ignored me. "Sheila took Shae to her parents, she might get there before me."

"I'll be fine," I repeated.

"Dani, take the 'S' off your chest. Let us help you." Andrea paused and I heard her sigh. "Gotta go, here comes Corey. Eat something. See you in a few."

There were only three Motrin's in the bottle. I took all of them. Not knowing what else to do, I took Jason's last letter from under my mattress and sat on my bed. I knew what the letter said – I read it again anyway.

February 14, 1997

My Dearest Danielle,

You are my one in a million and if I had the strength, this is the song I would sing for you.

As I look back over our lives together, I can only thank God. He gave me you and a wonderful son. We were meant to be a family. I pray you have felt loved and I pray Josh has felt loved and nurtured. I hope he always knows I did my very best.

I know I don't have long now, but I will cherish every memory. I only regret that it's much too soon. I want to see Josh graduate from high school, go on to college, get married and have a family of his own. I would have been a good Pappy. I also regret not having the chance to sit with him man to man and explain the adoption. I needed to let him know the word adoption is just a legal term but the love in my heart has always been genuine. One day when he has children of his own, show this letter to him, he will understand the difference between merely fathering a child and being a daddy. I am honored to be his daddy. I am honored that he carries my name.

Well my sweet, I am getting tired. I know this isn't the kind of love letter you were expecting, but I needed to make sure that you knew. If this is my last letter, know that it is sealed with all my hopes and dreams, love and kisses.

Forever yours, Jason.

After copying the letter on Monday morning, I scribbled a note on the back before placing it in the envelope:

> *'Josh, I know you're angry. I was young and did what I thought was best for both of us. Read this letter from your dad. Please call me, we need to talk. Love you much, Mom.'*

Over the next week, I raced home after work to check the answering machine. Every day there were no messages.

The phone startled me when it rang Friday evening. Sheila's voice was a welcomed diversion. "Hey girl!"

"Hey." The stress rendered me lethargic, and I felt like I hadn't slept all week.

"Shae is spending the weekend with Amber. I'll be over around 8:00."

"You don't have to do that," I protested. I needed an excuse to maintain my pity and solitude.

"Don't shut me out, Dani. I'm here for you."

"I'm sorry, I uh, I'm going to be terrible company. I should probably be alone," I continued.

"Wrong answer! You don't need to be alone! How long are you going to sit at home waiting by the phone?"

At that moment, I was willing to wait forever.

"You didn't go to Bible study on Wednesday, and I'll bet you haven't been out of the house except for going to work any day this week!"

"You're right," I whispered.

"Dani, you need a friend, and I'm all you got. I'll see you in a few."

She hung up and I smiled. Sheila was right. I wasn't in this by myself and I needed a friend. I was thankful she was coming.

Sheila arrived with a pizza from Vento's. We ate the whole thing and drowned our sorrows in cream soda. As I sat back on the couch like a rat that had eaten too much, Sheila kicked off her shoes and folded her legs on the couch.

"Dani, you need to know I'm not angry."

"I'm really sorry," I interrupted her.

"I'm over Sylvester," she interrupted me as she sat up, put her feet on the floor and rested her elbows on her knees. "God has sent me a good man and I can't wait to be Doug's wife. And God has made us friends for a reason..."

I interrupted her again, "I don't deserve your kindness."

"Forgiveness," Sheila corrected me. "That's the life lesson."

We sat in silence for a moment and then Sheila sat back and put her feet on the coffee table.

"I talked to Syd this morning," she began without looking at me. "You'll never guess what she did."

My heart palpitated. "What did she do?"

"She called Sylvester and asked him to come down so he could meet Josh."

"Are you serious?" I sat up and looked at Sheila.

"Girl, I have to go to North Carolina."

"No," Sheila was very matter-of-fact. "We have to go to North Carolina. I told Syd to let me know when her dad planned to visit them."

Another week passed and there was no call from Josh. Each of my attempts to call him resulted in talking to the answering machine I now regretted buying. My ulcer emerged in full force. Everything I ate made me feel like my stomach was on fire and my chest was going to explode. I was alternating between Tums and Maalox.

Monday, day sixteen, and still no call and no message from Josh. The one message on my machine was from Sheila. I changed my clothes and was getting comfortable on the couch when the phone rang.

"Did you get my message?" Sheila's tone was stern.

I sat up and put my hand on my forehead. I was afraid of any news she had for me.

"Sheila, is everything okay?"

"Yeah girl," she spoke quickly. "We're going to North Carolina Saturday morning. We need to leave about five — Sylvester is meeting the kids for dinner in Raleigh."

My mind couldn't handle the possibility of confronting Greg and Josh at the same time. I moaned into the receiver.

"Take a deep breath." Sheila's voice was calm. "We're going to get this taken care of."

I promised to call her later that evening. I called Andrea to inform her of our plans and then I called Alicia to see if we could stay with her. She had already talked to Josh and was meeting him at the train station Saturday afternoon.

The light was blinking on my answering machine when I got home from work on Wednesday. I pressed play and closed my eyes, praying the message was from Josh.

"I'm going to meet my father," his voice was filled with anger and escalated as he spoke. "You couldn't handle the truth but I can. You lied to me and then convinced Dad to lie, too. I got your letter and it didn't make me feel any better. You both raised me to be honest, but you were lying to me. You're just like your father – you want perfect. And your perfect was at my expense. Don't bother coming down this weekend. I don't need you to help me deal with this." There was silence and then the dial tone.

When Andrea came to get me for Bible study I was curled up on the couch unable to move. She took me to the emergency room and I was given a cocktail of Maalox and Lidocain. The doctor sent me home with a prescription for Pepcid. I wanted to call off on Thursday and Friday, but doing something other than staying at home thinking about the mess I created was essential to my mental stability. I contemplated calling my mom, then changed my mind. I wanted to call Isaac, just to hear his voice, but I was afraid I would only cry.

Friday was a clerical day so I left early to get ready for our trip to North Carolina. After my overnight bag was packed, I laid down and left a message for Sheila to call me when she got in.

The phone woke me. It was 8:20. "Dani!" Sheila was almost screaming and there was an urgency in her voice. "Dani, get up."

"What's the matter?" I suddenly had a sick feeling in my stomach. "Sheila, what's the matter?"

"Syd just called. She's at a hospital in Durham."

"Is she okay? Did something happen to Josh?"

Sheila spoke slowly. "It's not Sydney, it's Sylvester. He was in a car accident."

"What? He did what?"

"He was in a car accident on 85 and it doesn't look good."

"Does Josh know?"

"Yeah."

My mind raced. "Where's Josh? Was Syd with him when he crashed?"

"Josh is on his way to Raleigh. Syd wasn't with Sylvester. The state troopers found her name and number in his wallet and called her."

"Is she okay?"

"She's scared and confused. They told her it didn't look good when they took him to surgery."

"I'm on my way over," I said.

Sheila was standing in the door when I pulled into the driveway. "He's gone," Sheila announced as I got out of my car and walked up her front steps.

"What do you mean gone? He's dead?"

Sheila shook her head and Shae began to cry. I held them both and we stood in the doorway and cried together.

Fifteen

The funeral was scheduled for Thursday at eleven o'clock in Harrisburg. Sheila and Shae left on Tuesday to meet Syd and Josh. I didn't leave until Wednesday. There was no need to go to the wake, but I planned to attend the funeral. Josh was going to need me, in spite of his anger. Andrea thought it was a horrible idea for me to drive by myself. It was only three hours and I assured her I would be fine. After calling my mother, she volunteered to meet me in Harrisburg. Not knowing what to expect, I told her I'd be okay.

I packed Josh's navy suit and a pair of his dress shoes, not knowing if he thought of taking something to wear to the funeral. I also took my raincoat and umbrella. It always seemed to rain at funerals.

Sheila's directions to the Crowne Plaza were perfect and I arrived before eight o'clock on Wednesday night. Almost four weeks had passed since the last time I talked to Josh. Fear gripped me as I walked down the hotel hallway. What would I do first? Hug him or apologize?

I was relieved and angered when Josh wasn't in the room. I called Sheila's room, but there was no answer.

I sat nervously on the bed, staring out the window at the navy colored sky. My thoughts were racing and I needed to see my child's face. There was a knock at the door and tears swelled in my eyes as my mind raced to find the right words. It was Sheila.

"Hey girl, how was the drive?" Sheila asked.

"It was okay," I said hugging her and looking into the hallway. "Where's Josh?"

Sheila sat on the bed. "Now don't get upset."

"Upset about what?" I was standing in front of

her with my arms crossed.

"The kids stayed at the house with Sylvester's parents."

"Josh too?" I asked.

"All the grandchildren."

"Josh doesn't know them."

"He knows them now. And, they obviously knew about him." She paused to give me time to digest the information. "Josh asked me to bring his clothes to the house in the morning."

I sat on the edge of the bed fighting back tears. "He hates me, doesn't he?"

Sheila's voice sounded tired. "He doesn't hate you. This is a lot to deal with."

I didn't know how to respond. The skeletons in the closet were now tormenting me and I had no idea how to make them stop.

"Let me jump in the shower and I'll be back," Sheila said, heading for the door. "I've been in these clothes all day."

A shower seemed like a good idea. I stood in the shower and cried until my eyes hurt.

The church was only twenty minutes from the hotel. I left early enough to get an aisle seat before the family came in. I needed to make eye contact with Josh. His avoidance was heart wrenching as well as irritating.

The funeral director was hurrying people to get a final view of Greg before the family came in and I declined, going straight to a seat instead. The obituary listed Josh as Joshua Allen Henderson, which angered me. They had no right to pretend he was a member of their family! They did not know him, and his last name was Singleton, not Henderson.

My anger dissipated as the family processional began. Josh walked with Sheila and the girls. He was too far away for me to grab his arm. Sheila pointed me out and he waved. Then he walked down the aisle with the family and sat on the other side of Sydney. Everyone probably thought Sheila was his mother.

After the family was seated, the funeral director began preparation to close the casket. A thunder of wailing echoed in the church. Josh's head was down and I could tell he was crying. I didn't want him to weep for Greg. I cried enough tears for both of us after Greg discarded us.

Sheila held her girls close and it appeared she was crying, too. In fact, most of the people attending the funeral were crying. The numerous accolades of what a great person Greg had been were nauseating. I asked God to help me forgive him and not hate him. I wanted Greg to be the scapegoat for the mess I was in, even though my secret was the cause of my predicament.

"Please God," I prayed, "help me know what to say to Josh. Touch his heart so he can forgive me."

There was that forgiveness again. I was face to face with being forgiving as I was seeking forgiveness. No other examples needed — it was clear, too clear.

The pastor concluded the funeral by asking Greg's children to stand. Joshua stood with Sydney and Shae.

"Although your father is no longer here with you, he is here with you," he said putting his hand over his heart. "Remember him in what you do, in how you act, in how you carry out his legacy. People will remember him when they see you. What will you have them remember?"

The pastor motioned for the children to sit down. Joshua remained standing and I was afraid he would attempt to say something. He stood in that very same place and received a similar charge when Jason died. Josh sat down slowly and buried his face in his hands. I cried too, but for Josh, not for Greg. This was the third time I had been unable to comfort him in his grief – Jason, my dad and now Greg.

I was one of the last cars in the funeral procession and that was okay. I had no intention of going to the gravesite and didn't want anyone staring at me trying to figure out who I was. As I parked along the dirt road in the cemetery, I could hear the singing even with the windows up. I felt numb. "If His eye is on the spa-a-a-rrow, then I know, He is watching –o-o-over me." That was Nana's favorite song. "God," I sighed, "I don't feel like you're watching me right now and I need you. I can't do this anymore."

My stomach knotted as my eyes followed Joshua moving through the crowd. He walked to the front row and stood next to the grandmother he had only known for two days. Joshua reached over and held her hand during the prayer.

Staring at the faces of those around the casket, I easily identified Greg's brother – they looked just alike. His sisters resembled their mother. I avoided all of them at the church. What was there to say?

Joshua stood facing the casket with his back to me. I knew he really didn't hate me, he was just angry. My dad was right, my secret had come back to haunt me. The whispers in my shadows were now screaming. Joshua had the best of everything, including memories of a loving father. Jason loved him. Greg left him and me. The moment felt surreal. I attempted to get out of the car for air, but the door was too heavy. I let the window down and let myself sink down in the seat.

"I have planted seeds of wisdom in you," Nana's words resonated in my head. What had I learned? Life hurts. I hadn't learned that from wisdom, I learned that from pain. The sparrow had fallen and I wasn't sure God was watching.

"Ashes to ashes and dust to dust," the undertaker announced in his deep monotone voice.

Joshua picked up a flower and turned to hug Sheila. As he walked toward me, I wanted to run to him. I wanted to hold him and tell him how sorry I was for keeping the secret. I needed him to understand that I did what I thought was best. Holding back tears behind my sunglasses, I tried to make eye contact as he stood at the car door. Josh deliberately avoided making eye contact with me as he announced, "I'm going to ride back to the church with Miss Sheila. I'll meet you at the hotel later."

All I could do was nod my head because I wanted to demand that he ride with me. His words were suffocating and I was unable to speak.

Sheila put her hand on the window as it was going up. "It'll be all right." Her eyes were red and swollen. "I'll call your room later. Gotta go do this family thing right now."

The funeral procession was backed up and I got stuck at the gate. I regretted letting the silver car get in front of me. My tissues fell on the floor and when I reached down to get them there was a knock on the window.

"Mom, I'm sorry." Josh was crying uncontrollably. "I'm sorry. This hurts so bad. Why does everyone die?"

He was leaning on the passenger side of the car with his hand on the window. I don't remember shifting into park, or getting out of the car. Josh tried so hard to be strong for me when Jason died and now it was my turn to be strong for him.

"It's okay," I said as I held my son and let him cry. "I know it hurts."

Josh's words were marred by grief and I couldn't understand what he was saying. Holding him reassured me that he didn't hate me. If I had magical powers, I would have transferred his grief to me by osmosis. I couldn't, so I just held him.

Sheila and the girls joined us and we all hugged and cried. Then the woman in the black hat came and stood behind Josh.

"Joshua," she said with a deep Southern accent. "Is this your mama?"

Josh shook his head and I looked up to see her face beneath the veil.

"I'm Danielle Singleton." I extended my hand to shake hers. She held my hand tightly, and I noticed the tears falling beneath the black netting.

She said, "All I can say is I'm sorry. You have every right to be angry, but I would ask you not to. Today is sad enough by itself and I would hope that tomorrow we could all start over with the new day. I was hoping you would join the family for dinner so we could talk."

Mr. Henderson hugged Josh and then turned to face me. "Joshua is my only grandson. Please let us get to know him."

Although Mr. and Mrs. Henderson appeared sincere, Josh needed me. I scribbled my home phone number on the back of the funeral program and gave it to Mrs. Henderson.

"Please call me when you can," I said before

giving both of them a hug.

Josh hugged them, too, and thanked them for their kindness. I hugged Sheila and the girls and told them I would see them back at the hotel.

After everyone returned to their cars, Josh got in the car with me. "Why didn't you tell me?"

I exhaled slowly. "Sometimes when you don't know what to do, you do the wrong thing and you think it's the right thing."

Josh didn't respond.

"I was young and gullible when I met Greg, I mean Sylvester. I thought he loved me and wanted to marry me. When he dumped me after I got pregnant, I was devastated. I didn't know what I was going to do, or what I was going to tell you. Then Jason came along. It was much easier to say he was your father so that's what I did."

"I'm sorry about the message I left you," he responded, still looking at his lap. "You both should have told me when I was old enough to understand."

"You're right, we should have told you. Jason wanted to tell you when you were ten. I begged him not to. It's really my fault and I apologize."

"Did my father ever want to see me?" Josh asked.

"He never called," I responded.

"Would you have let him see me?"

"I don't know," I answered honestly. "I guess I would have." We rode in silence to the hotel.

Josh and I were up at 6:00 to have breakfast before going to the airport. His plane was leaving at 11:45, and I was getting on the road after I took him to the airport. I called Sheila to let her know I was leaving and to thank her. Whatever she said to Josh got through to him when

I couldn't.

"So now what?" Josh asked as he checked his bag at the curb. "What do I do with my feelings?"

"I wish I had the answers," I said.

We took our time walking through the airport. Josh's plane wasn't leaving for another hour. "I don't know what to say to Syd," he said breaking the silence.

"Did you get a chance to talk before the funeral?"

"No, not really. She was crying the whole time." He paused. "She's like my best friend. I told her everything about me. I guess it's okay to love my sister." Josh faked a smile.

We found two seats by the window in the waiting area. "Josh." I took his hand. "We're going to need to talk to someone."

"You mean like a counselor?"

"Yeah," I squeezed his hand. "I'll look for a family therapist. Maybe we can get two or three sessions in while you're home for Christmas."

He pulled his ticket from his jacket pocket. "Syd should probably come, too."

"I'll talk to Sheila about that tomorrow."

As we waited for his plane to begin boarding, I studied my child's face. His eyebrows meeting, his jaw tight, and the sighing — he had all of Jason's mannerisms.

He hugged me before boarding the plane. "I love you, Mom."

"I love you, too!"

When he got to the door, he turned and said, "I'm not mad," and he blew me a kiss.

While driving back to Pittsburgh, it was easy to

admit that my need to make things look 'right' defined me. After my brothers disappointed my parents, I tried to be the perfect daughter. Noah messed up in school, so I did my best to be an honor student. Joey never participated in church like my dad wanted him to, so I did. Everyone thought I had the perfect family, so I went along with the façade.

The most important thing was making other people proud of me and projecting the image of perfection. My inability to face the fact that I messed up led to this secret, and I realized that a skeleton had dictated my entire adult life. I hurt a lot of people. "God," I sighed out loud, "please help everyone I've hurt forgive me." I stopped in Breezewood just as I had done countless times before.

There were four messages from Andrea, and I called her before taking off my coat.

"What's up?" I asked, trying to hide my exhaustion. "Is everything okay?"

"Yeah, girl, I'm calling to check on you. I thought you would have been back hours ago."

"I waited at the airport with Josh," I explained.

"How is he?"

"I'm not sure the shock of it all has settled. Please tell Harvey to ask the Salvation Soldiers to pray for him," I requested.

I declined Andrea's dinner invitation and promised to meet her at church on Saturday. Then I called Sheila and left a message for her to call me when she got home. I was worried about Syd and wanted to see how she felt about all of us going to therapy over the Christmas break.

Josh decided to spend Thanksgiving in North

Carolina with Alicia's family. A part of me wanted to demand that he come home — a bigger part of me respected his wishes and acknowledged his efforts to grow up. He assured me he wasn't angry and that he just wanted to get his head together.

I called the Singleton's to let them know Josh and I would not be coming for Thanksgiving.

I started Thanksgiving Day thanking God. This thing called life wasn't easy. It took me through twists and turns and left multiple scars and bruises, but in spite of all the obstacles, I was still here.

"Thank You, Lord," I said out loud, "thank You for everything. Thank You for keeping me sane when I thought I was losing my mind. Thank You for caring about me when I didn't even like myself. Thank You for giving me Grandma Ida, Jason and Josh, and family and friends. Thank You for putting people in my life who love me."

The tears dutifully made tracks down my face. These were not sad tears, they were happy and thankful tears. I felt free. The secret was no longer in control.

"When God sets you free, you're really free," I could hear Nana saying. The wisdom seeds she planted were ready to bloom again. The weeds were being eradicated.

It was a brisk Saturday morning and only a few orange and yellow leaves were clinging to the branches of the trees on Sonny Street. Most of the leaves were now lining the street or piled in my yard. I took a deep breath and blew the air so I could see it. It felt good to be alive.

The women's ministry was having a potluck breakfast before our book club meeting and I baked a dozen carrot muffins using Nana's recipe. I had known for a month that we would be discussing *The Princess Within*, but put off reading it because I hadn't felt much like a princess.

We met in the Fellowship Hall and everyone shared their Thanksgiving stories: the turkey that didn't cook in the middle, the cake that fell, the burnt pies, the sticky rice and the potato salad made with potatoes and mayonnaise. We laughed and gathered together at one table so we could share testimonies while we ate.

Jennifer opened the group with prayer and Michelle blessed us with "Still I Rise". When the applause stopped, I was still standing and all eyes were on me. I stood amongst my sisters scanning their faces. Francis celebrated her fifty-ninth birthday and her eleventh year as a Christian after years of alcoholism, drug addiction and prostitution. Gloria's age was only evident by the crow's feet at her eyes, and she wore her joy like an aura, even though she buried her husband of thirty-five years less than a month ago.

Andrea planned to have at least four kids but was unable to conceive after having Corey. She continually praised God for giving her one miracle. Grace put her twins up for adoption when she was nineteen and at thirty-one was still not married. She remained confident that God would bless her with a family. During the height of her drug addiction, Michelle let a drug dealer have sex with Mikki, her twelve-year-old daughter. Mikki committed suicide when she was sixteen.

Theresa lost her son, her only child, because he was in the wrong place at the wrong time and bullets have no eyes. Paula had a reputation as 'the other woman' and then she fell in love with Mitchell. Fourteen years into the marriage, she found out he had three kids by a girlfriend he'd been seeing since they were married. Ava lived with the secret of being molested by her maternal uncle for thirty years. She never told because he was her mother's favorite brother. And Sheila, the best friend God blessed me with, was seated to my left.

We were all scarred from battle, but victorious. The devil was a liar and had been defeated. Satan could not have our joy or our souls. God had given us each other that we might praise Him for His keeping power and His many blessings. One by one, over the past year, the masks had come off. Everyone stripped the skeleton of its power, stood face-to-face with reality, and took a stand against the deep dark secrets that had tormented them for years. Everyone except me, and now it was my turn.

I focused my attention on the lamb so beautifully stained in the Fellowship Hall window and asked God to help me get through my testimony.

"I have lived with a skeleton," I began, wrenching my hands out of nervous habit. "The skeleton came out of the closet and hurt people that I love and care about very much, and now I have to destroy the power that the skeleton has held over me because I'm ready to be free."

I inhaled and exhaled slowly. "I had an affair with a married man after I graduated from college. I didn't know the difference between love and lust. I thought he really loved me. He proved that he didn't when I got pregnant with Josh. He left me. My pregnancy shamed my father but after I married Jason, he adopted Josh. I put my shame in the closet thinking no one would ever know Jason wasn't Josh's biological father. Even though he begged me to tell Josh the truth, I refused. The secret was my way of making it right."

My body shivered and I crossed my arms in an

effort to hold myself together. "A few weeks ago, Josh's father showed up. The world is so small and Josh's father was Sheila's ex-husband," I reported. "I hurt my son, my best friend and her children. My secret let my son fall in love with his sister."

Hard as I was trying to finish, my legs would no longer hold me. Sheila grabbed my hand as I was sinking to the floor. Then I felt the warm hands of my sisters. I could hear the hum of their prayers. My body felt light, like it would have floated away if they weren't holding me. I was free. No more weights, no more lies, no more secrets.

Later that evening, I called Mom. She knew my story and I wanted to reassure her that I was now free from the secret. I suggested a weekend get-a-way and she agreed. We made plans for a four-day cruise at the end of January. I would bring up the drinking because my mother needed to be set free, too.

Then I called the Singletons to thank them for loving me and Josh. I wrote notes of appreciation to Denise, Elaine, Maureen, Adrienne and Rhonda. For the ones who prayed, Jesus answered. For the ones who still didn't know Him, they needed to know that it was Jesus who made all the difference. Later that evening, I watched *The Color Purple*. In the end, Celie was victorious, too.

Andrea called me at work on Tuesday morning to remind me about the charter school meeting at Duquesne University. We planned to meet at her office so we could take one car.

I walked into the Board of Education ten minutes late and was caught off guard by his voice. "Danielle?!" He was just as surprised to see me. "How have you been?"

"How have you been stranger? It's good to see you!"

"Much better now." He hugged me. "Much, much better."

Tony was in town for a business meeting with the school district's fiscal director. We met later that evening for dinner and we talked until they began cleaning. It was almost as if years had never separated us. His smile was still inviting and his eyes still twinkled.

He told me about his divorce and his children. It grieved his heart to be apart from them, and he worked tenaciously to stay involved in their lives. His ex-wife was now remarried and living in Connecticut.

I told him about Josh and Jason. Then I told him about Greg. Tony stroked my face and held my hand, just like he had done at Nana's funeral. We reminisced about the stories Nana told us and I told him about the difference Jesus made in my life. As we waited for our check, I invited Tony to Bible study the following night. He declined, saying he had a dinner meeting. Driving home, I said a prayer for Tony. I asked God to open his heart to the wisdom seeds Nana planted in him, too.

Josh surprised me by coming home for Christmas break two days before I expected him. He wanted to go to Columbus to put a wreath on Jason's grave. I agreed and the three-hour drive gave us time to have a heart-to-heart talk about God, life, and love. It began to snow as we entered the cemetery.

"Dad always liked the snow," Josh stated while pulling over near the gravesite. "I remember when he taught me how to make angels."

I smiled at the memory. "He was a kid at heart."

"Remember the ET he made?" Josh asked with boyish excitement.

"Yeah, and I remember you falling asleep in the window because you thought it would melt overnight."

We laughed as we walked across the newly-fallen snow. I took Josh's hand and squeezed it as we approached Jason's headstone. Neither of us had been to the gravesite since we left Columbus.

"I love you, Dad," Josh whispered as he knelt at Jason's grave. "I know the truth. I wish you were here because this is kind of confusing, but I'll be okay. You made me promise to take care of Mom and I will. And I will love her forever — enough for both of us."

Josh stood and hugged me before taking the wreath from my hand. He placed the wreath on the ground in front of the headstone.

"Mom, did you always cry so much?"

"Yeah," I said wiping my face with the back of my hand, "but these are happy tears."

Josh stuck out his tongue to catch the snow and I smiled. Jason taught him to do that the first winter we dated. There was no sunshine, but I could feel Nana looking down on me and I knew Jason was watching, too.

"Love, kindness, goodness and peace," I said out loud.

"What?" Josh asked. "Mom, what did you say?"

"It's the wisdom seeds my grandmother planted in me a long time ago," I told him. "I'll tell you all about them on the way home."

Epilogue

Sheila and the girls joined us for two family counseling sessions in December to provide a safe place for everyone to share their feelings. I expected everyone to be angry with me, but the kids directed their pain at losing Sylvester instead of hating me for lying. I received grace and I was thankful.

Josh and Syd met with the pastor to help them sort out their feelings. Although they had flirted with each other, they were glad they had never kissed. By the time they returned to school in January, they were referring to each other as brother and sister.

Mom sold the house to the church in January of 2000 and knew my dad would be happy that it would be the parsonage. Two weeks after she settled into Joey and Stephanie's in Hampton, we met in Florida for our cruise. On our first night, we sat on the deck wrapped in blankets, drinking hot tea with a lot of lemon and honey.

"I know about the drinking," I said without looking at her.

"I'm sorry," Mom said meekly.

"Mom, I want to help you," I continued.

"I haven't had a drink in eighteen months," Mom said, with relief. She reached over and took my hand before she continued. "Your father came home one night in June and I was asleep in my recliner. He got concerned when he couldn't wake me and called paramedics. The ER told him I was drunk."

"You should have called me," I said, finally looking at her.

"When we got home from the hospital your father

held me, like he hadn't held me in a long time. He cried, Dani. I wanted him to cry out all the pain, disappointment and anger that was eating him on the inside."

I squeezed her hand.

"He was sorry that he hadn't been more loving. Sorry he hadn't been a better husband and father. And the next day he booked the cruise to Jamaica. He wanted to begin our 'better' since we had already endured our 'worse'."

We sat in silence. I was counting the stars.

"He was different after that. He was the David I fell in love with," Mom offered.

"I'm glad you got to have a few months of 'better'," I said sincerely.

"My mother planted the wisdoms seeds in me, too," Mom reminded me, and we recited them together.

On Valentine's Day, Doug asked Sheila to marry him and they set a wedding date – Saturday, November 24, 2001. They intentionally wanted to get married Thanksgiving weekend – they had a lot to be thankful for.

Josh spent the summer in Raleigh interning at Dennis' communications company. Sydney came home for the summer and worked at the church day camp. Shae struggled emotionally through the remainder of her sophomore year, but that summer she discovered her flair for fashion after being selected to model in the Back to School Showcase at the mall. She also met Khalid at basketball camp, and was looking forward to attending the Snow Ball with her first boyfriend.

I spent July writing the life lessons I never wanted

to forget. It was important to pen them so they could be an heirloom for our family. It felt good to know for sure that my wisdom seeds were deeply rooted and could no longer be washed away by my tears, trampled by my sorrow or strangled by the weeds of life.

In my journal, these are the entries I made about the wisdom seeds.

"For God so loved the world that He gave his only begotten Son, that whoever believes in Him should not perish but have everlasting life" John 3:16.

Love was the first seed Nana planted in my life. 'Love God with all your heart because He first loved you' was what she told me. Jesus loved me enough to keep me when I thought I could do it all alone. He didn't just keep me, He brought me through every storm and trial. After the darkest nights, He always sent a fresh new morning. After every rain, He sent the sun. Every time I wanted to give up, He gave me enough hope to hold on. In my darkest hour, it was the seed of love that sustained me.

"And be kind to one another, tender hearted, forgiving one another, even as God in Christ forgave you" Ephesians 4:32.

The second seed Nana planted in my life was kindness. I can picture her standing at the fence, telling me that love and hate can't live in the same heart. My heart has been set free from the captivity of anger and hate. I love my dad and am glad he didn't carry his bitterness to his grave. I only wish he had been set free sooner. I forgive

Greg. He didn't know God so he couldn't know how to love me, Sheila or his children. God forgave me. The people I hurt forgave me, too. There's only room for kindness in my heart.

"Do not be unequally yoked together with unbelievers. For what fellowship has righteousness with lawlessness? And what communion has light with darkness?" 2 Corinthians 6:14.

Nana wanted me to be happy and told me to make sure I surrounded myself with good people. God put good people in my life — people who love and care about me. My goodness cup continues to overflow — the third seed has been bountiful.

"A soft answer turns away wrath, but a harsh word stirs up anger" Proverbs 15:1.

The seed of peace was the final seed Nana planted in my life. "Make sure your words speak peace" was what she said. No more secrets, no more lies. My spirit is free and my words are pure and kind — they speak peace.

These scriptures had once been mere words that I memorized out of love for my grandmother. It took years to understand their significance. But the process helped me understand what Nana meant when she said God sees the sparrow when it falls. If He is watching over the sparrow then I know, that I know, that I know He is watching over me.